Crave All Lose All

A NOVEL BY

ERICK S GRAY

AUGUSTUS
PUBLISHING

This is a work of fiction. Names, characters, places, and incidents are products of the author's imagination or are used fictitiously and are not to be construed as real. Any resemblance to actual events, locales or organizations, or persons, living or dead is entirely coincidental.

ISBN: 978-0-9792816-1-7
Edited by Anthony Whyte
Design & Photogaphy: Jason Claiborne

First printing Augustus Publishing paperback January 2008

AugustusPublishing.com
info@augustuspublishng.com

Acknowledgements

I'd like to thank those who stood by me tall and strong over the years. Some from way back in the days and some of the new faces. I will never forget y'all. These are the people that pulled me up when I was down and made me smile when I wanted to frown. First, I got to thank God for everything. I know He's there, always watching, always listening and speaking to me when at times I just want to shut everything and everyone out.

As some know, I recently lost a few family members within the year, my younger cousin Pashad Gray, My Uncle Carl, Aunt Hanna, and another brother, Vincent E. Gray. You was coming home to us in August, but the day before your release, God took you to be home with Him. And I want to thank those that showed my family love, support and condolences through these trying times.

I also give thanks once again to my parents, Alinda Gray and Spencer Gray, for always being there for me, and the love they keep giving me. My sisters Tanya and Terry, my brother Pat for the strong siblings that they are—together, we will always remain strong. And Jean Gray, you suffered such a lost, but remember you are not alone—family will always be by your side during these troubling times.

K'wan, my brother from another mother, thanks for your support and love. You are my dawg for life, we gonna continue to grind and show this industry that we are nothing to play with. I lost three brothers over the years, but with you, Treasure, Mark Anthony, Anthony Whyte, Jay, and a few others y'all are my brothers for life. I lost three, but gain many. I wanted to let y'all know, that y'all are never forgotten and will never be taken for granted. Thanks.

Nakea, I always look forward your your guidance, thoughts, and inspiration. You know this business like O.J knows white girls. We all came a long way, and we been by each other side since back in the day, from doin' the wop at parties, but I'm comin' for your title, lol. But I don't know if you hear this much, thank you for everything.

Lady Scorpio, aka Kim, you are a true friend and very supportive of a brother. Thanks for your constant love and for constantly shouting me out on C2C. You are one in a few that don't forget about a brother online, where I be feeling so underrated in this game, you keep putting moving words in my ear and you always got time to check out my stories. That's why you're one of a few that will always get first shot at my books. I'm gonna stay showin' you love.

And I gotta show love to Tasha Herman, Linda Williams, Norma, Anna J and Azarel, the lovely ladies that are doing so many wonderful things, who keep enriching the lives of so many with their talents and trades.

Also to my cousin Petey, representing the south, keep doin' your thang down there cuz. You came a long way, and believe me, your story is comin' soon.

To my dude Kay, and his brother Jock, y'all keep your head up, and the two of you will never be forgetting. When y'all get home, we gonna do it up, believe me, good things are definitely coming y'all way. Much love to y'all.

And to my boo, Sequoia Hughes, you know I couldn't forget you. You are a beautiful and charismatic woman. I'm glad to have you in my life. You know I miss you, and believe me, things will fall into place for you really soon.

And the most important of all, my friends, my readers, and my fans who continue to support me and have supported me throughout the years, and a shout out to Tweety and Rah, for always showing me support and putting me in her collection. And to my dude, Hasheem, keep doing your thang.

But to everyone else, life is too short to wake up in the morning with regrets. Love the people who treat you right, forget about the ones who don't. And believe that everything happens for a reason. If you get a chance, take it, if it changes your life, let it.

Nobody said it would be easy, they just promised that it would be worth it.

Get at me via Myspace.com/ericksgray or email me at Writeone04@ yahoo.com 3

Special thanks to Augustus Publishing Manuscript Team, Tamiko Maldonado, Jason Claiborne and Ant Whyte-- The Dream Team

Go hard or go home...

Dedications

Sean Bell-1983-2006
Vincent E. Gray-1964-2007
Pashad Adache Gray-1991-2006
John Henry Grimes-1938-2007
Carl Willis Johnson-1945-2007
Kenneth Eric (Malachi) Daley-1957-2006
Alice Mae Cloud Smith-1926-2007
Gevondis Anne Whittingtondo-Gray-1956-2007
Hannah Latta Gray-1931-2007

Gone... but never forgotten...

Today I live, even though I found out that I will soon die, diagnosed with a touch of negativity in my system—soon my life flashes before my eyes. I wanna grip the stale air I inhale, exhale creativity and belief, pour out prosperity and richness through my daily deeds. Today I breathe, even though life is putting me in a choke hold, trying to detain my existence, execute my death mentally and physically, causing my mind to seize and doubt any good will come. My world shakes like an earthquake. My spirit darkened, like a moonless night over the sea—living with so much hardship, spreading like the vast deep-sea. I wanna breathe again. I wanna fly but feel rooted to the truth of reality. I wanna soar, see my dreams beneath me and dive into them with full force. Saturate the pessimistic thought with inspiration and dedication, overcome destitution with optimism. The spirit and faith that will surge throughout every negative and damaging point. Make all of me healthy and strong. Please make me loving and more understanding God. I wanna overwhelm myself with the thought of success and triumph over the adversity that forever would love to see me on bending knees, have me hateful to my own needs. I refuse to relinquish the thought of determination and might. Taking it one day at a time, being the best man I can.

Today, I want my intelligence to brighten and enlighten others, dispense knowledge to my brothers. I need for my people to understand, that what we truly own, is what we know, having an education is endless—a strong thought can't never be corrupt. A loving heart will never be distraught. And the mind is power and gold. I wanna drench my mind with limitless information, and then burst into my community with a rainfall of information. I wanna starve doubt, hate, jealousy and greed, plagues of this generation. Nourishing certainty, self-worth and self-confidence, spread education about our people's culture like everyday is Black History month. I want us to believe that we are truly rich in life and that all you need is the will, the spirit and the knowledge to thoroughly strive in life. I want us to grow, soar into unity—and be on one accord, fighting lies that's been told to our people, the things that separate us and contest the world that tries to lesser our race.

Today, I wanna reverse the Willie Lynch theory and unite the old with the young—bring together the old black pro for the young black male and the young black male pro for the old black male. We must benefit from the dark skin man, with the light skin man, and the light skin man with the dark skin man, understand that it is not the color or shade, but that we are still one man under God. We should trust and depend on the character of that man. And when we all are under that one accord of having attained the spirit, the determination, the integrity, the knowledge, understanding our history of where we been and where we want to go, and then wanting better for not only our race, but as humanity all together—it is then, that we are truly free.

Every man has by law of nature a right to such a waste portion of the earth as is necessary for his subsistence.

Sir Thomas Moore, Utopia II

Preface

There are two types of hustlers in the game—hustler number one is trying to survive to stay alive. Hustler number two grinds for the greed and thrill of the game.

The hustler that slings his drugs to survive has to feed and support his family. Maybe take care of home and pay his way through school. He doesn't have anyone else looking out for him.

This hustler never plans on being in the game for long. He makes that dirty paper, clean it up and keep it moving. For he knows the game ain't forever, so he invests his ends. Then he backs out, holding gwap never to return.

There's another dude hustling because he has a lust for power. An intense desire and craving burns his soul. Greed is his only motivation—the dollar is almighty to him and for power he hunger, the acquisition of which brings him closer to God.

When the soul is corrupt with lust for anything, there's a yearning—it changes you. You will kill to get yours. Hustler number two is in the new Benz, the latest Lambo, he's copping that new CL 600, rolling on dishes in Escalade. His soul burns for the possession of material things and the riches, the bling-bling. These things make him feel accomplished, influential over others.

The hustler with the lust for possession and power will kill, maim, destroying whatever's necessary to maintain greed. He will use intimidation and fear to have influence over the weak, the timid and the community. His only goal is to get money by any means.

A frail line exists between each level. If hustler number one is not careful and doesn't set a goal or have some moral respect for self, he will undoubtedly convert into hustler number two.

I was that nigga doing it to survive when I first started. Then I became hooked and suddenly I was in it for the thrill and self-indulgence. In a hustler's minute, I became trapped by my cravings. Slowly but surely I was killing myself and my community. The day I started in the game was the beginning of the end for me.

Prologue

1995...
Jamaica, Queens.

7:00 am on the dot Vincent's alarm went off causing him to rouse and interrupt the wonderful dream he was having of Janet. Ms. Jackson, if you nasty. They were both naked on a sunny warm beach somewhere in the Caribbean. He was dreaming that he was about to tap that pussy then he heard Method Man's rhymes coming through.

You're all that I need I'll be there for you...
You keep it real with me... I keep it real with you...
Loving your own seed they'd be in there too...
On top of that you got the good power U...

It was accompanied by the soothing voice of Mary J Blige. Vincent cursed, "Fuck!"

Ms. Jackson's curvy nude figure slowly disappeared. That was as close as he would ever get to having sex with her.

Still brooding over the miss, Vincent heard knocking on the door.

"Vincent, you up?" a male voice asked.

The teen rose up out of bed and rested against the headboard in an attempt to get ready for the day.

"Yeah, dad, I'm up," he finally shouted back while scratching his head.

"You know what today is right, boy?" his father asked.

"Yeah, I know," he answered.

"Alright now, get your behind out of bed and don't be late on your first day. Turn that music down, boy. You gonna wake up death one morning."

"Okay, okay" Vincent replied, slowly dragging himself out of bed, wiping cold out his eyes before turning down the radio.

He glanced at the calendar. July 10th, the first day of his new summer job at the Burger King that recently opened down the block. His father got him a job there right after high school graduation.

Vincent was reluctant because he thought that working at Burger King was a job for nerds and losers. He brushed his teeth and remembered what his pops had told him. "You think working at Burger King makes you less cool? You're a man for having a job no matter what job it is. If it's legit and will put some money in your pockets that's good. You gotta start somewhere in life…even if it means shoveling shit everyday."

He finished rinsing his mouth. If a man had to shovel shit for a living, then he might as well kill himself, Vincent thought. He showered away his drowsiness wishing he could sleep until noon. His father would be all over him if he was late for his first day. He left the shower thinking that this summer would be the worst yet. Instead of hanging out with his crew playing ball and meeting new girls, his three months would be wasted slaving over hot-ass grills flipping burgers at minimum wage.

Vincent quickly got dressed, throwing on some black Guess jeans, tan Timberlands, an Armani T-shirt, rocking a gold herringbone and a fitted Yankees cap. He threw his brand new work uniform in his book-bag and slung it over his shoulders. Vincent peered at his reflection in the mirror admiring how he looked.

"Vincent, you need to hurry up. Your breakfast is getting cold," his mother shouted, from the bottom of the staircase.

"I'm coming, ma," Vincent shouted back still standing in front the mirror. "I'm gonna be the best lookin' nigga they got workin' in fast food." He smiled.

He trotted downstairs and strutted in the kitchen. His father was already seated at the table drinking tea, the newspaper in his hands while his mother was near the stove scrambling more eggs.

Mr. Grey took time out from reading his paper and looked his son up and down.

"Where's your uniform?" he asked.

"In my book-bag," Vincent replied.

"In your book-bag…? Why?" he asked.

"Cuz, I'm gonna change into it when I get to work," Vincent answered.

"Oh God, please help me with this damn boy. What is wrong with kids today?" He shook his head before continuing. "You mean to tell me that you'd rather go into work dressed like some thug in baggy jeans and that damn chain around your neck than in your uniform. Are you too ashamed for everyone in the neighborhood to know that you have an honest paying job? Is that it? You wanna look like a damn hustler all the time and do nuthin' with your life!"

"Pop, you buggin' right know. That ain't even it in me. I just feel comfortable like this," Vincent retorted.

"Comfortable, huh…? That's why the police wanna throw you against wall and harass you. Cuz you and every other young black male wanna walk around with y'all pants sagging off your young asses and looking like trash. If you look like trash, then society and the police will treat you like trash," Mr. Grey stated.

Vincent sucked his teeth and glared at his pops. He knew he was far from trash in his sixty dollar jeans and two-hundred dollar chain. It was his style and he was against anyone trashing his style.

"You always got sump'n' to say," Vincent exclaimed. "Everything that I do is always fucked up in your eyes. You ain't even happy that I took this job."

"Boy what you say to me? You wanna be a man and curse at me in my home, in front of your mama and at this table," Mr. Grey shouted, rising up from the table.

Mrs. Grey had enough with their bickering. "Please, the both of you, enough already. Y'all are like children. Vincent eat your breakfast and enjoy your first day on the job," she shouted.

"I ain't even hungry right now, ma. I'll eat later," he said easing out of the chair and walking toward the backdoor.

"Vincent," his mother called out.

He ignored her and kept it moving.

"Let him go," Mr. Grey said. "Let him be a hardhead."

"Jason, why do you always gotta be so hard on him?" his wife asked.

With his anger cooling, he looked at his wife and said, "Because I love that boy so much, Jean. I want the best for him, and I know he's smart and has the potential to make more out of his life than I did. I don't want him to end up in these streets like so many of his friends."

Jean went over to her husband, sat on his lap with her arms wrapped around him and proclaimed, "You're a wonderful father to him, Jason. And you push for the best. With the love we give him, our son will turn out okay, baby. I trust him."

Mr. Grey stared up at his wife and smiled. "I love the both of you so much," he proclaimed.

"I love you too."

◇◇◇◇◇◇◇◇◇◇◇◇◇◇◇◇◇◇◇◇◇◇◇◇◇◇◇◇◇◇◇◇◇◇◇◇◇◇◇

Vincent hastily strutted to the bus stop. He was still angry at his father. *It never fails*, he said to himself. *All the time, he's gotta be on my ass about sump'n. He's never happy with anything that I do.*

Vincent was one block from Guy R. Brewer Blvd when he noticed a white four door Acura Legend with tinted windows coming to a slow creep towards him. He got a bit nervous, thinking about any previous beef that he may have with anyone. In the hood, it didn't take much for someone to get shot or murdered. A wrong stare at an individual could be a reason.

Vincent took a deep breath thinking *fuck it, if its beef then let them bring it*. He clenched his fist. The Acura pulled beside him and the passenger window came rolling down displaying a friendly smile. It was his boy Spoon who lived across the street from him. Tyriq was behind the wheel.

"What's up, Vince," Spoon hollered.

"Yo, why y'all creeping up on me like that? You lucky I ain't strapped."

"Nigga you ain't never been strapped," Tyriq shouted out.

"Yo man, where are you going this early?" Spoon asked.

"Work…"

"Work…? Your pops got you slavin'?" Tyriq asked.

"Yeah, he got me a job in the city. I gotta be there by nine." Vincent lied then quickly changed the subject. "What y'all doin' out here so early anyway? It ain't even eight yet."

Tyriq reached into his pocket and pulled out a phat wad of twenties and fifties. "Gettin' that gwap," he smiled. "You know the early bird always gets all the worms."

"Damn, you stackin' like that?"

"Twenty-four seven…"

"Is this your whip?" Vince asked pointing.

"My nigga, you need a ride?" Tyriq asked.

"We ain't in no rush," Spoon added.

Vince thought it over with the quickness. "Let's do it," he replied jumping into the backseat. He admired the soft, gray leather seats thinking of owning a car like this. His favorite whips were Acura's and Accords.

"The E or A train…?" Tyriq asked.

"E. What y'all dealing wit' today…?"

"Yo, we fit'n to see some white bitches out in L.I. We met 'em on the Ave last week doing their thang. They want ballers," Spoon said twisting a blunt.

"Oh word…damn, I envy y'all. I gotta go to this bullshit-ass job,while y'all get high wit' some white bitches," Vince said.

"Fuck the job. Roll with us ayyite my nigga," Tyriq suggested.

"Today is like my first day."

"Ayyite, I'll double whatever you was gonna make today. Have some fun, get some ass, my niggah, cuz these bitches are fuck-freaks," Tyriq said.

Vince smiled. His pops would flip out if he found out that he missed the first day. Vince knew he would get screamed on. But temptation was stronger.

"So what's it gonna be, Vince? You down or what…?" Spoon asked taking a long pull from the burning blunt and passing it to Vince.

"Fuck it, yo…I'm down with y'all," Vince said, taking the smoldering blunt from Spoon's hand. Pussy and partying was on his mind. "I'll just tell the people at work, I got lost. That's all. This is my first day. It ain't like they gonna miss me."

"Ayyite, that's what's up," Tyriq said.

"When you leaving for school, my nigga?" Spoon asked.

"Last week of August, kid..." Vince answered sucking on the blunt.

"Damn, college yo…you doing your thang, boy," Spoon said.

"Yeah, pops got me stressed about this job though, talkin' bout I need to save some money for books, food and shit while I'm there."

"I ain't mad at you, my nigga…do your thang my nigga," Spoon complimented.

"Fuck a college! I don't need no degree to get paid out here. Me, personally I feel school's a waste of time," Tyriq said, with his ignorance.

"Vince, don't listen to this cat. Keep doing your thang. He can't read anyway," Spoon joked.

"I know how to count my money, ayyite. And how to hold down these streets, that's all I need to know, ayyite?" Tyriq quickly retorted.

"Hey to each is own," Vince chuckled, feeling the affects of the weed. "Damn, this some strong shit y'all fucking round wit'," he coughed.

"Shit coming straight off the island boat. We got half a pound stashed," Spoon informed.

"Damn!" Vince was still coughing.

Tyriq continued onto Southern State Parkway. Weed smoke lingered in the car, and heads nodded in the rhythm to the sound of the Lost Boyz's, *Jeeps, Lex, Coupes, Beemers and Benz.*

"Yo, how far out on the island these bitches live?" Vince asked, work became a distant memory.

"Damn Vince, you thirsty like that?" Tyriq joked.

"Messing wit' this weed got me hornier than a muthafucka," he laughed.

Spoon and Tyriq joined in.

"Ayyite! But nigga don't leave any stains on my seat," Tyriq joked.

"Fuck you, nigga," Vincent said, his middle-finger held high. "Yo, I hope y'all got a bitch for me," he continued.

"Nigga, the way these bitches are, they'll fuck you, me and your pops," Tyriq stated, smiling.

"Leave my pops out. Just have a bad bitch for me to fuck wit'," Vince laughed.

"And you was ready to go to work, like a Herb? Now you can do your thang hard, nigga," Spoon said.

The three pulled up to a two-level bricked house in North Babylon. The tree-lined street was quiet, with manicured lawns and a silver Benz parked in the driveway.

"This is the real thang," Spoon said as he exited the car.

Vince and Tyriq followed closely behind. They paused checking out the serene neighborhood. In this serene setting of white America, the three stuck out like blackheads on a light skin bitch.

The doorbell sounded and Tyriq stood in front of the customized oak wood doors waiting for the girls to respond.

"I hope they're cute. Fucking wit' y'all made me miss my first day."

"Vince, be easy, ayyite? You here to enjoy yourself, man," Tyriq said, with a slight attitude.

The doors opened. Two beautiful blond girls stood in the foyer gleaming.

"Y'all made it," one said cheerfully.

"Y'all brought the weed?" the second girl asked.

"You know we do our thang," Spoon answered proudly.

"Ayyite, and we brought a friend," Tyriq said. "Sophia and Susan, this my nigga, Vince."

"Nice to meet you, Vince," the girls greeted with a naughty grin.

Vince smiled. Both girls were pretty. Susan was clad in a short ruffle denim skirt and blue bikini top. Sophia wore coochie-cutting shorts with a pink bikini top.

The three guys stepped in unaware that a nearby neighbor's eyes followed their moves.

"Ayyite, I know y'all can get a friend for my nigga," Tyriq suggested.

The girls smiled at each other then Susan said, "I know someone."

"Do that thang and call the bitch. It ain't no fun if my homie can't have none…" Spoon laughed.

The girls chuckled. Susan picked up a cordless and started dialing. Her parents were out of town for the week and she wanted to take full advantage.

The huge house was replete with Italian décor, imported pictures and a giant wide screen adorned the great room. There was a crystal chandelier suspended above the dining room table and outside in the back was a large patio adjacent to a swimming pool.

"It looks like money," Vince said.

"You like?" Susan asked.

"Nice, a nigga could get used to a place like this," he said.

Susan smiled. Vincent felt her flirting with him.

"C'mon on, let me show you around," she said taking his hand and leading him outside to the patio.

Sophia entertained Spoon and Tyriq in the sunroom while dissecting and licking a Philly blunt. Tyriq handed her a phat dime bag and she went to work twisting it.

These bitches had it made, Vincent thought as he stared at the pool wishing he could live like this. They had money in the bank, a Benz in the driveway and a phat ass crib. Going to college in September to study computers and accounting seemed like a dumb move. He blanked out the thought of his new job at Burger King.

"So, are you a hustler like Spoon and Tyriq?" Susan asked.

She moved closer to him and gazed into his eyes. Her feet were perfectly pedicured and her D cups looked like they were about to jump out of her bikini top. Her long blond hair blew stylishly in the wind.

"Nah, we came up together. They've been my boys since second grade," Vince stated proudly.

"That's cute. Y'all are best friends," she said gently grabbing Vincent by his shirt, pulling him closer. "Have you ever shot anyone before?" her tongue seductively swept over her lips.

Vincent chuckled, "Nah…you?"

Susan laughed, "No silly. But my father owns a few guns. They're upstairs. You can check 'em out if you want."

"Nah, I'm good wit that."

"Do you got a girlfriend?" she asked.

"Nah, you gotta man?"

"Not yet," she smiled.

He was turned on and wanted to fuck her good. It would be the first time with a white girl. That pussy was in the bag. Vince smiled.

Sophia rolled three blunts before the doorbell sounded. Susan excitedly ran to answer the door.

Vince remained chilling by the pool area thinking about pussy. Her juicy, white body was kinda sexy and her little ass was rounded at the right places.

"Everything's good out here? Y'all doing the down-low thang, huh?" Spoon asked stepping out onto the patio. Double-fisted, he had a blunt in one hand and a bottle of Dom in the other.

"I'm chilling," Vince responded.

Moments later Susan reappeared. Her friend was standing behind her. Vince and Spoon looked and nodded approvingly.

"Everyone, this is Asia," Susan said.

She was a cutie with titties that threatened to bounce up out of her blue, sheer top. Her faded blue jeans hugged her little ass. Her long, brunette hair was pulled back in ponytail. Asia nodded and smiled. Her stare rested on Vince.

"I don't want anyone to be a stranger here. My parents won't be back until Sunday night. So we got enough time to party! Yeah," Susan announced excitedly.

Sophia and Tyriq came from the sunroom and joined the rest. Three phat ass blunts were going around. There was more than enough liquor to service a bar for the night.

The hours passed and everyone got tipsy. Tyriq, Spoon and Sophia were fooling around in the pool. Sophia was now in only her pink and white panties while the duo finger fucked her under the cool clear water. The double team took turns sucking on her nipples.

Susan was seated in a lawn chair half naked clutching an empty bottle of E&J, sucking on a blunt.

Vince and Asia shared a blunt while in deep conversation. His dick was hard from the high and watching the scantily clad asses.

"Hmm…are you packing? Or are you just excited by what you see?" Asia joked.

"What you think? My lil' nigga is happy wit' things right now," Vince replied.

Asia smiled and they knew what time it was.

"Yo, I'm ready to check out the rest of this crib," Vince said hastily picking himself up from the chair and grabbing Asia's hand.

Tyriq and Spoon were running a train on Sophia. Tyriq was hitting her doggy-style by the pool, while her head was bobbing up and down off Spoon's dick.

Vince and Asia quickly found the master bedroom.

"Damn, this is fuckin' nice," Vince exclaimed. "Oh shit, they gotta fuckin' big ass TV embedded in the fuckin' wall. That's what I'm talkin' about."

Asia smiled and began unbuttoning her top while Vince quickly toured the room. He touched everything in his reach.

"I'm gettin' a crib just like this one. Fo' sho," he shouted. "Aw yeah, damn, you read my fuckin' mind," he said when he noticed Asia undressing.

Vince wrapped her in his arms and snaked his tongue down her throat. He shoved his hand down into her jeans and fondled her through her panties. Asia hastily undid her jeans and within seconds, Vince had her bent over the large king sized bed raw-doggin' that ass.

"Hmm…ah…just the way I like it," Asia closed her eyes and dreamily purred. His hard thrusting had her clutching the bed-sheets as she was ravaged by his thick black shaft.

"You like this big black dick in you, huh, white bread?" Vince laughed and teased grabbing her sides as he continued to tear into her.

"Ooh…ooh, I love it. Don't stop. Oh hmm… Yes…don't fuckin' stop!" Asia screamed.

"You wanna have a black baby wit' me, white bread? Huh. Ain't a white boy alive that can fuck you like me?"

"Hell no…oh God no…! I wanna have a big dick baby by you!"

Vince laughed loudly. Her pussy was tight sucking all of him inside. He came and didn't bother to pull out. Vince exploded deep inside her. They continued to put wrinkles and stains in the expensive, green, satin sheets.

As the day wore on, everyone continued to get more twisted. Vince, Tyriq and Spoon exchanged partners. Blowjobs were being performed and the girls even allowed anal penetration.

Dusk descended quickly. Vince peeked at his watch and saw that it was ten minutes after seven. He didn't care because his mind was cloudy with haze and the liquor in his system made him super-relaxed.

"Yo, we outta blunts," Tyriq said.

"Damn, I wanted to roll up another phat one," Spoon said.

"Yo, y'all niggas need to go to the store and get some more," Susan suggested. She was nestled against Spoon tickling his nuts.

"Yo, I'm fucked up right now," Vince said.

"Y'all niggas c'mon…I wanna get high again," Susan said. "Let's go to a bodega."

The fellows laughed. "Bitch, what you know about a bodega?" Tyriq said.

"Probably more than you, my nigga," Susan returned.

"This bitch doing her thang but she crazy," Spoon chuckled. "Fuck it, let's make this run."

"Yo, I ain't goin' no fuckin' where right now, ayyite nigga?" Tyriq stated.

"Nigga, get your bitch ass up and do this run to the store thang," Spoon said.

"Nigga, you a grown man…shit, take one of the bitches wit' you," Tyriq exclaimed.

"Yo, I'll roll wit' you Spoon," Vince said.

"I'll come with y'all too," Susan chimed.

"Yo, when I come back from this thang, I'm gonna fuck you up, nigga," Spoon said to Tyriq in a tipsy slur--clowning around.

Susan was loud and obnoxious as she strutted to the Acura. She looked high in her ruffled skirt, bikini top and her hair in confusion from the continuous fucking.

"My niggas...say what...my niggas...say what...we poppin' bottles and fuckin' models..." Susan sang offbeat, E&J strongly influencing her actions.

The same nosey neighbor watched them getting into the car. This was a proud neighborhood and the neighbor was not thrilled about this ruckus. Susan acting the fool while getting into a car with two rough looking black men. The cops needed to be notified.

Spoon started the car bumping *Eye 4 N Eye.*

As time goes by an eye 4 an eye...
We in this together sun your beef is mine...

so long as the sunshine can light up the sky we in this together sun your beef is mine…

"Oh shit! That's my niggas right there, Nasty Nas, Mobb Deep and Raqwon, the Chef. Pump that shit!" Susan shouted bobbing her head offbeat.

"Bitch, you ain't got no fuckin' rhythm to that thang," Spoon said.

"Yeah, but I had rhythm when you was in this pussy and I was swallowing your seeds," she countered.

Both men laughed.

Whoop-Whoop…

"Driver, pull your car over to the side," the cop shouted through a loud speaker.

"Ah fuck!" Spoon shouted.

Vince's high suddenly vanished when he saw the cops pulling them over. There was a drunk, scantily clad white girl in the backseat half-sleep and the parkway was a few minutes away.

Spoon knew there was half a pound of weed in the trunk, and a loaded 9mm under the driver's seat. Another patrol car pulled up, shining light on the dirty Acura.

"Yo man, what da fuck!" Vince shouted. His heart beating like he was running two hundred miles a minute. He tried to keep his composure.

Three male white cops slowly approached the car with their hands on their weapons. A bright flashlight was beaming.

"Driver, remove the car keys and drop them out the window," one cop instructed.

"Yo, we ain't do nuthin," Spoon shouted.

"Driver, remove your car keys and drop them out the window… slowly."

Too tipsy to put up a fight, Spoon sighed and did as instructed.

"Passenger, slowly put both your hands out the window and open the car door slowly."

Vince did what he was told and Spoon soon followed. Both men were soon thrown against the car and detained. Susan, high and drunk in the backseat opened her eyes and saw a cop staring down at her.

"Hey…what's up? Where my niggas at?" she hiccupped.

She was drunk, half naked with her nipple showing from her bikini top that was loosely untied.

"Ma'am, are you okay?" the cop asked, clearly disgusted by her behavior.

"She's doing her thang with us. Why y'all asking her some stupid shit like that? We just came from her crib," Spoon exclaimed.

"You shut up!"

Susan was asked to step out of the car. When she did, she staggered all over the place, collapsing into one of the officer's arms. Her bikini top became completely untied and her business was soon in view for everyone to see. Susan laughed, not caring at all.

Spoon and Vince were placed in handcuffs while the officers searched the vehicle. It didn't take long to find the gun and weed. Under arrest, they were transported to the station house.

"This is all fucked up. My pops is going to kill me and I missed work." Vince cried.

Susan's parents were called. She was free to go home when a relative came to pick her up. Spoon and Vince wasn't as lucky.

"Boy, have you lost your Damn mind!" Mr. Grey shouted, furious with his son for getting arrested in Long Island.

Vince was released on a ten thousand dollar bond. But he would rather be still in lock up than to deal with his father and his attitude. His father used a bail bondsman along with ten percent of the bail. Mr. Grey wanted his son home so he could kill him.

"It wasn't my fault; they were wit' some racial-profiling, pops. They had no reason to pull us over," Vince argued.

"Jean, I'm gonna murder him that fuckin' boy! You get caught with drugs and a loaded gun in a car with a naked white girl. You should have been at work!" Mr. Grey shouted furiously.

"She wasn't naked; she had on a skirt…." Vince countered.

"I don't give a rat's ass if she was dressed like a Pope. You shouldn't have been there. You don't give a damn about us or what you want to do with your life…do you?"

Jean was also disappointed with their son. She cried and wanted to calm him down. But understood the anger and rage he felt. She was furious too—but chose not to explode with anger and screaming like her husband.

"Jason, your blood pressure," she warned him.

"Damn my blood pressure! Is this boy retarded? I don't understand you, Vincent. You wanna end up like your friends? Boy, keep fuckin' up and you'll be out this house faster than these got-damn mice. I don't wanna even see your damn face…you make me damn sick."

"Jason," Jean cried out.

"This boy is goin' to straighten up, or get the fuck out my house. It's your choice."

"Don't worry, I'll be out of here soon and you ain't gotta worry wit' shit I do no more."

Vince stormed upstairs into his bedroom and was ready to pack his bags. He heard his mother crying out to him but ignored her and kept it moving.

Tensions were high in the home. Vince wouldn't admit it to anyone but he was scared. He had charges of gun possession, drugs and intent to distribute hanging over his head. It wasn't the first time he got into trouble with the law but the charges were the most serious he faced.

The days passed and Vince's lawyer informed him that Spoon confessed up to owning everything. Spoon would take a plea and the judge would give Vince a year's probation. His mother was ecstatic and so was Vince. Spoon took the heat and would do jail time. The news did nothing to relieve the strained relationship between father and son. Mr. Grey was still angry.

Spoon called Vince collect.

"Yo, why you confessed and copped a plea?"

"Cuz you don't need to be caught up in this system. I've been through it before and know how to do my thang. You about to start school this fall and got a lot going for you. If it wasn't for me and Tyriq you'd be doing your thang at your job. Do your thang, my nigga. Live life, don't worry 'bout me."

"I owe you, Spoon," Vince said.

"Yo, do your thang and stay away from 'em slutty, white bitches…

too much heat."

They both laughed.

Spoon got a five-year stretch. Vince tried to get on with his life. But when it rains it pours. Vince's pops died from a severe heart-attack two weeks before school was to begin. The passing of his father crushed Vince. He was unable to mend the hardship between his father and himself. He knew his father loved him so much and only wanted the best for him. The day he got arrested, he knew that hurt his pops so much. The experience haunted Vince and left him thinking if he would've gone to work, his pops wouldn't have been so stressed.

When they lowered his father into the ground, his mother held Vince tightly, sobbing. Vince stared at his father's casket and made a promise to himself to get his life right and do just.

Part One

Today... 2002

My alarm went off at exactly 6:10 every damn morning, indicating that it was time to get my ass up and ready for work. I didn't know why I was getting up to go to work. I had two weeks left then I'd be permanently laid off. I received my notice in the mail a few days ago. My job sent me papers saying *that they regret to inform me, but my employment status will be affected by reduction in workforce requirements in my classification*—which meant I was soon to be unemployed.

I worked for *American Airlines* for four years. Things started going bad after 9/11 happened. I knew it would be my turn soon. I'd hope and pray that the downfall wouldn't affect me, but it did. The economy took a nose dive and had a big domino effect. Businesses started closing down and lay-offs were next. Now it was my turn and soon I'd be out of a job.

I didn't fall asleep till two in the morning and was still groggy when I jumped in the shower. Unemployment was not an option. There weren't any companies hiring at the moment. I applied at Jet blue Airlines, the sanitation department, MTA, even the local Pathmark and was placed on waiting lists.

I started working for American Airlines when my girlfriend was seven months pregnant. I tried juggling getting my bachelors degree and working full time to pay the bills. That wasn't easy.

After pops died, I started helping my moms out. She was heartbroken. We fell behind on the mortgage payments and the bank foreclosed. My moms moved in with her older sister in St. Albans. It was a fucked-up situation.

Eventually I gave up my fulltime status at college to earn a steady paycheck. I was planning on going back full-time once I was back on my feet.

I met my baby moms five years ago while we were in John Jay college. Chandra and I had three classes together. We started talking at first, getting to know each other then we became friends. One thing led to another and a year later she was pregnant.

Beautiful with silky, dark skin, Chandra was charismatic with long, black hair extending past her shoulders. She was tall with a curvaceous body. Her legs were well defined, stretching up to the heavens.

Everything started changing after my son's first birthday. Chandra stressed me too fucking much about my lack of money and school.

I was already busting my balls with overtime at the job. We lived in a basement apartment and I was tired of living underneath everyone.

My job provided medical benefits and flight privileges. She never complained when I used my benefits to vacation with her in South Beach, Miami, Barbados, Jamaica, even Hawaii. She wanted a house with lots of windows and cars. She always whined about taking the train back and forth to work. Chandra was a fashion fanatic. She loved clothes and had more clothes than Macy's but she wanted more. Although she was a good mother to our son, we separated.

I moved in with my mother and Aunt Linda staying in the basement living an average life.

Two

My last day of work, I got drunk with a few fellows at a bar on Rockaway Blvd. It was the end of the day and I was in my uniform throwing back Coronas and E&J not thinking about unemployment. I stared at the TV watching a clip of President Bush as he spoke to the nation about Osama Ben Laden and the war on terror.

"Muthafuckas fucked up and we lose our jobs," Billy exclaimed. "Shit, they need to lay off Bush and that bitch, Rice. We the ones who suffer in the long run—the working man's always last."

"I hear that shit," Roger, my ex-coworker concurred.

"He got some fucking nerves being on TV talking about the war… that muthafucka is terror. They need to knock his ass down like they did the towers," Billy, my other ex-coworker joked.

"We gonna miss you and your lisp, Vin. We can still roll wit' you…" Billy said raising his bottle.

"You said that wit' just like Vince does," laughed Roger chugging.

I joined in the laughter.

Billy and Roger were white and been at the company two years longer than me. When the pink slips were handed out, it didn't matter if you were white or black. We were all in the same predicament—fucked.

I continued to down drink after drink. The news was too depressing to keep watching. Billy asked the bartender to change it. The Yankees were playing. I didn't like baseball so I turned my attention elsewhere. Scanning the bar, I did a double-take when I spotted a girl I went to high school with. Sharice was standing by the pool table with a couple goons.

I remembered wanting to hit 'em panties a long time ago. She was sexy, popular and everyone wanted a piece. Seven years had gone by but Sharice was looking good. She wore tight fitted jeans that highlighted her hips and a white top that left all her cleavage exposed.

She caught me looking. I smiled. Sharice was stuck on herself. From all the clarity in the ice she flossed on her neck, wrist and fingers, she had snatched up a baller.

I perked up and decided to holler at her as she strutted my way in five-inch stilletos. Her swagger could teach Beyonce a thing. Sharice snapped her fingers at the bartender while standing next to me without any acknowledgment. Her presence got my dick hard.

"Sharice, right…?" I asked.

"Do I know you, nigga?" she said with attitude.

"We went to high school together… had classes together during your senior year. I know you ain't tyrin' a play a nigga, now," I smiled.

"That ugly uniform you wearing, it's that easy for me to forget you," she snapped back. "What you make ten…twelve dollars an hour? You can't afford me, so step the fuck off."

Her response smacked the smile off my face. I was flushed with embarrassment.

"Oh, so you think you the shit now…bitch, you a fuckin' gold-digger," I barked. She had pissed me off.

"Don't get stupid. My peoples are over there and one word from me and they'll have you laid out on Rockaway Blvd."

"Vince, we don't need any trouble," Billy said.

"I'm tryin' to show this bitch some luv and she getting ill. Fuckin ho!"

"You 'bout to get fucked up," she said tossing the drink in my face.

"Sharice, you got problems?" one dude asked.

"This…piece-a-shit here just fuckin' dissed me," she said pointing.

"You got a problem, homey?" he asked with the pool stick clutched tightly in his hand. He was flanked by other goons who had his back. They grilled me like I was easy prey.

"Nah, nigga…but you need to teach this bitch some manners. Fuckin' ho, forgot where she came from. Maybe she needs some dick in her mouth for her to shut the fuck-up!" I barked.

It was suicide. I knew what they were about. Their deamonor and style of dress screamed hustler. I had just lost my job, had too many bills to take care of and my car was on the verge of breaking down. They had Benzs and Escalades parked outside. All were frozen in ice and had money to burn. I had twenty dollars in my pocket and no job. Tipsy I was and in no mood for bullshit. I didn't give a damn.

"Muthafucka, who you think you're talkin' to?" He was about six two, well dressed and well built. We were about the same size.

"Yo, I ain't got no beef wit' you, but your bitch is trash," I continued my verbal onslaught.

"Vince man, c'mon…chill out," Billy said fearing the worse. I needed to get hyped. There was nothing to lose and I haven't been in a fight in months. Sharice played me. I knew she was used to niggas kissing her ass.

I saw the pool stick coming my way, ducked and charged forward. My first victim caught the blow across his jaw. I hit the second nigga across his temple and I went for the third nigga. I hit that third nigga so fucking hard, that I felt his jawbone shatter. I was outnumbered, but going hard body and had the advantage for serveral moments. Then someone grabbed me in a chokehold from behind. His forearm pressed against my wind-pipe like a python left me gasping, trying to break free.

"Yeah, what!" one of the thugs shouted hitting me.

"You bitch-ass, my son hits harder…"

The next blow buckled my knees. I found myself on the bar floor in the fetal position being stomped.

"Yo, drag this muthafucka outside!"

"Yo, get the fuck off me," I yelled kicking.

My uniform was torn. My face was bruised and swollen from the blows bestowed.

"Yeah, talk that shit, fuckin' big mouth!"

"I'm calling the cops." The bartender shouted.

"We out…"

"I told you, stupid. Next time, you better fuckin' respect me," Sharice said looking down on me with a smug expression.

I was sprawled out on the floor, hearing them leaving. She followed her goons out the door.

"Fuck you! You still a ho!" I yelled.

I was hurting. My mouth was filled with blood and it felt like a few ribs were broken.

"Vince, you okay?" Roger asked coming to my aid.

"Thanks for the help," I said, slowly picking myself up off the floor and holding my side.

"You and your smart mouth, gonna get you killed one day," Billy said.

I looked at Billy thinking to myself, *fuckin' pussy*.

"I'd rather die on my feet than live on my knees," I said with as much conviction as I could.

Who was I kidding? I've been living on my knees in society since my mother lost her house to the bank. I dropped out of school to support my family. Now I've lost my job and my family. I just got disrespected by a bitch I went to high school with and her goons beat me down.

I sighed, licked my wounds and went to the bar for another Corona. I thought about dying on my feet and becoming a man in this world, instead of continuing to live on my damn knees.

Three

I woke up to the aroma of breakfast coming from the kitchen. Either my moms or aunt was cooking. They both were wonderful cooks. I glanced at the time. It was ten in the morning. I slowly got out of bed, nothing to do for the day but job hunt.

"Vincent, breakfast is ready," my moms shouted.

"I'll be wit' y'all in a minute."

I walked into the bathroom and looked at my reflection. My battered face from last night's fight stared right back at me—a blackened eye, a slightly swollen lip, yeah I was a piece of work. Some parts of me still hurt. But I knew I was able to get through the day.

I turned on the water and thought about my glory days. I remembered wanting to be a boxer and was training at a gym on Northern Blvd. I was nice and my pops was supportive. He always encouraged me to have a back up plan in case I didn't make it professionally. That meant keeping my ass in school and my face deep in the books, getting an education. Pussy and being stupid got in the way of me going to the golden gloves when I was seventeen. I got drunk and high with these two bitches the night I was supposed to leave on a flight to Chicago. My trainer was furious and barred me from his gym until I could get my act right. I never did.

Eight years later, I still had the physique of a boxer but my knuckle game was a bit rusty. My dreams were forever gone. I got dressed and went downstairs to enjoy breakfast. My mother was washing dishes and my aunt had left for work.

"Good morning, ma," I greeted, giving her a kiss on the cheek as she stood over the sink washing dishes with her back to me.

"Hey, sweetie did any one of them jobs called you back yet?" she asked.

"Nah, not yet," I answered.

"Don't worry, you'll find something."

"I hope so. I can't be sitting around the house all summer that'll be irritating."

"Be patient. Good things will come your way," she said. "Oh, Chandra called early this morning. She wants you to call her back."

"What did she want?" I asked.

"She didn't say. Call her back right away."

I sighed. Even though I was dead broke and she had a job making six hundred dollars a week that bitch wanted money. She'd have to wait.

"I'll call her back later."

My mother turned herself away from washing dishes and noticed my face. "Ohmygod, Vincent. What happened to you?" she shrieked.

"I got into a fight last night. It ain't nuthin' ma," I said.

"What do you mean, you need to be careful, Vincent. I already lost your father. I don't wanna lose you too."

"It was just a fight."

"Nobody just fight anymore, Vincent. Everyone wants to shoot each other."

"Might as well. The world's coming to an end anyway."

SLAP!

I didn't see it coming. My mother caught me unexpectedly, "You watch your mouth, Vincent and stop having this negative attitude about life. You think about the Lord and He will guide you."

"Ma, you didn't have to hit me like that…damn, you should've had my back last night. It would've been a fair fight then." I soothed the side of my face where she slapped me,

"Vincent, hush your mouth and eat your breakfast. I don't want you getting into anymore fights and talking silly."

I nodded, saying nothing.

My mother was a beautiful woman, fifty-six years old and still didn't look a day over forty. She worked at the hospital for thirty five years and was looking forward to her retirement. She was always there for me and I love her.

I heard the doorbell.

"I got it ma," I said and went to see who it was. I smiled when I saw Spoon standing at the door.

"Spoon, what's good?" I quickly opened the door and hollered.

"Came to talk to you," he said.

Spoon did a three-year bid at Clinton after the arrest in Long Island. I owed this nigga my life, because he had taken the heat.

He got right back on them streets with Tyriq hustling after coming home. Three years didn't stop him from becoming a paid man in the hood. He was a born to be a hustler. He was respected and feared in the streets, but we had love for each other like brothers.

"Come in," I said.

Spoon walked in and laughed when he saw the bruises on my face.

"I heard about that thang last night," he said chuckling.

"You should see the other guys' faces."

"What, they injured their knuckles?" he joked.

"Laugh, but I'm ready to get at their bitch-asses. Coming at me for a ho."

"Calm your ass. You don't need to get at anybody. I heard you were doing your thang, calling her trash and all," he laughed.

"Spoon, you should've seen the look on her face when I dissed her, it was priceless. Like I'm supposed to kiss her ass cuz she's fuckin' a baller. Yo I remember back in high school when Mel and them ran a train on her in the bathroom. She's trash fo' real."

"You would still fuck that thang," Spoon said.

"Hells yeah…her body is hmm…banging."

"C'mon Vince, you a working man … you know her thang. I ain't saying you ain't classy but Sharice always been about fuckin' niggas who doing their thang. You ain't about to spend a dime on that bitch."

"You right, I was a working man."

"What happened?"

"Laid-off as of yesterday…"

"Sorry, that thang hurts my nigga."

"Shit happens, right?"

"You'll be back on your feet doing your thang at a new job."

Spoon then looked around the place and his mood turned somber. "Vince, Thomas got murked last night," Spoon sadly informed me.

"What, he got killed. Get the fuck outta here! You fo' real, Spoon?" I asked in disbelief.

"They murdered that nigga on Supthin and Foch, shot him twice in the chest."

"You know who did it?" I asked.

"I heard he had beef with niggas from Hollis."

"Damn!" I muttered.

Thomas was Tyriq's younger brother. He was only nineteen and I remembered him growing up idolizing Tyriq and Spoon.

"Yo, I've known him since he was six," I said in a graved tone. "When is the funeral?"

"We don't know yet. We want niggas to show Tyriq and his family mad support."

"I'm definitely wit' that," I said hugging Spoon.

My mother came down the stairs in her blue scrubs, on her way to work. She saw Spoon in the living room and smiled. "Timothy, I haven't seen you in a long time. How you been?" she greeted Spoon with a hug.

"I'm okay Mrs. Grey."

"That's good. You're looking good, staying out of trouble?"

"Yes ma'am. Just stop by to say hello. How're you, Mrs. Grey?"

"I'm good, thanks for asking," my mother said, smiling. "Well, I'm off to work."

My mother hugged Spoon. Then she hugged me and kissed me on my cheek. "Remember, Vincent, it'll happen in Gods' time."

She walked to the door. Before leaving, she looked at the both of us and said, "I will keep the both of you in my prayers."

"Your mom's alright, Vince. You think she knows about me and the streets?"

"I don't know."

I knew she suspected that he was dealing. His style of dress wasn't as flashy but it was definitely expensive.

Spoon sported a diamond encrusted Presidential Rolex. In both ears he had huge diamond studded earrings that looked like golf balls.

"Vince, I need to be out. We'll get up later and talk."

"No doubt," I said.

I watched him get into a baby blue Range Rover and drove off.

Four

Thomas' funeral was large. It was held at J Foster Phillips funeral home on Linden Blvd. Hundreds of folks came by and showed support for Tyriq and his family. Thomas was loved and respected. He would be missed.

I showed up in a black suit and wing-tipped shoes, looking my best for his home-going. I was alone navigating my way through the crowd that lingered around outside.

Inside, I saw Spoon standing with a group of fellows wearing black T-shirts with Thomas' picture on the front. The picture showed Thomas with cornrows throwing up some gang signs. It was a quick memorial put together for him. Over two dozen young men were wearing the T-shirt.

Spoon nodded and I walked over to him. I hugged him and asked for Tyriq. He pointed inside. Folks were viewing the body. It was a full house.

I spotted Tyriq sitting quietly with his family staring at his brother in the casket. He was unflustered, sitting next to his mother in a three-piece suit. As I walked over to view the body, I remembered the last time I saw Thomas alive. It was six months ago at a club on Farmers Blvd. He was with his girlfriend and was happily spending money. He bought me a drink then we went our separate ways.

Lying inside a white sealer, gold cross casket surrounded by dozen of elegant, sympathy flowers and pictures, Thomas looked like he was sleeping. I glanced at Tyriq, he nodded and I went on my way. I wanted to talk but now wasn't the time.

The funeral went on and I thought of how my own funeral would turn out. Would there be as many people?

"You out…?" Spoon asked.

"Yeah, I'll be at the burial tomorrow morning."

"Take care," Spoon said giving me dap.

I stepped outside unloosening my tie and smiled when I saw two familiar faces standing on the corner. One was smoking a cigarette. It was Asia and Susan. I walked over. Asia was smiling and cheerful. She hugged me tightly. It's been seven years since I saw them. Susan was pregnant.

"Vince, you look so good," Asia greeted, her arms wrapped around me.

"How many months are you?" I asked Susan while still hugging Asia.

"Seven," she replied rubbing her belly.

"Tyriq's the father?" I asked.

She nodded.

They both looked good. Asia was wearing tight denim jeans and jacket while Susan wore a long teal dress. We talked for a moment. There were no hard feelings. Years had passed and pussy was on my mind.

I looked into Asia's eyes and she stared back smiling. We were both thinking the same thing. Asia turned to Susan and said, "I'm gonna catch up on lost time with Vince."

"Just make sure you don't end up like me." Susan smiled rubbing her belly.

I laughed.

An hour later, I had Asia stretched out in the backseat with one foot propped against the passenger headrest and the other against the backseat. I was pressed against her, sucking on her nipples, thrusting like a mad man and about to cum in her. It definitely felt like old times again.

The next morning, I stood quietly among the other three dozen mourners in Montefiore Cemetery and witnessed the burial of Thomas.

The pastor held a bible in his hand and proceeded with the burial. He was clad in grey suit and had a thick, white beard. He stood next to the casket and made the benediction.

"Now I have left you, for a little while. Please do not grieve and shed wild tears, and hug your sorrow to you through the years. But start out bravely with a gallant smile; and for my sake and in my name, live and do all things the same. Feed not your loneliness on empty days. But fill each useful hour in useful ways. Reach out your hand in comfort and cheer, and I, in turn, will comfort you and cheer holding you near. Never, never be afraid to die; I am waiting for you in the sky."

It was a sun drenched day. Thomas cousin, Latoya was next to me and she was sobbing quietly. The dark shades she wore could not hide her tears. Clutching my hand, she stared at her cousin's casket being lowered into the ground.

Tyriq was a statue, not moving during the entire ceremony. He wore designer shades and was gangster in a tailor-made black pin-stripe suit. His crew surrounded him and they all were dressed in black. The preacher continued.

"May Thomas Green rest in peace and find comfort in the Lord. Ashes to ashes and dust to dust, we return this body back to the dust…Amen."

"Amen," everyone said.

Crying and grieving was heard as the casket was lowered into the ground, with the women of his family wailing the loudest.

I kissed the rose in my hand and tossed it on the casket. Walking away, thinking death was an easy way out. I was in a fucked-up situation, out of a job and having to ask my mother for money.

I felt like a zero. Not being able to take care of my responsibilities was a hard nut to swallow. Tyriq walked over to where I was standing looking at black birds.

"Ayyite, thanks for coming, Vince. I appreciate it," he said.

"Thomas was like a brother to me too. I'm here for you, Tyriq." I said as we hugged.

"It's been a minute. What you been up to?" He nodded and asked.

"Unemployed…"

"You ain't at the airport?"

"9/11 fucked that up. I was one of the first to get cut. Goddamn Ben-Laden fucked shit up."

"Damn man, what you planning to do?"

"I can't call it. I've been job hunting. Ain't nuthin' happening so far."

"I got a proposition I wanna holla at you about. Vince we family …you being here today at my younger brother's burial mean a lot. If you need anything, get at me."

"Cool, I'll keep that in mind."

"Ayyite my nigga, we'll talk," he said hugging me and walking away.

Spoon appeared in the backdrop watching me and Tyriq. I nodded and he returned it before walking away.

Five

After the funeral, I headed over to my baby mother's place. It was Saturday afternoon and I missed my son. I needed his joy and spirit to uplift me. Between the lay-off and Thomas' funeral, I was going crazy and needed to escape.

Chandra opened the door, but there was no welcome smile. She was unconcerned and distant.

"I missed you, too," I said with attitude.

My sarcasm matched her frown. I walked into the two-bedroom apartment and closed the door. Chandra walked into the kitchen and I followed. She was looking good and I was still attracted to her. I still had love for her that burned within me when I came around her. We had been apart for a year and a half, but only stopped fucking for six months.

She cut me off from the pussy, cold turkey. I speculated it was because of someone she was fucking and got jealous but it wasn't my business. We weren't together.

"Where's my son?" I asked.

"In his room sleeping," she said brushing me off.

She was making fries and had burgers cooking on the Forman Grill. I eyed her for a short moment. She was in blue-jeans and black T-shirt. Her long hair was styled into a pony-tale. A new diamond bracelet adorned her wrist and her earrings were new. They had to be from some nigga she was fucking. And by the gleam in the jewelry, he must be stacking paper like that.

She was acting like I wasn't there. Chandra busied herself going back and forth to the cabinets and stove. She suddenly stopped with a frustrated looked and said, "Your son needs some sneakers. And he needs some summer clothing. He only has winter clothing and it's like eighty degrees outside."

"Chandra, I know that but I bought him a pair two months ago."

"Yes, but he's a child and he goes through them fast, always running and playing," she said.

"Damn, Chandra, I ain't made wit' money. Why can't you buy him what he needs for now? You're making six hundred a week. I ain't working right now."

"You're his father and can help out with something."

"I do help out, so don't come at me wit' that shit," I barked.

"Whatever!" she spat.

"Yeah, whatever," I exclaimed.

"So, you ain't found a new job yet?" she asked sounding judgmental.

"I'm trying."

"Well you need to try harder, Vincent. You knew the Airline was going to lay you off and you should've been looking for another job months before. I can't do this by myself. Your son needs a ton of shit by next week and I can't get that for him. I just paid rent and went grocery shopping. I'm broke."

"What's up wit' all that bling…?" I asked.

"A friend," she quickly replied.

"Nice gifts from a friend."

Chandra cut her eyes, rested her hand on the kitchen countertop and placed her other hand on her hip, "Yes, I'm fuckin' da niggah, if that's what you was about to ask." She exclaimed.

I grunted trying to control a rage that could lead to me slapping the shit out of this bitch. Before I could respond Chandra was in my face.

"And don't ask the nigga that I'm fucking to do for Vinny. He's your son and you need to handle yours."

"I wasn't gonna go there, because I don't want no one taking care of my responsibility. Don't fuckin' play yourself, Chandra. Remember, I've done for my son. So don't be throwing shit in my face, 'specially 'bout some nigga you fucking. I ain't the one for you to be fucking play wit' right now…"

I reached into my pockets and pulled out my last twenty. "Here, you need money, take it," I shouted tossing the bill at her.

"Vince, I don't need petty cash," she said.

"You need it more than me, so take the fuckin' twenty," I spat.

She sighed and replied with, "You're getting loud and ridiculous, Vincent. Please lower your voice."

I looked at her feeling angry and hurting on the inside. It was sad. I felt low bending to pick up the twenty dollar bill. I could tell she was staring as I stuffed it into my pocket. It was as if I had given myself a handout.

"Yo, fuck this, I'm out. Just tell Vinny that I love him and I'll see him tomorrow."

"Vincent," Chandra called out.

"What?" I turned and asked.

"Can you or your mother watch him next weekend for me?" she asked.

"Why?"

"I got plans," she replied.

I wanted to tell the bitch no, go fuck herself because I knew her plans were to get at some nigga and get fucked. But I loved spending time with my son.

"Cool, I'll take him," I said.

"Thanks," Chandra smiled.

"I'm not doing it for you. I'm doing it for my son. I love him regardless of you being a bitch. I'm gonna be there for my son," I proclaimed.

I was in the hallway when I heard her say, "Vince, please get a job, not a hustle."

"What do you mean?"

"Vinny's gonna need a father in his life, not one that's behind bars, or dead. Have you given going back to school any thought?"

I chuckled and left thinking she was acting like she cared for a nigga.

I sat in my car for hours outside Chandra's building thinking who was doing more for her than I could. It bothered me that another man was being a father to my son. He was able to afford clothes and toys for my son's birthday and holidays.

I spotted a burgundy Escalade with 24" chromed rims pulling up. A six-three, stocky dude with long dreads wearing a white and black tracksuit, and sporting new Jordan's stepped out. A baller and definitely a nigga Chandra would fuck with, I started grilling him.

Slowly driving in his direction as he walked to the building, I eyed him like there was beef between us. He turned and looked at me with a scowl. Our eyes locked.

"You gotta problem, brethren?"

He was Jamaican and Rastafarian.

"Nah dreadlocks, I thought you was someone I knew, that's all."

I smiled and drove away, blocking the thought that this punk-pussy-ass, nigga could be fucking my ex, my baby mother.

Six

That same night, I was on one of the rooftops of the buildings in 40 projects smoking, drinking. There were couple of niggas from the way enjoying the night reminiscing on Thomas and how it was coming up back in the days.

I clutched a forty-oz malt liquor bottle and stared down at 107th Avenue from seven stories up. Watching life in the hood, one nigga laid to rest and it keeps going endlessly like space. We mourned and hurt but our days never stop. I thought about what the pastor said at the burial, about starting out bravely with a gallant smile; for my friends 'sake and in his name, live and do all things the same. I chugged the forty.

I found myself wishing that my days wouldn't go on. It seemed easier to be dead. *But damn, when I'm dead, who's gonna look after my son and my moms…?*

I took another swig from the 40oz and continued to look down at society. There was a row of trucks parked on 160th street, nothing but tricked out Escalades, Yukons and Range Rovers, all sitting on huge chromed rims right across the street from the bodega.

The owners of the lavish rides were up on the rooftop, enjoying the night and trying to escape reality off beer, Hennessy and weed. I tried to trick out my '89 Mazda 626 with cheap alloy rims and tinted windows. It wasn't close to what these niggas pushed.

"Vince you good my nigga…?" S.S. asked me. He was Spoon's cousin. We went to high school together, were the same age and fucked the same bitches coming up.

The only difference between S.S. and me was that he owned a sixty thousand dollar truck and always stayed with a knot.

"Yeah, I'm good, just thinking about some shit," I replied casually.

"Here take a pull," he said passing me the dro.

He poured beer on the rooftop and said, "That's for my nigga, T. May he rest in peace. He'll be missed."

The rest followed doing the same thing. S.S. pulled out a .357 and said, "Yo we need to send my nigga, T out right. The niggas who murdered him is still breathing."

"My nigga, I'm down. Your beef is mine." Someone shouted.

"Fuck it; let's give this nigga a twenty one gun salute right now," S.S. said aiming his .357 into the air with his arm outstretched.

More guns were pulled and aimed at the night's sky. I waited for shots to start ringing. S.S. let off and soon an explosion of gunshots followed. I covered my ears and waited for the salute to end. It sounded like war on the rooftop. Seeing residents running, ducking and looking around made me laugh.

Empty shells covered the rooftop when it was over. S.S. and his niggas were high and ready to get into whatever.

Tyriq appeared on the rooftop soon after the shooting. Everyone gave him respect.

"Yo, it's sounded like Iraq up here," he joked.

"What's good?" S.S. greeted him with dap and a hug. "We lighting up the night for your brother."

Tyriq strutted around the rooftop clad in a Mitchell and Ness Jets throwback Jersey, jean shorts with beige Timberlands. He rocked a diamond platinum chain that gleamed brightly like the sun itself.

"Ayyite, Vince, what's good? You acting a fool with these niggs too?" he laughed.

"I'm wit it, came up to chill and get my thoughts together," I smiled.

"Ayyite, been a stressful, fucking day," he said.

I swallowed another mouthful of brew and stared at the neighborhood. Tyriq and the rest stood behind me.

"Yo S.S., y'all niggas bounce for a minute. I wanna have a word with my dude, ayyite?" Tyriq requested.

When the door shut, Tyriq stood next to me.

"What's on your mind, Vince?"

I had a lot on my mind, money, the funeral, my son, my baby moms, struggling to stay afloat.

"Nuthin' much, just enjoying the night," I responded.

"Ayyite, let me get a taste," he said pointing to the beer. I passed it and he took a mouthful. "Look at these muthafuckas here, late as usual."

I looked down and saw three police cars drive hastily up 107th Ave and five uniformed officers got out.

"Clown ass pigs," Tyriq laughed and pulled out a small wad of bills. "Let me give them a lil' sump'n for their efforts," he said tossing the wad of bills into the streets. Hundreds, fifties and twenties floated into the night's air, falling loosely to the ground.

I laughed.

"Look at that money. You think I give a fuck. I own this shit. The fucking world is ours for the taking. Who's gonna stop us?"

I peered at the lay of the land that was South Jamaica, Queens. These niggas have it lovely, I thought.

"C'mon, before I end up busting my gun," Tyriq said.

We walked down the piss-ridden, staircase and heard commotion. In the lobby, the police were harassing S.S. and his crew.

"Why y'all fucking with us?" S.S. shouted. "We ain't strap."

He raised his shirt. They got rid of the gats knowing the police would be around.

"Word, this some bullshit…!" Macky shouted.

He was pressed against the wall, looking upset. The cops tossed everyone against the wall. S.S. resisted.

"Fuck y'all! I ain't doin' a damn thing. Shoot me, muthafuckas!"

Two officers tried to tackle him to the floor, but S.S. swung and punched one in his face causing him to stagger and almost fall. Couple cops hit S.S. in the back with batons. He winced and collapsed.

"Yo, is that fuckin' necessary?" Tyriq shouted.

The crew was getting rowdy watching S.S. getting roughed-up by the NYPD and stepped forward to help him but were greeted by police issued Glocks.

"Back off!"

I witnessed the fire and prejudice in the eyes of the police. One more step could cause an explosion.

They put the iron bracelets on S.S. and brutally carried him outside. The officer who S.S. punched took pleasure in twisting S.S. arm making the 'cuffs tighter.

"You going to jail, nigga!" he cursed at S.S.

"Fuck you!" S.S. spat.

He was five-eight but tough and took shit from no one, not even the cops. His knuckle game was fierce and he had an itchy trigger finger to match.

The cops took away S.S. satisfying their adrenaline rush for the night. The lobby cleared out and quiet down soon afterwards. We were seething over the arrest but shit like that was common and we were used to it.

Tyriq looked at me and said, "Let's ride, too much drama round here, ayyite?"

"I'm wit' it…"

◇◇

Traffic was light on Hollis Avenue but the corner boys were out chilling in front of the bodegas gambling and peddling drugs to the fiends. It was a balmy night and besides the drama earlier, everything was peaceful. I sat in the backseat of Tyriq's burgundy Escalade listening to a mix CD. The air in the truck was saturated with weed smoke. I was quiet for most of the ride and listened to Tyriq and Tip talking about pussy. They didn't discuss too much business around me. I was high, chilling in the backseat. They were cautious.

Tip slowly drove slow and easy through Hollis. I was paranoid at first. Tip had a reputation and was known to be violent. He was one of Tyriq's top enforcers and was feared in the hood like the virus.

Tip was twenty-two with long cornrows to his back. In the summer, he wore tight fitted tank tops exposing dark chiseled physique. Past murders made his eyes cold. He was a loyal underling to the game.

Earlier we stopped at the USA diner on Merrick Blvd and eaten. Tyriq picked up the tab. After that we went to see one of Tyriq's bitches on Linden then ended up here in Hollis.

My nervousness subsided after we were high. He joked with Tyriq. I never heard him laugh and when he did, it was kind of cynical.

"Why you quiet back there, Vince?" Tyriq asked turning his head to get a view of me.

"I'm chillin," I said.

"A nigga almost forgot that you were back there," Tyriq said.

"I'm high as a muthafucka," I laughed.

"Yeah, ayyite, that's that bomb shit right there. I got pounds for sale," Tyriq informed.

"Yeah, this shit gotta nigga wanting to fuck," I said.

"You need pussy nigga?" Tyriq asked.

"I could fuck wit' a blowjob or sump'n," I said, slouching down in the back.

Tip turned and cracked a smile.

"What's up? That nigga need to ease his tension?" Tip asked.

"That nigga is craving pussy. Shit, he needs to take his mind off pussy for a moment, ayyite? And think about business," Tyriq said.

"Yeah, we gotta talk," I said.

"Yeah, we gonna talk, but not tonight. Tonight, we're gonna party like rock-stars. My brother, Thomas is in the fucking ground right now, but we gonna live and do us for that nigga," Tyriq proclaimed. "Yo, Tip, take us to that spot in Mt. Vernon where the bitches be at."

Tip smiled and drove the truck toward the Grand Central Parkway.

Seven

Sue's Rendezvous in Mt. Vernon was a haven for high class pussy and big money. The place was not only infamous for the exquisite ladies who danced but also the celebrities from the music world and gangland passing through in search of a good time. Tuesday nights were special. The spot would be crammed with pussy, money, and ballers.

Tip parked and three of us walked into the club expecting the best. Pussy relaxed me, and tonight was no different. The only thing that was scary was being in Sue's with dozens of beautiful women dancing topless and having broke pockets. I kept my composure while following Tip and Tyriq inside. *Freak me baby*, by Silk blared through the speakers.

Tyriq gave the bouncers dap and fifty dollar tips. He was a regular and we were led to an empty booth in the back that easily sat a dozen people.

R. Kelly's *Honey Love* blared through the club. I sat and gazed at a beautiful honey-brown, topless stripper seductively clinging to a pole, her thick hips gyrating to the smooth tune. She was clad in a string thong, clear six inch wedge heels, rich, thick, black hair flowing from under a white cowgirl hat. The hat was different and that did it for me.

"Ayyite, you like that?" Tyriq asked nudging me.

"I could get wit' dat ass," I replied.

"You lookin' like you ready to spend some money," Tyriq said.

I laughed embarrassed that I had no money and continue watching the stage. Money sprinkled everywhere and the music switched up from R to Jigga.

A waitress came over and placed two bottles of Cristal along with champagne glasses in front of us. Tyriq gave her a c-note. She smiled and asked if we were good. We nodded and focused on the other girls surrounding us.

"I know you had Cristal before, right Vince?" Tyriq asked.

"Nah," I said.

Tyriq popped open the bottle and began pouring.

"Ayyite, tonight we getting fucked up," he announced drinking from the bottle.

Tip sat back casually, his black tank-top showing off his physique, huge ice around his neck, with a deadly gaze fixed on the crowd. I was hanging around ballers. But the lint gathering in my pocket was the only thing balling on me. My thoughts were soothed by Allure's, *My love is the Shit.*

From the ballers to the working man, there were all types in the club. I took a few sips of Cristal and decided I needed something else.

Tyriq whispered something to Tip. He reached in his pockets and passed something to Tyriq.

"Here you go my nigga," Tyriq said leaning close to me.

I saw a wad of bills held together by a few rubber bands in his hand.

"What's wit' dis?" I asked.

"Just take it," he offered.

"For me…?" I replied skeptical about taking the money.

I didn't want to owe him. I was always my own man and never needed handouts from anyone except my mother.

"Yo Tyriq, I don't wanna owe you, man." I stated.

"Don't insult me, Vince. We fam, ayyite. I'm looking out."

"Nah, I can't…I'm not wit' that."

"Take it and have a good time. I got plenty, ayyite?" he smiled.

Temptation, I knew what that was about. I was surrounded in a sea of pussy. Money was the bait used to catch a lap dance and get some pussy. I felt the urge but knew someday it might cost me more than I could afford.

I stared at shorti with the cowgirl hat. She twisted her lithe body around the pole like a pretzel. Her titties freely bounced. My dick got hard.

"Fuck it!"

I opened my hand and Tyriq passed me a wad.

"Do you, just don't give it all to one pussy," he joked.

"Let the games begin," I nodded not caring.

The thought of my father and the principles he expected me to live by flew the coop. I had climbed in the nest with Tyriq.

The huge wad of cash felt good in my hand. My heart raced as in a hustler's mile I went from nothing to the top of the devils' advocate. I didn't have to give the money back. It felt good.

I removed the rubber-bands and counted hundred after hundred-- four thousand dollars. Tyriq pulled out another wad and placed it on the table next to the champagne bottles.

He continued drinking. Among the ballers in the spot, Tyriq was a big man. His younger brother was buried this morning and he was acting nonchalant about it. This was his way of easing the pain, probably all part of a game.

The money in my hands had me thinking about bills that I could pay, clothes I could buy my son. Four thousand dollars may not be a lot to Tyriq, but it could do wonders for me. I thought about spending little and pocketing the rest for a rainy day.

But as the night went on, I ended up spending like I had it coming continuously. I got caught up in the hype with Tyriq, drinking and having pussy in my face like I was Hugh Hefner. Twenty-five hundred was burned in two hours. I had lap dances and spent half of the money on Star, the thick chick with the cowgirl hat. I bought her drinks, fondled her as she sat on my lap and tipped her with twenties.

I left the club with Star around three in the morning. She had her own ride, a black Honda Accord, and lived in Mt. Vernon. Once we were in her apartment, the both of us went at it, tearing at each other clothes with a keen lust to fuck the shit out of each other. I wasted no time throwing her into the doggystyle position and making waves out of that ass. For an hour strong the sex was crazy and I ended up passing out afterwards in her bed. Star went to sleep with my dick in her mouth.

Eight

The next morning, I awoke to the ringing of my cell. Forgetting where I was for a moment, I looked around the strange bedroom and was on the verge of freakin' out. Shaking the cobwebs from my brain, I quickly came to my senses. I felt Star's warm, butt-naked naked body next to me. Slowly I got it together and answered the call.

"Who this…?"

"Wake your ass up, nigga. That pussy good but we need to be out, ayyite?"

"Yo, I'm still in Mt. Vernon."

"Yeah I know where you at, I'm parked outside," he said to me.

"You outside…? How da fuck you know where she stay at?" I asked baffled.

"Yo, you think you the only baller that ho done fucked. Her pussy gets around faster than the latest Jay Z track. You wore a hat, right?"

"No doubt my nig," I replied.

"Good, cuz me and Tip ran a train on her couple weeks ago," he snickered.

"Word…?"

"Get dressed and come down, don't keep me waiting long, my nigga."

I jumped out of the bed. Star was asleep on her stomach, with that phatty in my view. She was eye candy fo' sure, but not wifey. I gathered up my clothing and threw on my jeans, T-shirt, and searched for my boots.

I went into her bathroom and washed that smell of pussy off me. Star yawned and looked up at me when I came out.

"You leaving, baby?"

"Yeah, my peoples are waiting for me outside," I said rushing.

I was about to walk out the door when I heard Star say, "Baby, before you leave, can you leave me a lil' sump'n?"

"What, you mean some paper?"

She nodded.

I stared at her full thick figure, with her big titties in my view, and thought about getting that number for a second round someday.

"How much you need?" I asked.

"A few hundred, maybe five," she said.

After I done spent about twelve-hundred on her in the club last night. I went into my pockets and pulled out the dwindling knot of money I still had. I looked at her and tossed a hundred dollar bill at her.

"That's it?" she replied with attitude.

Gold-digger fo' sure, I thought. I snickered, collected myself and kept it moving.

Outside, Tyriq was waiting in his Escalade.

"What's good wit' you?" I greeted him with a dap.

"That bitch asked you for a tip, right?" He asked.

"Yeah, how you know?"

"Yo, she a thirsty-ass bitch always got her fuckin' hands out. Shit, as much money my crew done blown on her, I need to drag her ass fuckin' downstairs and have her work a corner for me," he laughed.

"Where's Tip?" I asked.

"Takin' care of sump'n," he said driving off. "I know you hungry, nigga?"

"No digga…"

◇◇

We ate at a nearby IHop, chatting up old times. He updated me on Susan's pregnancy and their situation.

"Yeah, her pops definitely didn't like no nigga like me running up in his baby girl. Yo, Vince man, I got that bitch in pocket sump'n serious. She's made a few runs down south for me in the new Benz her daddy bought.

She was sneaking around, but once that bitch got pregnant, she came clean to her father about me. He deaded that bitch, trust fund gone and everything. Fuck her daddy. I got that bitch still makin' ends."

"Damn!" I said.

"But I saw you gettin' cozy wit' Asia. You fucked her again?"

I smiled.

"Ayyite, pussy is like a fuckin' drug to you."

"Best thing for a nigga to relax wit'," I joked.

Tyriq laughed. "Nigga, how many bitches you done fucked since we were kids?"

"Enough..."

"That's why you broke now nigga, always spending fuckin' papers on bitches. You should be gettin' that money, ayyite."

"Yeah, I know. Live and learn, right."

"I'm learning how to get fucking paid right now, locking shit down out here, ayyite?" Tyriq said.

"I'm wit' you."

Tyriq took a few bites out of his pancakes and I dined on waffles and eggs. I wished Spoon was with us, it would've been like we were all eighteen again.

It was reaching afternoon when we headed back to Queens. The sun shone brighter as the day wore on. I needed to shower and a nap.

"Yo, Vincent, how's your son doing?" Tyriq asked driving down the Grand Central.

"He's good."

"Ayyite, how old is he now, four?"

"Yeah, he's my lil' soldier," I stated.

"What about Chandra, you still fuckin' her?" Tyriq smiled.

"Nah, we been done wit."

"Word...? I remember she used to be at your crib all the time. Damn, I thought y'all was gonna get married and I was gonna be your best man and shit."

"Shit changed. She's doing her and I'm doing me."

"Ayyite, I hear that. But you could be really down, Vince. What you tryin' to do? You tryin' to find another nine to five or you want some serious paper in your pockets?"

"I'm trying to survive and I wanna take care of my son," I said.

"I respect that. But you need to step your game up, ayyite? In this world, you're either a somebody or a nobody. To put it simply, you either gonna be a hawk, or a fucking duck. A hawk takes what it wants, by swooping down and snatching up its prey quickly and fuckin' shit up with 'em claws and those big ass wings. Ducks, they lay around like a prey to everything. You living like a duck, Vince. Falling prey to society, you letting these fuckin' crackers make decisions for you."

"I hear you," I nodded.

"Me Vince, I'm an entrepreneur. I run these streets. Ain't no cracker telling me how to handle biz, Vince?"

"I'm wit' you."

"This game, the hustling it's *my* American dream right. I didn't have to go to no college and take out loans to get what I got. I don't owe no-fuckin'-body. Muthafuckas out here–they owe me."

"I'm wit' you."

"You my nigga Vince…"

"No doubt…"

"We like fuckin' brothers. You always had my back and I always have yours. You like the one nigga I trust out here, cuz I don't trust no-fuckin'-body. Shit, my moms and your moms went to church together. Ain't that some crazy shit?"

"I know," I replied.

"I hate to see my brother struggling. You're better off without that job anyway. In Africa, we had mutha fuckin' dynasties. We were the first peoples to live like kings. The fuckin' Europeans stripped that away from us. They made us their bitch, had us slaving in their fields. I refuse to be anybody's bitch," Tyriq stated.

I nodded.

"I'd rather die on my feet, than…"

"… Live on my knees…" I said finishing the statement. He looked at me, smiling.

"Ayyite my nigga, I follow that rule every fuckin' day." We exchange dap and Tyriq continued. "You tired of living on your knees, Vince? I know you want mo'-better."

I quietly peered out the truck thinking about what Tyriq was saying.

"Why you need me?" I asked.

"I need a nigga to make a few runs out of town for me," he informed.

We got off the Van Wyck expressway. Tyriq continued to talk, trying to coax me. He reached into his pockets and pulled out a wad of hundreds.

"See this here, Vince," he said waving the knot, "this is what it's all about. This is power right here. With money like this niggas and bitches are gonna be on their knees ready to suck your dick for a piece. This is chump change right here. I'm getting mines."

I saw a baby-blue Lexus pull up beside us with two fine females sitting in the front seat. I smiled flirtingly at them. To my surprise the driver smiled waving politely at me. We stared at each other for a few.

"See, that's what the fuck I'm talkin' about! You getting distracted by pussy when I'm tryin' to put some paper in your pockets," Tyriq shouted.

"I was just lookin'…"

"Fuck them hos and do you."

"You right," I said.

The light changed, and soon we were on the block again. I pulled out the money left over from last night and handed it to him outside my crib.

"Here, yo…thanks," I said.

"What's this? Fuck you think you're doin', Vince?"

Tyriq looked at me as if I had disrespected him.

"I'm giving you back what I got left."

"Yo, do I look like I need that shit back?"

"I'm sayin wit'…"

"Take that and buy your son some toys."

"You sure…?"

"Vince, that's your money, ayyite?"

"Thanks, yo," I said, stuffing the knot back into my pocket.

"Holla at a nigga…"

"No doubt, one," I said giving him a loud dap thinking a nigga gotta live. I walked to my mom's crib.

I was about to take an afternoon nap when I heard the phone ring. I picked up.

"Hello?"

"Hello, can I please speak to Mr. Vincent Grey." A woman's voice said.

"This is he…"

"I'm calling about your job application to UPS. We're giving out a courtesy call to let you know that your application is on file."

"Oh, good, so when are y'all hiring?" I said excitedly.

"Not until the end of the year, November."

"When…?"

"November… we usually hire more help around that time, to help out with the holiday season, and we'll give you a call around then."

"November…? Why the fuck you called me for if y'all ain't hiring right now?" I barked.

"Excuse me…" she was shocked.

"Lady, I need a fuckin' job now. Fuck I'm gonna wait five months for y'all to call," I said hanging up.

I fell back on the bed. After a few winks, my moms came in and told me Tyriq was on the phone. It was five in the evening.

She passed me the cordless and raised her eyebrows before walking out the room.

"Tyriq, what's up?" I asked.

"You sleep?"

"Nap," I said.

"I don't know what you do most, ayyite? Fuckin' with da bitches or sleepin'. Meet me in an hour," he said.

"An hour…?"

"Yeah, at the corner of your block…"

I hung up and started getting ready. My mother came back in the room.

"So, you and Tyriq are best friends again?"

"We always been cool," I replied.

"How's that boy? I haven't seen him in a long time."

"He's good," I said, throwing on my Tims. I knew where the conversation with her was going.

"You know, Vincent, I heard a lot of things about that boy. Is he into drugs?" my mother asked. She already knew the answer. "He's always driving nice expensive trucks."

"I guess..."

"Boy, don't lie to me. I still talk to his mother. You think that I don't know?"

"Why'd you ask me then?"

"I know he's your friend, and y'all grew up together, but don't let that boy get you into any trouble. You hear me, Vincent? You're a good man. If your father was alive, you know what he'd say. He loved you and wanted nothing but the best for you. Don't disappoint him."

"Yeah, I'm wit' you, ma."

There was a short pause as both of us reflected on the memory of dad.

"I miss him, ma. Sometimes it seemed so much easier when he was around."

My mother came closer, pulled me into her arms, embracing me.

"I know baby. I miss him too. But you have to be strong for me, for the family. I know things are hard now, Vincent. In due time, baby… God speed…"

Nine

I waited for Tyriq on the corner of my block smoking a Black & Mild. It was boiling outside, and I felt like I was about to melt in my wife-beater, denim jeans, and timberlands. My mother's words were eating me up on the inside as I waited for Tyriq to show. I had to do this one thing, make a couple thousands, put myself above water and shit.

Around six in the evening a burgundy Escalade pulled up.

"Get in, Vince," Tyriq said.

I jumped in giving him dap and he pulled off. He was sporting a fresh throwback Bulls Jersey and a matching fitted.

"Damn, nigga, you don't sleep, huh?" I joked.

"I'll sleep when I dead," he responded.

"Yo, I'm in," I said feeling my heart race.

"Now you bout ya biz," he nodded.

"I just need to make some quick paper, get me back on my feet and then I'm goin' back to school," I added.

"Yo, ain't nuthin' wrong wit' that. I need some educated niggas having my back in this game. Yo, some of these young corner-niggas that I got workin' for me, they bust guns and can hold it down. But when it comes to simple math and some intelligent shit, they dumb as rocks, Vince," he stated.

We drove down Supthin Blvd.

"You hungry?" he asked.

"Nah, I'm good."

"Ayyite, tonight I want you to meet some of the fellows."

"That's cool. But Tyriq, one thing, I don't have shit wit' this game.

And I ain't no killer. I just wanna make some money, that's all. I ain't out here trying to kill anybody."

He stared at me before replying.

"What da fuck you mean you ain't a killer? Shit Vince, everybody's a killer. You just don't know it yet."

"What'd you mean by that?"

"Everybody's got two fuckin' sides to them…good, bad, slut, wifey… fuck it. Everybody's got that twin self they try hard to contain. You just ain't brought yours out yet."

"What, you tryin' to kick psychology now?"

"Ayyite, if a nigga come after you… better yet, if a nigga come after Chandra or your son, your mother, what you gonna do?"

I hesitated and Tyriq answered for me. "Yo, I tell you what you're gonna do, Vince. You're gonna take that nigga out before he come get at you and your fam. No doubt about that, right?"

I shrugged.

"You'd be a fool if you didn't lay that nigga out. You feel me?"

"Yeah, I feel you."

"That's how it is with this game, Vince. If a nigga threatens your family, your money, your business, you gonna lay him down and make sure he stays down. That's survival. That's how it's played out here, we family. We ride together and we die together. My shit is tight, ayyite? Strong, cuz out here, only the strong survives… ayyite? It's like the jungle, Vince. We lions, the cannibals in this fuckin' concrete jungle and them junkies, the competitors, the haters, and even five-o, are prey. They are weak. If they try to come at us on some disrespectful shit, we tear and shred them like muthafuckin' lions in Africa. In this here game you better fuckin' respect strong and hard, cuz if you don't, then this shit is gonna come back and bite you on the ass… I came up in da game strong, cuz I put my heart into this shit. I don't care if you're peddling drugs on some dirty ass street corner day after day. Be the best hustler on that corner. Sell them rocks like your package is the last package on the earth. That's what I expect. You do this with heart, go at it a hundred and ten percent or don't do it at all. A hundred and ten percent…?" Tyriq asked.

"Yeah, my nigga I'm wit' you," I replied.

"Let's go shopping, tonight, you rolling fresh."

◇◇

Tyriq, Spoon, and I got out of Tyriq's new Yukon sitting on 24" spinning chromed rims. It felt so good, as the three of us approached Occasions on Merrick Blvd. Dressed in Jockey waffle crewneck shirt, denim jeans, and suede shoes, I was feeling like a don. Tyriq sported a Mitchell & Ness '65 Philadelphia 76ers jacket, denim jeans, and white Nikes. Spoon rocked a green Pelle Pelle jacket, T-shirt, matching limited edition Air Force Ones and Enyce sweat pants.

Hordes of people were waiting to get in. The ladies were all looking sexy. We walked through the thick crowd heading for the front. No one said a word to us. Two brawny bouncers let Tyriq and Spoon through immediately. It became a problem when I tried to follow.

"You gotta wait," he told me in a stern voice, pushing me back.

"Tyriq, what's good?" I called out.

"This Vince, he down," Tyriq said.

"I'm sorry…ah, I didn't know." The bouncer nodded.

I eyed him as I passed. The nightclub was on and popping. Music bumping and the ladies were looking good. I followed closely behind Tyriq and Spoon to the VIP. where bottles of Cristal, Moet and beautiful women flooded the room.

I never experienced anything like this. The love and respect was overwhelming. Everyone greeted Tyriq, especially Spoon with mad love.

The ladies stuck to them like white on rice. I was excited but nervous. I knew a few but many didn't know me. It was a new world for me.

Tip was clad in his usual wife-beater, flexing his biceps and having a shortie on his lap. I smiled when she started nibbling his ear.

Tyriq threw his arm around me, while clutching a bottle of Moet.

"Yo, this my nigga, Vince, right here. He's family, ayyite? So y'all treat this nigga with respect."

The deejay had the spot jumping with jams and I was right up on the ladies getting my game on.

During the course of the night, I became familiar with the crew and bitches. Tip, Killer Ty and Bones were Tyriq's main enforcers. John-John,

Malik, Red, Loc and Spoon were lieutenants.

John-John was a huge gorilla looking linebacker mutha fucka, who was six-three and two hundred and seventy-five pounds easy, with a lazy eye. Red, was a high yellow slim looking nigga with short curly hair. Malik was a stout looking muthafucka, with a thick black beard and heavily tattood. Loc was a light skinned, pretty boy. His hair was styled like Snoop Dogg and he had gray eyes.

Tyriq was lounging, sipping Cristal with a bitch. Tip walked over and whispered something in his ear. The look on Tyriq's face changed. He got up with a sense of urgency.

"Yo, Tyriq, everything good…?" I asked when he was close to me.

"I gotta go handle sump'n. Enjoy yourself Vince," he said rushing from the VIP with Tip, Killer Ty, and Bones following.

"Vince, let me holla at you in private for a moment," Spoon said.

"No doubt," I said following him out.

We walked out for fresh air. I looked at Spoon and was shocked when he suddenly rushed me and threw me against a wall. His forearm was pressed against my windpipe. His grip around me was tight.

"What the fuck is wrong wit' you nigga!" I shouted.

"What the fuck is you doing?" he barked.

"Fuck you talkin' about?"

"You think this thang is glamorous, muthafucka?" He exclaimed.

"What?" I asked confused.

Spoon let up on his grip and backed off.

"Tyriq shouldn't have brought you into this thang. It ain't you, Vince," Spoon said.

"What da fuck you mean this ain't me?"

"Nigga, you think this thang is just about money, ho's and clothes. You were doing good, nigga. You got your son. You had a job, yo. You're a civilian. This shit here will change a man, Vince. I don't wanna see you get caught up in this thang and get killed. You my nigga from back in the days and I respected you cuz you never got caught up in this thang we do. You weren't out here frontn' like most these niggas be doing. Your thang was tight."

"C'mon, Spoon, what else am I supposed to do? I got laid the fuck off and ain't no other jobs out there calling me. I gotta live and eat too, right? I'm just trying to make my money and do me."

"Not like this, Vince. You understand that once you get involved in this thang, ain't no going back. When you in, you're in deep."

"Spoon, I know how to handle myself. I ain't pussy."

"Vince, let me tell you something. See me…? I was born into this thang. You used to live across the street from me. Remember how my moms got down when I was young—three different niggas in the crib every night. Punk-ass niggas fuck my moms so she could score drugs. Yo, they used to shoot up right in front of me. My moms ain't give a fuck. As long as she got her drugs, she was good. But when everythang wasn't cool with her, yo, that bitch used to whip my ass, take out her frustration on me. That punk ass, Rolla move in with us, shit got even worse. You remember all 'em nights, po-po used to come to my crib, cuz the nigga beat my moms and me."

"What you trying to say?"

"I used to envy you, Vince. You ain't had to go through the thang I went through. Why you think I liked spending time over your house so much. I was able to get away from that hell hole. Your moms and pops were like family to me. I used to want to run away and move in across the street with you and your family. Growing up, all I knew were the drugs and the dealers. You don't need no thang like that."

"Yo, I'm just trying to make ends, get my shit right then get the fuck out."

He snickered and said, "Yeah, that's what they all say then they get greedy."

"That ain't me, Spoon."

"We'll see. We ain't kids anymore," he said walking away.

I remained outside for a moment, thinking. *Am I getting over my head in this thing? Nigga, just get yours and get out*. I sighed.

Ten

Tyriq

Tyriq and his crew of three drove into Hollis. It was ten minutes passed two in the morning and the streets of Hollis, Queens was quiet and peaceful. Tyriq gripped the 9mm riding shotgun. He peered out the window thinking about his brother's death. He knew the culprits responsible for his brother's death would come out of hiding soon--and they did.

Sham and Marlon were knuckleheads from the neighborhood. They dabbled in everything from hustling, grand theft auto, pimping and murder. Thomas was killed several days ago beefing over money and pussy. They hid in Connecticut after the murder with bitches they'd met a year ago. Young, dumb and full of cum, they smoked, drank, fucked, and didn't have a second thought about dropping bodies for quick cash. They made fast illegal cash, and spent it on pussy, drugs, bling and sneaks.

Sham and Marlon always hung out at Wave carwash on Springfield Blvd. It was no surprise that on their first night back in town, they were chilling in front of the carwash. Sham stood in front of his prized '68 red Camaro holding a beer in one hand and smoking on a joint with the next. He was a thug who felt he had something to prove to everyone, while Marlon was a developing crack-head, who loved to get high and be with his boys.

Several men stood around the two, as they gambled, drank, and shouted out obnoxious remarks to the ladies that passed.

"Your roll, nigga," Sham shouted out, taking a mouthful of the brew.

Seth shook the dice in his fist and quickly let them lose. He rolled a straight four, losing a hundred dollars to Sham.

"Yeah, give me my money," Sham hollered.

Seth handed over five twenties to Sham.

"Yo, run it," Seth suggested.

"Ain't nothing," Sham said.

The dice game continued. Marlon waited for a pick up. He was fidgety, looking around for a quick high.

Seth looked at Marlon and shook his head in disgust.

"Yo, why do you even fuck with that nigga?" He asked Sham.

"We go way back. He always got my back," Sham answered. "Just roll the fuckin' dice."

"You buggin' having a crack-head watch your back," Seth said shaking the dice.

Marlon saw the black BMW pulled up near the light and he quickly walked over.

"Why you late?" he asked the driver of the car.

"I'm here, right!" barked the driver.

"Fuck it, let me get two," Marlon said, leaning into the car and handing him the cash.

Marlon quickly snatched the rocks and wandered off to enjoy his high somewhere private. He was crossing Springfield Blvd without looking at the black truck speeding down on him.

"There's one of them right there," Tip shouted. He gunned the truck in Marlon's direction.

"Hit that muthafucka!" Tyriq said. He cocked the 9mm.

Marlon was like a deer caught in headlights when he saw the truck speeding in his direction. Within seconds, flesh and bones collided with metal and speed. There was a loud thud and Marlon was pinned under the vehicle with great intensity. His head split open like a melon.

"What the fuck!" Sham shouted rushing from the dice game when he heard the chaos.

He saw his man crushed under the truck and became enraged.

"Oh shit!" he screamed.

The doors to the truck flew open. Sham tried to reach for his .357

and was seconds too late. A burst of gunfire from two Mac-10s violently greeted him. He tried to run but the bullets tore into his frame like it was paper causing him to shake. A few rounds ate at his face.

Killer Ty and Bones enjoyed the massacre, squeezing death into Sham and Marlon like it was open season. Their eyes were darkened with murder.

Tyriq watched his two henchmen quickly throw the streets of Queens into chaos. Sham and Marlon's people fled when they heard gunfire.

Sham was sprawled out on the cold concrete. His body contorted from the vicious attack. Marlon wasn't any better. Killer Ty and Bones jumped back into the truck and sped off.

"Bitch asses! Ayyite, now my brother can rest in peace." Tyriq sat back holding the 9mm.

Eleven

My first run had me nervous a bit. I was transporting a mule carrying a few kilos to Albany. Tyriq had an operation brewing. He needed someone who could speak Spanish and I could. My grandmother on my mother's side taught me Spanish since I was six years old. But she died when I was thirteen. Tyriq also needed me because I had a clean driver's license and was a new face on I-95 and to State police, if pulled over.

We linked up at one of Tyriq's stash houses in Queens. Tyriq had just received a sizeable shipment from the Jamaicans and was ready to distribute the product.

There were three girls and I was introduced to Shae, the mule going to Albany. She had a honey brown complexion and long, brown hair. The other two were going to Kansas City, and Charlotte. I watched as they readied the work for delivery. It was a surprise that Spoon or anyone of Tyriq's lieutenants weren't present. Twenty-four kilos of cocaine were on a large extended table.

"Y'all get ready to carry this work, ayyite," Tyriq said.

The three girls started undressing. They were down to their underwear. I was the only one who seemed distracted by them. Everyone else stayed focused on shipping out the product. I was seated in a chair, flipping through a magazine trying not to stare.

Three padded white suits were handed to each girl and they began putting them on. Shae strapped herself into one. The fat suits were made out of soft fiber clamped around the body by two straps. She looked pregnant.

Each suit was padded with a special lining that concealed six kilos apiece. Everything was done and the girls started to get dressed again. They came in wearing tight jeans, stilettos, and sexy tops. They walked out clad in sweatpants, large T-shirts, and sundresses.

It was ten in the morning and we were looking at a three hour ride. I was ready to get into the rented silver, four-door Pontiac Grand Am and get shit over with. I had all the information needed for the trip.

"Vince, let me holla at you for a sec," Tyriq said.

I nodded.

"Rule number one, keep your fuckin' mouth shut. Rule number two, be about your business and keep sharp. Rule number three; never mix business with pleasure. And rule number four; get that money and do it right."

We locked eyes for a minute and then he said, "Ayyite, be back here tomorrow, my nigga."

I nodded again. We had to stay the night in Albany because Tyriq felt it was safer. Cameras were everywhere and he knew big brother was watching.

Tyriq didn't want guns in the car, and everything was handled with latex gloves, so there wouldn't be traces of drug resedue anywhere on the car. I was to meet up with one of Tyriq's men at a certain location for protection and dependable transaction. Shae already knew the area and the man.

Ten thirty we were into the Pontiac and soon traveling to Albany.

Shae was quiet the entire ride. She looked beautiful pregnant. I listened to Biggie and Pac and thought about what I'd do with the ten grand Tyriq was paying me. I arrived in Albany at three in the afternoon.

We were to immediately meet at the Bus terminal over by Hamilton and Green with this dude called, Giant.

I pulled up by the bus station and Shae made a call. She told me to pull to the side and wait. I parked on Hamilton Street, across the street from the Ramada Inn and waited.

"I'll be right back," Shae said getting out of the car.

I started looking around, trying to be observant. The area wasn't busy. A few people waiting for the scheduled buses arriving and departing.

Tilting the seat back, I turned up a biggie track and nodding my head to *Notorious Thugs,* trying to remain calm.

The sudden knocking on the passenger window scared the shit out of me. It was Shae waving her hand, gesturing for me to follow her. I got out and she led me to the Ramada.

We walked in together, heading to the elevators. There was a small, frail white girl at the front desk that looked uninterested in us. She was too busy on the phone and barely glanced our way. Once in the elevator, Shae let out a sigh.

"You okay?" I asked.

She looked so real that for a second I forgot it was a stunt and I thought she was pregnant. We got off at the second floor and I followed her to room 204. She knocked on the door three times and waited. The door opened and a hefty man, in a sleeveless dark T-shirt, who was about five-nine came into view. He had braids, a thick goatee and sported wire-rimmed frames. His arms were huge and his chest stuck out like he was about to explode.

He moved to the side, we entered and he locked the door behind us. There were two 9mm's with silver handles on the bed and a shotgun in the corner. Giant looked like he didn't take any chances.

"How many…?" Giant asked Shae removing his glasses.

"Six," Shae responded rubbing her belly.

Giant nodded, "Yo, your boy good?" he asked.

"Yeah, this is Tyriq's homeboy."

Giant stared at me for a moment, sizing me up. His arms were inked with tattoos and he kept a scowl on his face. "Yo, what happened to S.S?" he asked.

"The other dude got locked up for hitting on a cop," she said.

Giant let out a stressful sigh and shook his head like he was annoyed. Then he went over to the bed, picked up a gun and slid a clip in.

"Ozone gonna meet us up on Clinton Street tonight. We got a few hours to chill. This is y'all room, so act normal and don't go anywhere but from here to the lobby until the package is dropped off. Understood?"

"Yeah," I said.

"Don't fuck this up," Giant said glaring at me.

"Yo, I'm good," I repeated. He was aiming his attention toward me when he said it and I didn't like it.

I knew none of the key players in Albany and was only a driver. I knew to mind my business, get shit done and be out back to Queens in one piece. I didn't give a fuck about Giant or Ozone. Once I got back to Queens, I'd be ten-thousand dollars richer and it'd be all good.

Giant stashed his guns in a holster and placed the shotgun in a duffle bag. He then casually walked out the room.

I yawned, stretched and sprawled across one of the twin beds, trying to relax. I watched TV while Shae began making a call on her cell. I thought about fucking her. Staring at her back, I knew it wasn't happening.

I flipped through different channels. There wasn't shit on. Shae finally got off the phone.

"You could come out of that suit, ain't you hot?" I asked.

"I'm okay. I'll feel more comfortable when this shit is dropped off," she said.

"How long have you been moving shit for Tyriq?" I asked.

"Long enough," she returned, being short with me.

"Okay," I said.

It was clear that she didn't want to be bothered. I wanted to fuck that smart ass attitude out of her, but let it be. Shae took a nap and I watched some TV to kill time. Three hours later there was a loud knock at the door. I got up and went to the door.

"Who is it?" I asked.

"Giant…"

It was time. We gathered up our things and followed him to a white Tahoe sitting on 24" chromed rims. Half hour-later, we were on Clinton Street ready to link up with Ozone.

Clinton Street was in the grimy section of town. It was littered with run down row houses and looked like a bomb had hit some parts of it. Crack-heads and hustlers sprinkled up and down the block conducting business in the midst of the dilapidated structures.

Giant parked and I helped Shae out from the backseat. Holding her hand, I guided her to the location. It was another badly maintained row of houses with thugs lingering out front.

Sunlight was coming to an end bringing dusk. I didn't want to be caught here when night covered this hood.

"You speak Spanish?" Giant asked me.

"Yeah…"

"Good."

One of the young thugs approached us. He was shirtless with his upper body covered in tattoos. He rocked a big chain around his neck, a doo-rag and Timberlands. His demeanor said he had juice in the hood.

"Giant, what's good?" he greeted.

"What's poppin, Everyday?" Giant replied.

Everyday looked over at me with a screw face and asked, "You gotta problem with me, puta!"

"Nah," I replied.

We followed him down some tattered wooden stairs into the basement. This was a large factory where six workers were readying the work for street distribution. Wu-Tang's *Protect ya neck* blared out a portable radio. My heart race as we went to a room in the back. Ozone was there. He was ghetto-rich. Ozone's attention was on a fine mamacita with thick hips like J-Lo and long braids.

"Ozono, el paquete está aquí," Everyday announced.

"Everyday, ¿Quién es este nuevo mutha fucker, y donde esta S.S?" Ozone asked.

Everyday shrugged and said, "No se, nunca he pedido."

Ozone wanted to know what happened to S.S. Everyday had no idea.

I answered Ozone's question. "Sorry for the trouble on my behalf, S.S. got caught up in a situation in Queens. So I'm here to replace him. ¿Hay un problema con eso?" I asked.

Everyday and Ozone looked taken aback. Ozone looked at me and said, "So you speak Spanish."

"Si," I replied.

Ozone smiled. "Please, let's get down to business then." He looked at his female companion and said, "Jessica, nos deja por un momento."

She walked out the room. Shae undressed removing the suit and placed it on the table. Everyday undid the suit carefully pulling out keys out of the lining. Everyday smiled, holding two keys in his hand. "Pure white gold," he said.

When the product was removed, Ozone handed a black duffle bag to me.

"A hundred and fifty-thousand upon delivery," Ozone said.

I took the bag and counted the cash.

"That's what's up," I said.

We stacked the money into the lining of the suit and Shae put it back on.

"What's your name?" Ozone asked.

"Vince…"

"I like your swagger. Tell Tyriq, business is good up top and I'll be giving him a call soon," he said.

I nodded and walked out. We left for the Ramada.

"I need a shower," Shae said, walking into the bathroom. I was sprawled out on my bed staring at TV, thinking. The package was dropped off and I was ten-thousand dollars richer. It was easy money for once. At my old airline job I couldn't make ten-thousand dollars in one month, even with overtime.

I smiled. I was in Albany, alone in a room with a beautiful woman and I had some money to spend. I heard the shower running and thinking about Shae's beautiful, petite figure wrapped around me got my dick hard.

I removed my shirt exposing my six -pack. It was a humid night and the air conditioner in the room wasn't making the room any cooler. I sat at the foot of the bed thinking about finally being able to do for my son.

Shae stepped out the bathroom with a white towel wrapped around her. Her hair was wet and I couldn't help but admire her.

"You got a problem with your fucking eyes?" she barked pulling out fresh panties and bra out of her bag.

"Yo, why you giving me such a hard time, beautiful? What you think I'm about?" I asked.

She glared at me and said, "I know your type, cocky, arrogant and you probably got women all over. What, you wanna fuck me! Just because we're sharing a room doesn't mean i'm giving you some pussy. Y'all niggas are all alike"

I chuckled. "Luv, you don't even know what I'm about. You're working for Tyriq just like me."

"I don't have a choice," she replied.

"That's bullshit, we all got choices."

"Well, you don't know my situation," she said.

"And you don't know mines," I spat back.

She was shocked at my comeback. I dug her attitude and respected her.

I stood and said, "Listen, This here is temporary for me, until I get some dough saved and get back on my feet."

I began telling her about my situation, from the troubles with my pops and how he died, with my moms losing her house, to losing my job and needing to provide for my son.

I threw my shirt back on and slid into my boots. I needed a walk. Shae was quiet as I walked by her and had my hand on the doorknob.

"My son has autism," she said.

I slowly made my way back into the room and caught her gaze. Her eyes were sad and her mind seemed troubled.

"I'm sorry to hear that."

"He's three and he needs a lot of treatment, and that cost money. I had him when I was sixteen and his father doesn't care for him at all. He says it's my fault that our son is retarded. He called his own son retarded. His father makes tons of money in the streets, but don't give me a dime, cuz he doesn't make handicap kids, that what he tells me. So I gotta do for him, alone."

Shae started getting ready for bed. She was young and scared, I understood.

"I'm going to the store, you want anything?" I asked.

"No, thanks," she said.

"I'll be back."

I stared at her before walking out the room.

"If the world didn't suck, then we'd fall off."

She smiled.

"You have a beautiful smile."

I walked out the room feeling good knowing that I wasn't the only one with problems. Some problems are much greater than others. I took a quick walk searching to forget about my situation in Queens. Tonight I wanted to be new.

Twelve

It was like a breath of fresh air when Tyriq handed me the small envelope filled with hundred-dollar bills. I wore a huge smile on my face. So much money in my hands, now bills could get paid and the many things I could get me and my son, clouded my mind.

"Ayyite, Vince, you did good," Tyriq complimented.

We sat in his parked truck, watching the night, puffing Black & Mild, I stuffed the envelope in my pocket.

"I'm gonna need for you to do another run for me soon."

I was feeling dubious but never let it get in the way. "Where to…?"

"Philly."

"Never been there," I told him.

"You'll love it out there, it's only about an hour and half ride," he said.

"Shae coming…?" I asked.

He smiled, took a few pulls and said, "You feeling that, huh."

"She cool," I smiled nodding.

"You fucked her in Albany?"

"Nah, we kicked it," I said. My mind started wondering if Tyriq had fucked Shae. I was too scared to know the truth. I let it be.

"Talk…?" Tyriq said.

I was ready to hop out his truck and get some sleep.

"Yeah, I'm gonna give you call. And be ready for that trip."

I got out not trying to even think of another trip. Tyriq looked like he wasn't gonna take any shorts. Another ten grand in the bank wouldn't be too bad, though.

◇◇◇◇◇◇◇◇◇◇◇◇◇◇◇◇◇◇◇◇◇◇◇◇◇◇◇◇◇◇◇◇◇◇◇◇◇◇◇

It would be a week before I'd leave for Philly. The following day I stashed some of the money under my mattress and went shopping on Jamaica Avenue with the rest. I picked up some things for my son, and myself. It felt good not worrying about pricing shit. Whatever my eyes rested on, I was able to afford. I hit up so many sneaker and clothing stores, that the money felt endless.

I went into the Coliseum mall on 165th street and walked downstairs into the jewelry exchange. Soon the owners were calling me to booths, each offering to give me a better price on any piece of jewelry. I had eight grand on me and kept reminding myself that *I'd pay bills, saving the rest for a rainy day*. That thought didn't last long.

I spotted an expensive necklace that would fit perfect around my neck. The last piece of jewelry I bought was back in '96.

"That piece right there…?" I asked the Hindu man behind the glass counter.

He removed the piece I was pointing at. "I'll give you good deal, my friend."

I examined it closer. It was a heavy white gold necklace matching 18K diamond cross pendant which would look impressive around my neck.

"For you, fifteen hundred…"

Treat yourself for once, Vince, I told myself. "I'll take it."

I walked out the mall feeling like I was on top of the world.

I knocked on Chandra's door carrying bags of clothes and toys for my son. I couldn't wait to see the look on my son's face when he saw me. I heard the radio playing so I knocked harder. The apartment door opened and Chandra stood in front of me looking so good in a pair of tight blue jeans and a tight T-shirt that highlighted her thick breasts.

"Vincent," she said, wide eyed. "Why didn't you call?"

"I was in the area. I got some stuff for my son." I held up the bags.

"Oh…but I got company."

"Yo, I'm here to see my son," I blurted.

"And you should've called first," she repeated standing in the doorway and blocking the view inside.

"Chandra, I don't give a fuck who you got in your apartment, I'm not here for you. I'm only here to see my son and give him the gifts that I got for him," I said. I was lying. I wanted to see her.

She sighed and stepped aside, allowing me entrance. I walked in and was upset to see my son sitting on the lap of the same dreadlock dude I had the stare-down with from before.

"Daddy," my son shouted jumping up and running to me. I scooped him up in my arms hugging him tightly.

"What's up lil' man. You miss me?" I asked.

"Yes, daddy," he said hugging me.

"Guess what."

"What?"

"Daddy's got some gifts for you."

"Yeah…" My son beamed with joy when he saw the three bags.

I remembered that Chandra had company and wished the nigga would disappear. He was in a black and gray tracksuit. His long dreads tied together neatly in a ponytail and sporting a nice Rolex and diamond studs in his ears. It felt awkward with him being there.

Chandra felt the tension and came over to introduce us. She stood between us, glanced at him and me and said, "Vincent, this is Jamal…Jamal, this is Vincent, my son's father."

He gave me a slight head nod, but I didn't return it. I tried to let his smirk not affect my mood. My son tugged at my shirt and then went digging into one of the bags.

"Daddy…daddy, you got me toys?" he asked excitedly.

"Daddy got you plenty of things." I said squatting next to him pulling out a remote control car.

"Wow!" my son exclaimed.

It was like Christmas day for him. I bought Vinny name brand clothes and top of the line toys.

"You must've found a great job," Chandra said bewildered.

A look of disproval greeted her. She backed off knowing what my stare meant. Being around my son, I kept my cool. It made me beam with joy watching my son pulling out toys.

"Thank you daddy," my son said.

"Well ain't you the Santa Clause," Chandra said. Her arms were folded across her chest and she was eyeing me suspiciously.

Vinny reached into the bag with the PS2 game system and screamed. "Wow! Mommy, I got another one," my son hollered.

"Another one…?" I questioned.

"Yeah, daddy…Uncle Jamal bought me one too."

"What?"

I was furious.

"Mi heard, lil' Vinny talk about di PS2, and mi took da time out ta buy him one," he said in thick Jamaican accent. He got up off the couch and walked over.

"You his fucking father…?"

"Vincent," Chandra shouted.

I glared at him with hatred.

"Bredren, mi respect ya position…mi ain't tryin' to intrude."

"Like hell you ain't nigga!"

He shrugged and walked over to Chandra. "Chandra, tell ya bloodclaat friend, him want no trouble fi mi…mi a real shotta bwoy, mind ya nah get cap inna ya rassclaat face," he said.

"What da fuck you sayin'!" I shouted getting closer. "Speak fucking English, nigga; this fucking America, not some third world town in Jamaica."

"Vincent, shut up!" Chandra yelled getting between us like a referee.

Tears were forming in my son's eyes and I said to him, "Everything okay, lil' man. We're just adults in a small dispute, nuthin' ain't gonna happen."

I looked up and saw Jamal pulling Chandra to the door by her arms. He back stepped, open the apartment door, and I heard him say, "Mi gwan go before mi get vex." I peeped them hugging and kissing before he walked out. "Ya no wah vex a man like me."

I couldn't wait for him to get the fuck out. When he was in the hallway, Chandra slammed the door and shouted, "Vincent, what's wrong with you?"

"What's wrong…?" I retorted. "I come up in here and see my son sitting on that nigga's lap. And he's been buying gifts like he's daddy. What's wrong with you?"

"I needed help and wasn't getting shit from you. What else am I suppose to do? He's looking-out. Now you wanna flip on me cause you gotta a little cash to spend? You wanna scream on me in my own place. I told you that I had company. And I told you to call before you come here," she screamed.

"That ain't no excuse to have that nigga around my son," I barked.

"You could be so damn impossible to deal with!"

We were screaming at each other and forgot our son. He was crying for us to stop fighting. I felt bad. I hugged him but resented what Chandra did. She was looking for a man who could give her financial security. Jamal looked like he had plenty of finance. I had to get my grind on.

Thirteen

I was alone on this trip crossing the Ben Franklin Bridge. It was nine pm., and fifteen kilos were stashed in hidden compartments in the car. I was to meet a man at a club in north Philly, near Broad Street and exchange car keys.

It was my first time in Philly. I didn't want to get lost and had mapped out the area. The ten grand coming to me wiped any nervousness away and put some pep in me. I was determined to get the job done.

Driving down Broad Street gazing at the structures and people I smoked a Black & Mild cigar. There were cuties outside Temple University, waiting for the bus. And seeing that, I knew Philly had a lot to offer me.

I was in a blue four-door Intrepid, bouncing to Biggie Smalls. The further north I traveled, the more gully it got.

A few Philly heads were hanging outside a run down looking gentlemen's club on Germantown Avenue. I didn't want to park the car too far away. So I quickly surveyed the area, driving around the block a few times and parked a few cars from the club.

I got out, secured the car and walked to the place. There weren't any lines. A bouncer doing a lousy search for guns charged me ten bucks to get in.

I took a long pull from the Black & Mild as I walked in. Ho's, tricks and dancers sprinkled the dimmed and seedy establishment. Beanie Sigel's *Stick 2 the Script* blared throughout the club. I eyed the two dancers on stage and smiled. They were butt-naked in stilettos sweating from shaven pussy, shaking their asses.

Money over bitches nigga stick 2 the
script…fuck a dirty bitch…

we cop we flip re-up get back on our shift...

The lyrics reminded me. Pussy could wait. I had too much money parked on the streets to be distracted by a bitch's smile. I scanned the area. There he was wearing a Jets Jersey at the end of the bar with a beer in his hand. The barstool next to him was empty. I quickly took the seat.

We both were quiet for a moment. I continued to smoke my black and he sipped on his beer. We kept our eyes peeled on a Hershey, nude thick ass doing it on stage.

"You need anything?" the bartender asked.

"Corona," I said.

A short moment later, she returned with the beer. I gave her a ten.

"Keep the change," I said.

"¿El esta aquí para el trabajo?" I asked in Spanish without turning to look at him, which meant, *is he here for the pick up*.

"Si," he replied.

I took a sip from my beer and subtly handed him the car keys. He nodded and passed me his. I informed him in Spanish that it was the blue Intrepid parked five cars down from the club on Germantown, and he said his ride was across the street, a white Honda Accord. He got up, took out his cell and quickly took a picture of me.

"Insurance," he uttered and then walked out the club.

I put the keys in my pocket, took a few more mouthfuls of beer and eyed the stage. One caught my eye. Her curvaceous, thick figure was wrapped in skin like night. When she moved her body shimmered, glistering like baby oil. Her long sensuous black hair tickled her back, her smile was golden. The tattoo on the small of her back, made her even sexier.

Our eyes locked briefly. She smiled liking what she'd seen. I drifted closer pulling out a wad of bills tipping her big Willie style. Tens, twenties rained on her. I quickly caught her attention.

She spread her legs like wings to a jumbo jet. Then took her fingers parted her sugar lips and played with her pussy. I watched, enjoying the show letting ten dollar bills chase her.

"That's right, baby, make it rain on me," she said moving around mischievously under the rainfall of tens.

I ran my hand up her thigh and rested it in between her legs and massaged her pussy. She moaned as my touch entice her.

I fondled her tits, thighs, and her sweet ass. She had my money all around her, butt-naked in six inch heels.

"What's your name, beautiful?" I asked.

She came closer to me, took my chin into her hand, molested my earlobe with her tongue and her lips, and seductively whispered in my ear, "Cashmere." She then stuck her tongue in my ear again.

"I like that."

...Sexing you is all I see...freak'n you is all I need...what must I say what must I do to show how much I think about freak'n you...

Her moves were accompanied by Jodeci. The song crept in my mind, alcohol and her body did the rest. Another twenty, another round and I asked her to leave with me. I wanted to fuck her. My dick had never been so hard. Cashmere was down but wanted me to pay for it. Her fee was two-hundred. I had the bread and took her offer.

We left around one-thirty. I found the white Honda Accord parked across the street and deactivated the alarm to the car. Soon I popped the trunk to see if there was anything inside, and it was empty. The money was concealed somewhere in the car. I wasn't worried.

We were soon on our way to get a room at a nearby motel. Once inside the room, we went at it hard-body—fucking and sucking, contorting each other like pretzels. Cashmere had good pussy and let me come in her mouth. She swallowed my kids effortlessly.

"You a freak," I said sounding breathless and looking spent. She put the pussy down on me.

"You enjoyed it though. You wanna go for two for half?" she asked.

I glanced at the time and saw that it was four in the morning. "I'm good."

"You coming back soon?" she asked.

"Of course," I smiled.

Then storing her number in my phone, I quickly got dressed, leaving Cashmere naked under wrinkled bed sheets. I hated leaving but had to get this car and money back to Tyriq.

I was alone in Philly with a hundred and fifty-thousand dollars concealed somewhere in the trunk, without any protection. It was bad enough I left with the bitch to get a room.

It was five in the morning when I got on the New Jersey Turnpike. I hit Tyriq on the horn and told him that everything was cool.

◇◇

I got to Queens around seven that same morning and drove the car to a chop-shop on Liberty Ave. There were three men present dressed in blue overalls. Two men were Haitian and the third was Jamaican. They looked like mechanics and ordered me to leave the car parked and wait.

No one touched a thing until Tyriq walked in with Tip a hour later. Everyone stood up at attention like a general was present. The Jamaican said something to Tyriq and he ordered them to take the car apart. After that, he came over, and gave me dap.

"You did good," he said handing me the envelope with ten grand.

I smiled, put the bulky envelope in my back pocket, and was ready to go home and get some rest. I had no interest in knowing where the money was hidden.

"I'll see you around, Tyriq," I said walking away.

"I'll call you, soon, Vince," he said.

I was on my out the garage, when Tyriq hollered at me.

"You had fun at Motel 8, huh?"

"You had me followed?" I asked.

"Don't take it personal. That was a lot of cash and you was in one of the worse hoods out here. I trust you but them niggas in Philly, I don't trust. I have to cover all areas of my business, nigga. I know you handled yourself out there. Next time don't let the pussy distract you from business, ahight, nig—let the bitch wait for the dick. Get your paper right."

I nodded.

"Get some rest. There's a cab waiting for you."

I got in and gave the driver my destination. I sat back feeling ten-thousand dollars richer. It was reassuring to know I wasn't alone in Philly. Then a thought overwhelmed me. Was his boy watching my back, or was he watching me to see if I would cross Tyriq by stealing? In this game, you never know anyone's true intentions.

Fourteen

The money kept coming. I was in involved in the trafficking of kilos state to state, and my life was getting richer. In two months, I made more money transporting drugs for Tyriq than working at the airline for two years. The cash was coming nonstop. On a daily, I'd have about four grand on me, spending effortlessly on whatever. I started to acquire jewelry, clothes, shoes, sneakers, even cars.

August '02, I purchased a Range Rover for thirty-five thousand cash off the lot in Jersey. Tyriq knew a dealer who owned a leasing company. He hooked up Tyriq with cars and got him around reporting transactions. He hooked me up the same way. I didn't trick out my ride with huge spinning rims, deafening sound systems, and custom paint jobs like most hustlers did. I didn't want that kind of attention.

I had family to think about and wanted to have a low profile. Besides I was staying with my mother and damn sure didn't want her to know anything. I parked the truck around the corner and walk down a block to my home. I hid all my jewelry, cash, and even the .45 Tyriq gave me in a stash box in the truck. My mother thought that I had a job at a trucking company in the city that paid me decent.

I paid off bills that were in my name, and treated myself to whatever I wanted, even pussy. I was soon on the same status as S.S., Tip, and the crew, with what seemed to be having never-ending riches, cars, bling, and bitches. I had the money but respect of the streets I had to earn that. Pay my dues. A reputation meant everything. Without it you were open to violence and confrontation with stick-up kids, rival crews, even with peers. I had the money but still didn't have the respect on the streets yet.

I wasn't an enforcer or a heavy weight. I was only a transporter making runs out of town for the crew. The system was flawless. We never kept money and drugs in the same place. The pregnancy runs were untouchable. No one knew about the suits lined with half dozens of kilos, except for connects out of town. The girls were subtle, reliable and street smart. I was making weekly trips and was meeting with plenty of Tyriq's out of state connects and they got to know me. They were getting comfortable seeing my face, especially Ozone from Albany and Tango from Philly. They knew I was Tyriq's main man, and I reliably showed up on time with everything ready.

The months passed with me in the drug game. Money I was making and status I was building made going back to a nine to five, living from paycheck to paycheck, seemed redundant. I felt myself growing accustomed to the lifestyle I now live. Having thousands and thousands in my pockets, a truck that I loved driving and ladies loving me, was a dream that I hated to end. Everything I wanted was within my reach. Money was not an issue.

I wanted to splurge on my family, especially my son. The first day of school was looming. He was starting the first grade in a new school. I went on Jamaica Avenue and spent five-hundred dollars on clothing and items on him for school. Along with shopping for him, I went shopping for myself, Chandra, even my mother. I knew it'd be hard to explain where the money came from. I bought her a few gifts and kept them in storage.

The next day I went to see Chandra and my son. I knocked on her door, looking like I just stepped out of the pages of GQ. Clad in Gucci black striped wool- silk, two button suit with flat front trousers and a pair of polished black wing-tip shoes. I sported a diamond ring and had a large diamond earring in my right ear.

I remember Chandra complaining that I hardly dressed in nice suits, shoes and slacks. I was always looking like a thug in Tims and baggy jeans. I wanted to surprise her. The suit cost me four figures. I had three more like it.

When Chandra came to the door, she was taken back by my sharp appearance.

"Wow," she uttered, eyeing me up and down.

"You like?" I asked.

"You look good, Vince," she said.

"Thanks," I smiled.

"I remember twisting your arm to get you into a suit, now what is that, Armani?"

"Gucci, and like you said, I needed to change my style a bit."

"Work must be really good," she said.

"I'm doing good."

"I see," she said, dryly.

I knew she had her doubts about me having a legit job. Shit, I really didn't give a damn what she thought. I was finally taking care of my son and that was the only thing that mattered.

"Where's my son? I bought him some things for school," I said holding up the three bags I had in my hand.

"He's not here. He's with his godmother for the day."

"Oh, well can I come in and show you some of the things that I bought for him?"

At first Chandra looked hesitant then she let out a sigh.

"Sure," she said.

I walked into her apartment and it was free of the Jamaican nigga. Mary J. Blige was playing and incense burned in the living room. She was getting high, it was the only time she lit incense. I eyed Chandra loving how she was looking in tight fitting blue shorts, showing off her legs, a wife-beater and wearing white ankle socks. She looked good. My heart was burning for her.

"All this?" she asked.

"What can I say, I love my son," I stated.

I started removing certain items from the bag. I showed Chandra some of the school clothes I bought him, hoping I got the right size. I got him some sneakers, a new Spider-man book-bag, lunch-box and tons of arts and craft materials. I got him a few toys and some new games for his play station.

"You really outdid yourself, Vincent. How much did all this cost you?"

"Don't worry about it. I took care of the school shopping this year, so for once treat yourself," I said.

She showed me a faint, mock smile and said, "Should I be concerned?"

"About…?"

"Your sudden cash flow and the Gucci suit you're wearing. You must've landed some high-end job at some huge paying firm in the city. Congratulations, baby…you're finally on your way," she said to me in a scornful tone clapping her hands slowly.

"You making fun of me?" I said, tightening up my face.

"Take it as you want, but I ain't stupid Vincent," she replied.

I wasn't trying to hide my involvement in drugs from her. I wasn't concerned about what Chandra thought. I still wanted her to love me. We were no longer together. One of the reasons was financial.

"I know you're not a stupid woman, Chandra. What else you want me to do?"

"Keep looking," she said.

"So easy for you to say…"

"I told you earlier, Vinny needs his father around and with you into this shit, who knows what's going to happen?"

"I can handle myself, Chandra. Look, that Jamaican muthafucka you keep having around my son, what you think he's about?"

"Don't worry about him, he's not Vinny's father. You are. And besides, Jamal owns a few businesses and he's out of that lifestyle."

"And you believe that shit? C'mon Chandra, don't be pulling that moral shit on me. You and I know what you're about, nice things, designer seams and as long as you're getting yours, it's easy to look the other way, right?"

"You don't even know me, Vincent," she replied bitterly.

"What? I was fucking you long enough to know a lot about that ass, bitch," I shouted.

Slap!

"Fuck you!"

"Get the fuck out my house," she screamed.

I knew I was wrong for saying that to her and I didn't want to leave with her angry.

“Chandra, look…I’m sorry. I ain’t mean to say it like that.”

“Don’t ever disrespect me like that, Vincent…especially in my own home,” she warned.

“And I’m sorry. Look, let me make it up to you.” I went over to one of the bags and removed the gift I bought for her. “I got you a little sump’n too,” I said handing her the long black case.

She seemed uncertain taking it. Chandra looked at it and then at me. I wanted her to love the gift. I wanted to win over her heart again. Maybe start over. I loved her so much and wanted a future with her. I thought that the gift I purchased for her would hopefully be a start to our reconciliation.

“I don’t need anything from you, Vincent,” she said strongly.

“Nah, that’s yours to keep,” I said.

“You don’t owe me anything.”

“Chandra, when was the last time I bought you sump’n nice, huh? Now take the gift and open it up. Don’t insult me by denying it,” I said firmly.

She looked reluctant but opened the case and caught sight of the 18k white gold pendant necklace that suspended a black South Sea cultured pearl. I paid four grand for it. Chandra loved pearls and I knew it’d be the ideal gift.

“Ohmygod, Vincent,” she exclaimed. Her eyes were wide and fixated on the necklace.

“I assume you like the gift,” I said smiling.

“You remember… it’s beautiful,” she smiled.

“I’m glad that you like it. Put it on.”

I removed the necklace from her hands. Standing behind her, I gently fastened the necklace around her neck. Chandra rushed to the mirror and looked at the necklace sparkling around her neck.

“For you my queen,” I stated.

“How much did you pay for this?”

“Don’t worry about it, Chandra; it’s no dent in my pocket.”

She turned and looked at me, and her face suddenly looked worried “I can’t take this from you Vincent. What will Jamal think? It’ll condone what you do in the streets,” she said unfastening the necklace.

“Chandra, don’t do this to me. The shit is yours, keep it. I’m no leaving this apartment wit' it."

"Why does it have to be so difficult with you?"

"Why does it got to be so damn difficult wit' you? You can't take a simple gift from me?"

"This is not a simple gift."

"You do what you want with it. I'm not taking it back. It's cool that Jamal could buy you nice things and you good. I try and do right by you and you throw it back in my face. Fuck that nigga, yo. He can't be me, Chandra. I can finally afford to buy you sump'n nice and you trash me."

"It's not even like that, Vincent. You know how I feel about you hustling. You gonna break your mother's heart."

"She doesn't know what the fuck I do. And she ain't gotta know, unless you fucking tell her."

"I don't even wanna be the one to break that poor woman's heart like that. You're her only child and God forbid something happens to you. Her husband is already in the grave. Now you want her to lose a son."

"I didn't come here to fight wit' you. I wanted to do sump'n nice and be there for my son. But if it's gonna be like this, then I'm out. I got too much shit to worry about, than to come here and beef wit' you."

I began walking to the door, Chandra was behind me.

"Vincent…"

"I'm tired and need some rest," I said.

"Why do you gotta be like this, huh?" she asked glaring at me.

"I'm being my own man right now. You was beefin' wit' me when I was broke, about we ain't got this and we need that. Now you're beefin' wit' me when I'm paid. What the fuck you want from me? I'm trying! It's fucking hard out there!" I barked.

"You think I don't know that? I'm here trying to raise our son, working full time and hold down my own. Despite what you think of Jamal, he helps out somewhat. But he ain't there like that. And I don't want any shortcuts in my life, so the law or cops could snatch it away from me. I want a stable foundation and a home for Vinny. A home, Vincent, not a house…a home, there's a difference, Vincent. And when I finally get mines, it's gonna be for keeps."

"You finished," I replied sarcastically.

"Ohmygod, you could be such a little boy sometimes. Here, take your gift and leave and do what you do, cause your hard-headed Vincent," she said, handing me the necklace.

"Like I said, you keep that. I don't want it back, enjoy the shit. Tell my son I said hi."

"You're gonna learn the hard way," Chandra said then the door slammed.

Fuck her, I thought. Black women, I didn't know what the fuck they wanted from a man. I wanted to impress her, but shit got thrown back in my face. I wanted to go back and talk to her but pride got in the way. I kept it moving. I didn't want it to look like I was sweating her and left the building.

My life along with my personality was gradually changing. I was feeling like I had some control of my life. It felt stable. But the riches I was making had to get my hands muddy soon.

Fifteen

It was Iris's twenty-first birthday. Tyriq was throwing a huge birthday party at Club A, a swanky club on Farmers Blvd near the Airport. It was popular and the revelers there were mostly teen, sprinkled with a few male knuckleheads and wanna-be gangsters.

Iris was Tyriq's wifey. Her curvaceous figure, balloon tits and honey brown complexion belonged between the pages of a Black-tail magazine. Tyriq loved them young and sometimes naïve. He sometimes got them pregnant just as fast as he fucked them.

His white bitch, Susan, gave birth to a healthy baby boy two months ago. I heard, he's only seen his son twice. He was too busy being a playboy, getting money and fucking bitches.

I pulled up to the club in my truck and noticed the winding long line outside. The cuties were looking like XXL's eye candy models. Majority of the folks were waiting for Nelly to show up and perform his hit song, *Hot In Here.* Tyriq had real juice with Nelly's manager and Iris was a huge Nelly fan. It was the perfect birthday gift.

At midnight, I parked my truck and walked to the club entrance. Confident, I was skipping the long wait and getting in without any hassle. I sported an Aem'Kei T-shirt, Evisu jeans and suede shoes by Clark. I had five grand in my pockets.

My diamond chain swung from my neck and the ladies were looking and admiring. I walked up to three bulky bouncers and said, "I'm here for the birthday party."

I pulled out my wad of hundreds and gave the main bouncer a hundred dollar bill because I could. He took the c-note and said, "Yeah, I know you, you're with Tyriq's crew?"

I nodded.

"Yeah, it's poppin in there my nigga, you good." He removed the velvet rope that stood in between us and allowed entry into the wildest party in the city.

"Oooh, take me with you," a brown-skin cutie in a jean skirt and tight T-shirt pleaded.

I looked at her and liked what I saw, because she came with two more friends that looked just as good.

"Yo, they wit' me…" I said handing the bouncer an extra c-note.

He shrugged.

"C'mon, y'all wit' a real baller now," I said. They rushed past security and quickly followed behind me.

We walked into club A, hearing the deafening sound system blaring some Mobb Deep and Lil' Kim. Moshe, Kimberly and Azarel were cousins visiting from B-more, staying in Crown Heights with family. We moved through the crowd, heading to the VIP section where the real party was taking place. I had two ladies, arm-in-arm.

"Vince, what's good my nigga?" John-John greeted. We became real cool through the months.

"What's good my nigga?" I gave him dap.

He looked at the three lovely ladies I was escorting, smiled and said, "You the man, Vince."

I nodded and walked into Iris' private birthday party. It was cluttered with ballers and hustlers. The high-end bitches were leaches to the money in the room. Cristal and Moet was everywhere and it looked like a scene out of New Jack City, fashion, jewelry and money flaunted.

Moshe and her cousins were rapidly impressed by the lavish scene and got real comfortable with a few hustlers. I spotted Tyriq seated in the middle of a large red sectional with Iris sitting by his side. He was surrounded by friends and business associates on both ends. He downed a bottle of Moet like it was Kool-aid, and there was money scattered everywhere, from the tables to the floors. It seemed like decoration.

“Ayyite, there goes my nigga right there,” Tyriq hollered raising the Moet bottle and gesturing me over. I gave a few niggas dap as I made it to what looked like the cool kids table.

“Happy birthday, Iris,” I said leaning forward and kissing her cheek.

“Thank you, Vince,” she replied smiling.

She looked good in turquoise sleeveless hooded jacket and corduroy Capri pants, with white leather boots. Her hair was styled in long braids to her back. She had a thin waistline, thick hips, along with her huge tits and ass. I couldn’t help but stare.

Lucky muthafucka, I thought.

“Yo, take a seat and have a drink,” Tyriq offered.

I sat between him and Tip. He sipped his drink and had his arm around a beautiful brunette. The party was off the hook. DJ Clue got the crowd poppin’ with hot mixes. Spoon came through with his girl and it was like one big family. We laughed, got tipsy, and fucked with the finest bitches in the place.

Around two in the morning, Nelly finally came through with his huge entourage and performed his hit singles on the stage with his hype men. The ladies went berserk, rushing the stage to be near him and desperate to feel the sweat drip from his arms and chest, only to be pushed back by security.

They were screaming, pushing, and in awe over that country nigga and his country-ass rhymes. I mean, I gave him his respect because he was doing his thang, but myself, I was a Run DMC, Biggie, 2pac, and Nas listening nigga.

Iris was standing a few feet from the performance in complete amazement. Tyriq was next to her downing a bottle of Moet. Nelly came to Iris, took her by the hand, having Tyriq’s permission of course and pulled her onto the stage to celebrate her birthday in style. Iris looked like she was ready to jump on that nigga but Tyriq was watching.

I watched the performance holding a bottle of Grey Goose, laughed and then it dawned on me that I was wearing almost the same jewelry as Nelly. His diamond long chain was almost similar to mines, except a different pendant. I felt good inside. My bling was the status of a mega rap star and in my mind I was doing something right.

Spoon threw his arm around me and asked, “You having a good time, my nigga?" He was a bit tipsy.

"Yo, this shit is poppin," I replied.

"You doing that thang," Spoon said hugging me.

Tyriq came by all smiles, clutching the half-empty bottle of Moet. He was dancing and looked like he was having fun. He grabbed me and Spoon in a close hug, and said, "Y'all my niggas… nah fuck that, y'all are my fuckin' brothers for life." He then looked at me and said, "Ayyite, I'm glad to see that finally all of my brothers are gettin' that money. We doing our thang and the future is fucking ours. We the new Supreme team... Ayyite…"

Tyriq raised his bottle and proclaimed, "To us. Let us continue to hold these streets down for many years to come and get this money."

"To us," Spoon and I joined in, raising our bottles and clanking them, signified union.

I was happy with the family. Spoon and Tyriq were the closest to having brothers.

"Yo, yo, y'all mind if I snap a picture of y'all three?" the photographer asked. He'd been snapping pictures all night and finally got us together.

"Go ahead and snap that pic," Tyriq proudly said.

We gathered closely together our arms around each other, bottles raised in the air posing like we were gangsters. The photographer took five pictures of us in different poses then passed us his business card.

"I be putting them on line, on this website I got," he said.

"Fuck that, send me like a dozen copies," Tyriq said giving the photog a hundred dollar bill.

"Yo, I want copies too," I said.

"Same damn thang here," Spoon said.

We both reached into our pockets and passed him c-notes. He smiled telling us the pictures would be available tomorrow.

What we had was a brotherhood. Over the years, I drifted from Spoon and Tyriq. Now it was fun hanging out with them again and making money. I felt equal.

Around four in the morning, I left the party with Moshe under my wing. I was thinking pussy and knew I had the right bitch for the night as I staggered out the club tipsy. Moshe two other cousins were wasted from the drinks they consumed throughout the night and were soon about to become jump-offs for a few of my niggas. I didn't give a fuck about them, because I already had my piece.

I drove to the nearest motel to get a room for the night. Grey Goose and Moet flowed through my system. I was high and felt so fuckin' horny, that I was ready to spread Moshe's pussy open wide like the Grand Canyon.

It was nearing fall and the money I was making with Tyriq, the holidays were going to be good for my son, family and myself. I had a birthday coming in December and knew that I wanted to celebrate it. Styling with money, bitches, champagne and hordes of celebrities, I wanted to do what music moguls and rap stars do. *Couldn't afford* was no longer in my category—drug money was soon to become my only currency.

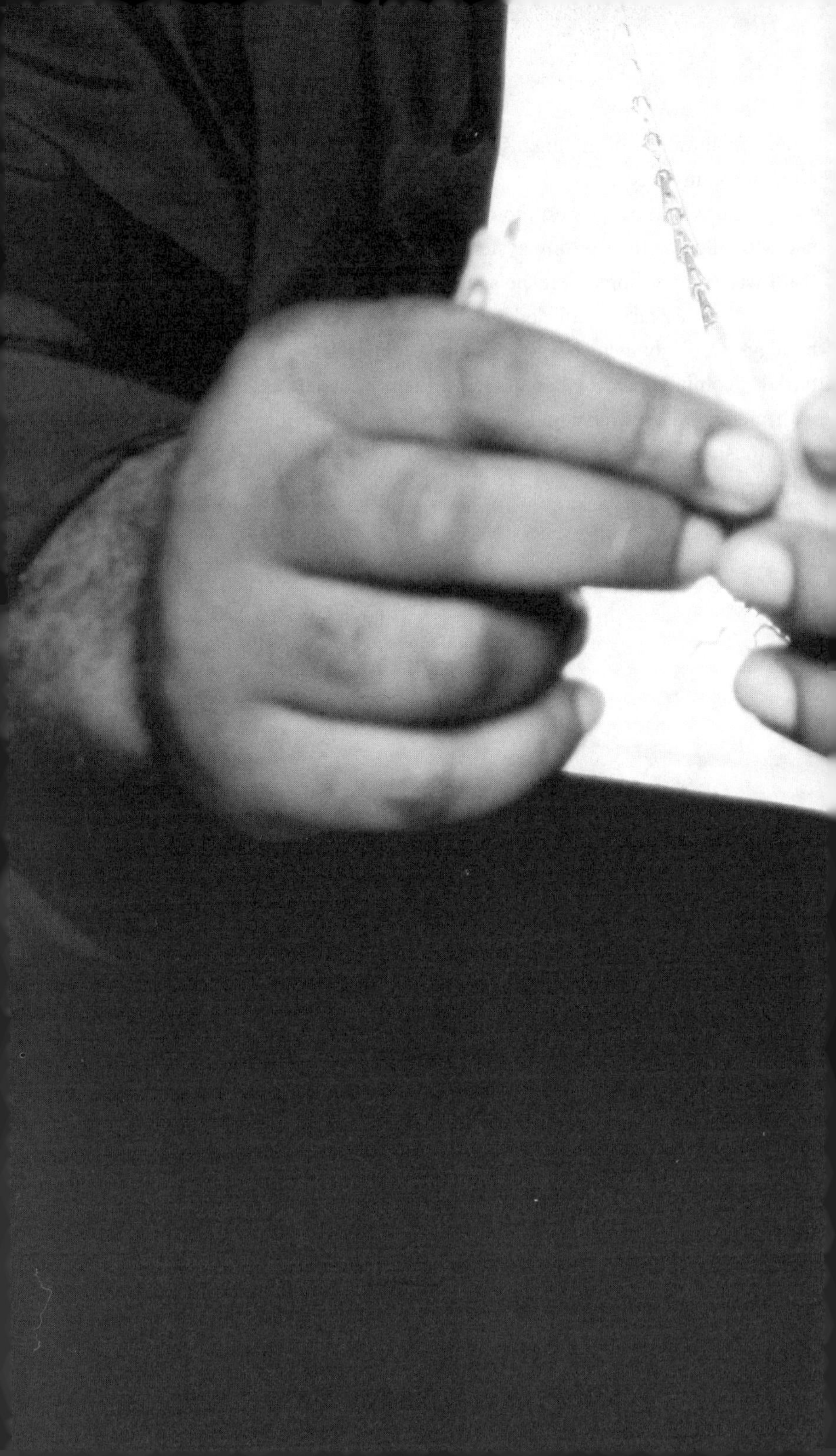

Part Two

Life is a gift,
how you choose to live it,
is your choice.

"I love you, daddy," my little man proclaimed over the phone.

"I love you too," I returned smiling.

It was his first day at a new school and he was excited about going to kindergarten. September 8th was his fifth birthday and his mother threw him a nice party at Chucky Cheese in Long Island. I offered to help with the party but she argued that she didn't want her son's birthday to be funded with drug money. That made me upset and we had an argument about it. Chandra was cool with taking the gifts I bought for him for school but it became a problem when I wanted to help with the party. The bitch was contradictory and it was pissing me off.

"You gonna become the next Albert Einstein, right?"

"Daddy, I ain't that smart," he said.

"Yes you are Vinny. You're smart, so never doubt yourself. You're my little genius," I told him.

After my talk with my son, Spoon knocked on the door. I let him in.

"You ready do that thang?"

"Yeah, give me a minute," I replied.

"Early bird gets it," he said.

"Gimme a second…"

"Where's your moms?" he asked.

"At work, seven to five shift."

"You in the game four months and your moms don't have a clue?"

"I got my ways," I said.

"Still parking 'round the corner, huh? You think your neighbors don't talk?"

"Yo, they ain't in my business like that, Spoon," I said.

"It's all good, you do your thang, I ain't telling. Besides, I'm hearing, you're about to be promoted. I'm hearing good things about you."

"Tryin' to stay focus, Spoon," I smiled.

"On what…?"

"What you mean?"

"Is this long term for you? I mean, you still got your dreams right?"

I knew where he was going. We locked eyes for a short moment.

"I ain't forget," I said.

"You had enough saved when you bought that truck."

"Spoon, don't criticized me. Cuz you been in this game long before me and you ain't going nowhere. I know you looked out for me when that shit went down wit' that white bitch in LI and I ain't never gonna forget. I'm grown. Don't baby me. I made my decision and I'm gonna live wit' it."

He nodded and said, "Vince, you right. I ain't trying to baby-sit. I'm looking out."

I took a sip of tea, "I trust you to have my back."

"That's my thang then I got you," he countered.

I finished my tea and we were out the front door. I got into Spoon's Range Rover and we headed to Brooklyn.

We ended up in East New York. Spoon made a few stops, talked to his peoples and kept it moving. I was chilling, listening to the radio, when I heard Spoon say, "You gotta make your bones soon."

"What you mean?"

"You planning on stepping up, you gonna have to make your bones."

"I already told Tyriq I ain't down. I'm just trying to make my paper."

"It don't matter what you feeling. If you wanna be trusted, you gotta do that work thang. Work can get ugly," he said. "If you refuse then you'll labeled a snitch, weak and believe me, you don't want to be neither."

"What am I supposed to do?" I asked.

"You still want me looking over your shoulders while you do your thang?" he asked. "I mean, it's your decision, right?"

"You gonna throw that comment in my face?"

"Vince, you're in deep. No matter what Tyriq got you locked in the crew. You know a lot about our organization. If you don't go through with it, it's gonna bring suspicion on yourself. When niggas doubt you… You're a smart man. You already know the outcome."

"I know. How soon…?" I sighed.

"Like tonight, yo."

"What?"

"Yo, just get in do your thang and get out, no hesitation. I got your back on this, Vince," he assured.

"Who is it?" I asked.

"You'll find out tonight. Let's just chill," he said pushing the Range down Atlantic Av.

My heart was racing. I was worried. I knew Spoon had my back. But murder was a whole new ball game for me.

"When was the first time you killed someone?" I asked. When it came to violence, I heard Spoon was a nightmare on the streets. He was a cool nigga willing to give the shirt off his back, if he liked and respected you. Spoon stopped at a light, looked at me and advised, "When you kill a nigga, shut the fuck up about it and act like it never happened."

I nodded.

Around three in the afternoon, we were at one of his baby-mamma cribs. Melissa was a beautiful woman, who gave birth to three of Spoon's children. Ryan was seven, three year old Octavia and Aaron, one year. There was Wendy, his other son's baby mother. Jaime was four. Spoon got around with the ladies, but loved his kids even more. He enjoyed spending time with them. I was Jaime and Ryan's godfather. I loved and treated Spoon's kids like they were my own.

Melissa cooked steak and eggs for us. I chowed down on her cooking like the homeless. We spent about two hours over Melissa's place. I played Play station with Ryan and laughed it up with Melissa and Spoon.

We left Melissa's crib and ended up in Flatbush, near Kings Highway. We rolled up to a nice looking four story brownstone on a lonely, tree-lined street. Spoon parked and stared at the place.

"What we here for?" I asked.

"That right there is the future," he stated.

"What, you moving?"

"Nah, I copped that three months back, paid half a million. It's on the market for 1.4 million. How you like it?" he asked.

"It's nice."

"I got four more thangs going in Brooklyn just like this one. I want to rent 'em out to families and businesses, make a profit. You can never go wrong with owning a piece of nice real estate, especially a brownstone or some land. In this country, you need some kind of ownership. People gotta live somewhere and this country is gonna continue to build. I'm trying to get mines and have something for my kids."

The only other time I saw Spoon beaming so much, was when he was with his kids.

"A lot of these young'ns think having bling and tricked out cars is life, that don't even compare to this right here." He pointed to the brownstone. "You wanna go in and check it out?"

"No doubt..."

We got out. The building was in good shape. I followed behind Spoon and checked out the polished hardwood floors and high ceiling. It was huge and empty, with an original staircase and a huge backyard.

"You know I always had dreams of getting into real estate. I don't care how I fucking did it," he said admiring the place.

"It's definitely nice."

After seeing the place, we drove to Queens and linked up with Tyriq at his lounge on Linden. It was still early and the place was empty. Tyriq had live-in quarters above the place. It was where he liked fucking bitches.

We walked up one flight of stairs to meet with Tyriq. I noticed Iris coming out of the bathroom tying a small robe around her. I caught a quick glimpse of her glistering nude body and my dick jumped. She caught me staring and smiled.

"Hey Vince..."

"What's good, Iris," I replied.

She was scantily clad, not giving a fuck, and her eyes stayed locked on me. I kept my composure, knowing she was wifey to the boss. My eyes watched her ass cheeks that were barely covered by the short thin robe. Tyriq emerged from the bedroom wearing some brown shorts and sporting a six pack.

"Ayyite, my niggas," he greeted.

"What's good," Spoon and I both greeted, giving Tyriq daps.

"Spoon talked to you about tonight, right?"

"You already know how I feel," I said.

"Hold on," he said. He went over to the bedroom door and closed it.

"Ayyite, you trying to come up...? This is how you do it if you want respect. Vince, we boys but in this game we on some different shit. I want you to prove your manhood. Let these niggas know what you about on these fucking streets." Tyriq proclaimed sternly, locking eyes with me.

I was still unsure when I nodded and asked.

"So who you want got?"

"We don't talk on that here. I just need to know you ready. You're doin' good out there, my nigga. It's time for you to step your game up. So you wit' us?"

"Yeah," I reluctantly answered.

"You a soldier Vince," Tyriq said. He gave me dap, looked at me and said, "Us, right?"

"Us," I said, and the embraced became a bear hug.

Doing the hit would solidify my position with Tyriq, and the crew. Like them I'd be a murderer and it would be official between us.

◇◇

I rode back home thinking about tonight. Spoon dropped me off and I walked through the front door trying to get my head right. I was nervous as fuck. *You need to do this, so they won't do you*, I kept telling myself.

I walked into the house and saw my mother seated on the large brown sectional, with the photo album on her lap, and listening to Bootsy Collins' *I'd Rather Be with You*, staring at old pictures of the family, my pops and us when I was young. She seemed burned out from her daily ten-hour shifts at the job.

"Hey mom," I greeted her with a quick kiss on the cheek.

"Oh, hey how was work today, sweetie?" she asked.

"It was cool, getting more overtime."

I hated lying to my moms.

"See, I told you…all you needed was to be patient, have your trust in God and things would work out for you," she stated proudly.

"Yeah, you did. I see you got the photo book out," I said, trying to take her mind off of me and work.

"Yeah, just looking through some old photos of the family," she said.

I noticed a picture in her hand that was of herself and my father captured in a loving hug.

"Your father was such a handsome man, like you, Vincent," my mother said looking up at me.

"Yeah, he was. And you're still beautiful, ma."

She smiled. "Are you in for the night? You want me to cook something? Your aunt Linda should be home soon. I should start making dinner."

"Nah, you get your rest ma. I'm 'bout to head back out soon, meet up wit' some of the fellas and get a drink or two," I said.

"You be careful, don't be out there drinking and driving."

"Nah, you know I got better sense than that."

"Okay, Vincent. You know I always trust you," she said.

"Yeah…I know," I replied coyly.

I was about to head to my room, when I heard my mother say, "Oh, Vincent, this Sunday, come with me to church. You haven't been to church in a long while."

I smiled. *What the fuck*, I thought, of all the days to bring up church. My moms must have a sixth sense. Maybe it was a sign about tonight.

"Alright, I'll think about it, ma," I said.

"You need to come. The pastor asked about you. He wants to see you," she said.

"I'm gonna see him soon. But I need to run to my room and change for the night. I don't wanna be out too late," I said.

"Okay, sweetie, but we'll talk," my mother said refocusing on the photos.

I rushed in my room, closed the door and took a deep breath. Was this really me about to do the unthinkable tonight? Defy my father's beliefs about human life…? He taught me that no man had the right to take another's life. He believed that every man should treat each other as equals.

When I was out in the streets, I loved it. But when I walked in through the front doors and had to face my mother, I hated it. I was lying to my mother about everything. The guilt sometimes ate at me. I was her son and always her baby boy. The Vincent she once knew was changing to someone she didn't want to know. I had to do this to prove myself. If I didn't there'd be doubt about me. When there's doubt death was soon to follow.

A little after ten, I jumped into Tip's burgundy Escalade. I was wearing black sweat-shirt and jeans. Tip had on wife-beater, jeans and Tims. It seemed he didn't want to be bothered with me. There was a job to be done. It felt like some kind of initiation. He drove in silence until we were about ten blocks away from my home.

"Who we gettin' at…?"

"You cannot fuck this up," he said coldly.

"I understand."

"This dealer, P.R. from Hollis feels that because he's down with Law, he can cut into our cheddar coming from Liberty and 177th street. He robbed a few of our dealers from around there. He's a pain and he's gotta go down."

Tip was on Liberty. When we came to a red-light, he reached under his seat and handed me a fully loaded, black .9mm.

"The safety's already off, just point and squeeze, drop the nigga. Be out," Tip instructed.

I gripped the steel and nodded. It was like a bitch about ready to lose her virginity. My hands were sweaty and the closer we got to the area, my heart was racing so fast and hard. I thought Tip heard it.

We came to the corner of Farmers Blvd and Murdock Av. P.R. fucked with a bitch in the area. The bitch he was fucking had juice with Spoon. She instantly gave up P.R. for a few G's and a pound of haze. She called Spoon and set up the hit.

Tip parked the truck near her crib on the residential block. He shut off the lights and engine. Tip knocked out the bulb to the streetlight and we sat in the truck waiting in the dark. After an hour, P.R. emerged from the shabby, two-story corner house on the street. We had cover and concealment from the many trees and shrubberies on the block.

But P.R. didn't come out the house alone. He was with another dude who looked just as shady. They were heading to an old Toyota Camry out front. I held the 9mm tighter in my hand. They were talking and laughing without a clue.

"Here, put these on," Tip said, handing me a pair of white latex gloves.

I put them on, and Tip made me wipe the gun down before I popped off, making sure there were no prints on the weapon.

We watched P.R. get into the car on the driver's side and Tip said,

"Do you. Pop the driver first then his boy after."

"Both?"

"Yeah, muthafucka," he exclaimed.

I got out the truck. The nine at my side, I trotted over to the Camry using darkness to hide my approach. I heard the engine idling. P.R was in my sights as I got closer.

"God, please forgive me for this."

I raised the gun to P.R's chest and fired.

BLAM BLAM.

The night around me lit up in two quick blue flashes. P.R. slumped over the wheel, two shots in his chest. The car suddenly rolled forward.

"Oh shit!" His boy screamed.

The car crashed into a tree. P.R.'s boy tried to make a quick exit. I ran up on him and fired three shots into him, dropping him face down on the concrete. Tip raced up to me in the truck. I jumped in and he peeled off.

My heart thumped like I was having a panic attack. I was sweating, my hands were shaking and I couldn't breathe. The nine was in my grip. I wanted to get rid of it with the quickness. I leaned back against the headrest wanting to disappear.

"Relax, just breathe…you did it, nigga. The first is always the hardest. But once you get past that, it gets better."

They actually want me to do it again? I already proven myself. What more was there? There was no turning back. I just committed the ultimate sin. How could I repent—I didn't know. I knew my father was spinning in his grave. And knowing my life would no longer be the same.

◇◇◇◇◇◇◇◇◇◇◇◇◇◇◇◇◇◇◇◇◇◇◇◇◇◇◇◇◇◇◇◇◇◇◇◇

Tip pulled up in front of Tyriq's sports bar on Linden. We dumped the gun in a distant sewer drain. I was a bit calmer. The place was crowded. I followed Tip pass security as we made our way upstairs into one of Tyriq's private rooms. When we walked in, Tyriq and some bitch was counting money and Spoon was on his cell-phone. Tip gave them a head nod, and Tyriq nodded back.

"Ayyite, welcome to the family, my nigga…" He got up, came over and embraced me. "You good…?"

"Sure…"

He pulled me closer and whispered, "I told you, everybody's a killer. You just gotta know how to bring that animal out."

I looked over at Spoon and he had no words for me. He just gave me a head nod, and took a puffed on a Black & Mild.

Tyriq called the bitch over counting money. She walked over with a bulky white envelope and passed it to Tyriq. He placed it in my hands.

"Vince, here's twenty grand, you did good."

I took the money.

"Yo, I want you to leave town for a minute, until things blows over," Tyriq suggested.

"Go where?" I asked.

"I don't give a fuck; you paid. But get your mind right and don't even think on what went down."

"I'll do that."

"But yo, I need you to make another run out to Philly," he said.

I nodded.

After that I left the club. I wasn't in the mood to stay. I wanted to go home, pack my bags and go somewhere far. It was a good idea to leave town, because the more I stayed in my people's crib, the guiltier I got. It was making me angrier. I couldn't live pretending that it was one thing in my mother's eyes, when I was totally the opposite. Something had to give.

Seventeen

New Jersey Turnpike- 11pm,

Two FBI agents sat waiting in a black four door Caprice parked in an all night rest stop on the Turnpike. Agent Pena and Smith were thirty miles from Philadelphia. They munched on peanuts, sipped on hot coffee and talked about baseball and the upcoming World Series.

Agent Smith glanced at the time on the dashboard for the umpteenth time in one hour, and said, "Where the fuck is he?"

"Give him time, he'll show," Agent Pena said tossing a handful of nuts into his mouth while peering out the window.

"He better…"

"So, who's gonna win the World Series?" Agent Pena asked.

"My money's on the Giants, that Barry Bonds and Reggie Sanders gonna take them somewhere," Agent Smith proclaimed. "And you?"

"I'm a diehard Yankees fan from the Bronx, Smith, can't go wrong rooting for my Yankees," Agent Pena said.

"Yankees are overrated."

"Explain the twenty six world series titles."

"Luck..."

"You my friend know nothing about baseball."

Agent Pena was born in Santa Domingo and moved to the Bronx when he was ten. He'd been in law enforcement since he was twenty-one and saw what drugs, gangs, and violence could do to a community. His older brother was gunned down in a shoot out when he was seven. The only right way to avenge his brother's death was to work in law enforcement.

Pena was in his early thirties, married with two beautiful offspring.

Agent Smith was six-one and handsome African American. He was in his early thirties and graduated with a criminal justice degree from John-Jay College. He had a hard-on for upholding justice in the city of New York.

They had their eyes set on Tyriq and his crew. He knew Tyriq was making millions from drugs, extortion, prostitution, and had a murderous crew at his command. South Jamaica, Queens was being torn apart by drugs and violence. But Agent Smith knew that Tyriq was small fish, compared to his number one target, Demetrius.

Demetrius was a descendant from the Jamaican Shower Posse, and was responsible for eighty percent of the drugs coming into Queens and Brooklyn. Demetrius ran with a fierce Jamaican crew called, Shotta's, who were from Kingston and Tivoli Gardens, in Jamaica. They killed, extorted and shipped tons of drugs into dozens of communities in New York. It was estimated that Shotta's were sitting on a hundred million dollar empire.

It was a big case for both agents, and with the help of their confidential informant, they seemed closer to making a major bust. It was a career case, bringing down the ruthless Jamaican drug cartel.

"I told him ten O' clock," Agent Smith angrily shouted. "It's eleven fuckin' thirty. He thinks we got time to wait around. I'll shove his ass into the prison ground if he screws us around."

Agent Pena tossed another handful of peanuts into his mouth. "We'll give him another fifteen minutes. Maybe he got stuck in traffic."

"Stuck in traffic my ass," Smith remarked.

Five minutes later, headlights were approaching the sparse parking lot. They sat up in their seats and observed the red Accord.

"Think it's him?" Pena asked.

"It's him," Smith responded.

The Accord parked parallel to them, and then a male figure got out from the driver's side and quickly got into the backseat of the Caprice.

"You're late," Smith said.

"What the fuck you want me to do? Traffic was a bitch in New York. It took me damn near an hour to get over the Verrazano."

Smith turned to look at him and asked, "What you got for us?"

"Nothing new…"

"What the fuck you mean nothing? It's been two months since you checked in," Smith barked.

"It's the same thang like last time I saw y'all muthafuckas. Tyriq ain't changing up a damn thang. He don't trust niggas like that. He watches everythang."

"Yeah, but ain't you suppose to be his right hand man?" Pena asked.

"I know, but he's cautious."

"What about the Jamaicans, when is he meeting with them again?" Smith asked.

"Don't know, the last shipment we received from them was five-hundred kilos two months back."

"From where…?" Pena asked.

"Jersey, but them Jamaicans are careful. They never do a deal in the same spot. They switch up a lot, and Demetrius ain't never there when the deal's going down. His man, Jagged takes care of that."

"We need something useful, Spoon. It's been months and we still ain't any closer. What good are you, huh? We're giving you a chance to do right but you ain't doing Jack."

"I'm trying."

"Try harder, or your black ass is going to jail for a long time and you can forget about ever seeing your kids again," Smith threatened.

"Fuck you, Smith and leave my kids out your mouth."

"No fuck you, cuz you're giving us bullshit!" Smith shouted.

"Alright, everyone chill out!" Pena shouted and tossed some pictures on Spoon's lap. "Who's the new guy?"

Spoon looked through the large glossy photos of Vincent and the crew then sighed.

"He ain't nobody," Spoon said.

"You sure, he looks like a major player," Smith said.

"We came up together. He just likes to be around the life. He ain't no thang, y'all ain't gonna get not a damn thang outta him."

"You better be real with us, Spoon…no more games," Pena said.

"I know."

"What about the drugs, how's he still shipping them out of state?" Pena asked.

"I told y'all before. He got bitches trafficking that shit for him and if he ain't using his bitches, then he got cars with compartments. You never know with him, he's got a routine, sometimes he switches it up on the humble to be safe."

Pena looked at Spoon.

"We need something on audio."

"Fuck that. No wires. I get caught wearing that shit and that's my life. My kids, my family," Spoon said.

"You scared of your boy?"

"Fuck Tyriq! The Jamaicans find out and they'll kill not just me but my kids, their mothers and whoever the fuck I know."

"We can protect you," Smith assured him.

"It ain't going down like that," Spoon said.

"You don't have a choice, Spoon. We need something concrete," Pena said.

"When the shit hits the fan, Spoon, think. You'll do time, not life. With your priors, that's a damn blessing. Five years will be the most you'll do for helping out. Then you can see your kids have a future and your real estate that you love so much, can be saved too. You fuck up on this and I guarantee, everything you love will turn stink shit," Smith warned.

Six months ago, Spoon got busted with 20 kilos of uncut cocaine in Connecticut. While locked up in Connecticut, a witness linked him to a murder he committed a year back in New Haven. His back was against the wall and the feds flipped him when they threatened to take away everything he loved. They wanted to also lock up his baby-mother Melissa and charge her with conspiracy. They threatened to take away his kids, even put them in different group homes. The authorities were going after his family, his businesses and his real estate. Spoon was a major player and the feds offered him a deal because they were after much bigger fish. After his rendezvous with the agents, Spoon drove back north on the Turnpike.

Eighteen

I spent three weeks, shacking up with Cashmere in her one bedroom apartment in south Philly, near Tasker Street. I kept a low-profile. Cashmere loved having me over and we fucked everyday. We couldn't get enough of each other. I helped pay her bills, her rent and took her shopping at the Gallery mall on Market St. I treated her like a queen, thinking she was wifey and spent over eight grand on her.

I was in contact with Tyriq. We talked nothing about the murders. But I couldn't stop having nightmares about the two lives I took. There were nights when I'd wake up in cold sweat, short of breath, ready to flip. Cashmere would be there, comforting me, massaging my shoulders then giving me brains.

The night I drove from New York, I moved thirty kilos in a secret compartment of a Ford Taurus. I met with Tyriq's connect at a bar in West Philly. We exchanged cars and then both went on our way. An hour later, I met up with one of Tyriq's people from New York, exchanging cars again. He took the green Acura I picked up with the money and I got into a cream Lexus GS, fully loaded. It was my ride while I was in town.

I was missing home and my son. I told my moms the reason I was leaving town for a few weeks, was to train for my CDL in a different state. I told her that my job was putting me through the course so I could advance to becoming a driver at work. She looked at me skeptically. Once I got back to Queens, it would be time to move out. I needed to get my own place.

I got to know Cashmere better. In the club she knew how to work the crowd, her sex appeal was crazy strong. I knew she even began to trust me. We left the club one night with her saying, "Baby, I want you to meet my cousin, Inf. I've been telling him about you," she said.

"Telling him what about me?" I asked. I didn't know her cousin and didn't want to know her cousin. I was only in Philly for a short while and I wasn't trying to get with niggas down here.

"I told him you cool peoples. He just came home and trying to get shit poppin for him," she mentioned.

"What he want wit' me?" I asked.

"He just wants to meet and talk to you. Inf is cool peoples, Vince. He's real and he' ain't no joke when it comes to the street."

"What he about?"

"Just meet and talk to my cousin, Vince. I'm telling you, he got some shit brewing and you need to get down with it. Trust me, ain't shit gonna happen to you, I know you don't know him, but take my word, he's cool, and he's about that paper."

While driving south on Broad street, I thought about the meeting.

"Ok, I'll meet wit' him."

"I'll set it up."

◇◇

Two days later, I met with Inf. He wanted to rule the projects again with drugs and fear. I walked into the heavy, crime ridden Tasker homes of South Philly with Cashmere and a .45 in my waistband. The battered dilapidated row houses and buildings looked like they were about to crumble. The corners were drug infested. Abandon cars lined the streets and graffiti marred the walls. The streets were littered with empty crack vials and nickel bags. Wide-eyed, skeleton-like zombies peddled their mother's television, camera and VCR or whatever else they could come up with to pay for their next hit. I didn't feel comfortable parking the Lexus out front.

Cashmere led me into a run-down building with shady looking niggas out front. They glared at me like I'd fucked their mothers.

"Yo, this nigga with you, Cashmere?" one asked with a screw face.

"We here to see, Inf."

"He up there…who this?" he asked.

"This my, boo, Joker. He gonna get y'all paid out here," she said.

"Oh word, what you a connect?"

"I'm here to talk," I said.

"Where you from…?" Joker asked.

"Up top," I said.

"Fuck New York…y'all couldn't even protect them towers up there. We hold our own down here, nigga," Joker laughed. He lifted his stained T-shirt revealing a Glock in his waistband.

"C'mon, we ain't got time for him," Cashmere said pulling me into the building.

We got to the seond floor and walked down a narrow littered hallway. Cashmere knocked on an apartment door that had loud thunderous music coming from it. She smiled at me.

No knowing what I was walking into made me nervous. It could be a set-up. I'd known Cashmere for a few months. I was a better friend than a foe to her but I learned never to trust a bitch. That was the reason for the .45.

The door opened and a tall, stocky nigga with dozens of tats on his arms, emerged.

"What's good Cashmere?" he smiled.

"I'm good, Shakes. My cousin in…?"

"Yeah," Shakes said.

He gave me the screw face and looked like Joker had downstairs.

"Who's this nigga?" Shakes asked in an unfriendly tone.

"Chill, Shakes. I already told Inf 'bout him," Cashmere said.

Shakes continued the screw face even after Cashmere told him about me. I knew I had out-of-town written all over me. My Yankees' fitted, jewelry, fresh white-on-white uptowns and my up-top swagger, I didn't let the angry stares get to me, though.

We walked into the apartment and excessively strong weed smoke filled the air, loud rap music was playing, and half dozen goons loitered in the apartment. They all knew Cashmere and showed much love but I was standing in the middle of a lions den.

Inf was seated on a tattered brown sofa twisting a blunt. He was wearing a tight wife-beater, had a shaved head and rocked a thick groomed beard. He was a stocky beast with bulky arms and large stomach. He had juice in Philly and did ten years for drugs and attempted murder. Before his incarceration, he controlled drugs and gang movements from Morris and Tasker streets and Schuylkill Expressway to Lanier Park and 29th. He was thirty-four and ready to reclaim his throne on the streets and needed my help.

"What's up, cuz?" Inf hollered raising up off the couch and moving toward Cashmere.

"Inf," Cashmere answered giving her cousin a hug.

"I already told you about Vince. Vince this Inf, my cousin…"

"What up?" Inf greeted me with a dap.

"What up," I said, halfheartedly.

Inf looked at me with cold, hard eyes and said, "Yo, hold on," he looked at his boys and shouted, "Yo, turn that fuckin' shit down. I'm tryin' to talk."

His boys turned down the loud rap and then Inf focused his attention on me. "I know you don't know me, and I don't know you but my little cousin speak very highly of you. She says you be doing your thang in New York. I can respect that. Check this, I just came home from doing a long bid. I need to get my money up and I need a connect that's gonna supply me some heavyweight. Are you the man to talk to? If not, don't waste my time. I only deal with real muthafuckas, and if you ain't real, you gonna find yourself leaving in a trash bag."

"I'm the one."

"Let's talk."

I took a seat on the couch next to Inf. Cashmere sat next to me. Inf continued to roll a blunt and asked if I wanted a smoke, or a drink. I declined.

Inf informed me that he had the territory, the soldiers and the juice to move up to thirty kilos in his hood. It was a gold mine for him. His old connect caught a federal charge. He didn't want the streets to dry up and needed a line on quality shit.

"Tell your peoples to ask around about me. These streets will tell you I'm good money," Inf boasted.

"I'm gonna get back at you, and let you know what's up," I said.

"You do that."

I stood up and we shook hands. Inf's eyes told me he was hard to the bone and was ready to murder to control money, power, and respect.

When we left the apartment I was feeling like I had a ghetto pass in south Philly. Inf assured me that nobody would fuck with me. I wasn't worried I had protection in my waistband.

Out on the street, I saw Joker and his goons out front. He looked at me and said, "Everything good?"

"Yeah we, good," I replied.

"It's gettin' late, dog, you don't wanna get caught out here after dark. That's when the wolves come out," Joker laughed.

"Joker, shut-up," Cashmere said.

"Just tryin' to give your boy some advice…"

"Yeah, whateva…" I said.

We exchanged stares. I was hoping he wasn't going to be a problem. I could tell he was a knucklehead.

I got back to the Lexus. It was untouched. Cashmere was happy she'd made the connection. She wanted something out the deal. The bitch was money-hungry but was definitely about her business. She saw an opportunity and went for it knowing that her roughneck cousin had her back.

When I got back to her apartment, I put in a call to Tyriq and Spoon. Spoon was the first to call me back.

"What up?" he asked.

I didn't want to say too much over the phone so I said, "Yo, I got a line out here in S.P…some big fish came at me, and is ready for sump'n."

"Yo, we sent you out there to keep low and you doing business. What you think this thang is? Yo, I'll get at you when you get back up top." Spoon hung up leaving me baffled.

"Baby, what your boy say?" Cashmere asked.

"I'll talk to him when I get back to New York," I told her.

"That's what's up," she said excitedly.

That same night, I sweated out the bedroom sheets, stretching that pussy out like I had no sense. It got my mind off shit. I twisted and turned that bitch into several positions and busted a nut in her. The second nut I let loose on her back. Afterwards, I collapsed next to her and stared up at the ceiling. Cashmere nestled against me, sucking my nipples and tickling my skin with her soft touch.

"You okay?" she asked.

"I'm good."

"What's on your mind?" she asked massaging my chest gently and toying with my nipples.

"I need to get back to New York and handle this thing."

"When are you trying to leave?"

"Tomorrow…"

"So soon…? I'm gonna miss you."

"I'll be back to deal with your cousin."

I felt her enticing touch move down under the sheets. She gripped my flaccid dick and began stroking it thick.

"Besides money, I'm gonna give you another reason why you need to bring your ass back to Philly."

She moved her head south under the sheets and wrapped her lips around my shaft. Her tongue coiled around the tip and she began sucking me.

"Damn…hmm, oh shit," I moaned holding onto the sheets for dear life. Cashmere bobbed her head, sucking my dick for twenty minutes. I busted off in her mouth and she swallowed my kids. She wiped her mouth and said, "You better not forget me, baby."

"I definitely got you," I said spent.

She smiled and nestled again. I held her in my arms and closed my eyes.

Nineteen

The next day I crossed the Verrazano and it felt like I never left. I hit up Tyriq and Spoon to let them know that I was back. Tyriq wanted to meet with me right away. I wanted to stop off at my place first to see how my moms and aunt were doing.

I pulled up to my crib around nine pm. There were lights on in the house. I was in the cream GS staring at the front porch. I got out, walked into the place and shouted, “Mom, Aunt Linda, I’m home. I heard nothing. My room looked like someone had gone through my shit. I went to my drawers and looked for the ten grand I had stashed but it wasn’t there.

“Is this what you’re looking for?” my mother asked standing in the doorway, glaring at me and holding a bundle of hundred dollar bills.

“Where’d you get that?” I asked.

“Boy, don’t play stupid. Where did you get all this money from?” she asked angrily.

“Working,” I replied.

“I called the job. They never heard of you. You’ve been lying to me, Vincent. Is this what you went out of town to do? Are you selling drugs?”

“C’mon mom,” I said.

“Then explain this, Vincent,” she shouted.

“Why are you in my business?”

“Boy, what’s wrong with you? Talking to your mother like that,” my aunt Linda said walking into the room. My aunt was in my face. “Vincent, you need to get out this damn house if you wanna sell that shit. I’m not having that here.”

"Whateva…!" I shouted.

My mother rushed up to me and slapped the shit out of me. "Vincent, how dare you come into our home and defy everything me and your father believed in and worked so hard for?" She began ripping the money to shred.

It was sad to see her crying.

"If you needed money, you could've come to your mother and me," my aunt stated.

"We trusted you," my mother said.

"I did what I had to do, ma. It was only temporary, and besides, you can't say I didn't try. I bust my ass going to school and holding down a job to support a family. What I got in return? A job that don't give a fuck about me and the unemployment line..."

"You watch your mouth in my house," my aunt shouted.

"I'm out anyway. I don't need this shit!"

I scrambled around the bedroom, tossing clothes in a bag.

"Get out of here and don't come back into this house until you get your act together Vincent," Aunt Linda shouted. "You're a grown man, Vincent; you need to be on your own."

"I'm good," I stated.

My mother tossed the money at me and it went flying everywhere—ten-thousand dollars spread all over my room.

My mother and aunt were standing by the doorway, watching me get my shit together. I then heard my mother cry out, "Do think about your son, Vinny? You're doing wrong, baby…you're doing wrong. This is not you."

I tossed the bag over my shoulder and went for the front door.

"Y'all can keep the ten grand," I said.

"Get out my house with that damn drug money!" my aunt screamed.

I rushed pass them, the exit my only focus. I was in the living room.

"Noooo! Don't go, baby. Don't go!" My mother screamed grabbing my shirt and pulling me from the front door.

"Ma, let me go…let me go," I said.

"No…ooh!"

"Jean, let that boy go so he can leave out my house. He's a man now. Let him do what he wanna do," Aunt Linda said.

"He's gonna get himself killed out there, Linda. I don't want my baby dying out in the streets. I love him," my mother cried.

She tugged on my shirt but I relentlessly moved forward, ignoring my mother's wailing. It hurt to see her in pain but it was for the best. I couldn't continue to do what I do, and still live under my people's roof. It was the only thing that Aunt Linda and I agreed on.

Outside on the porch, my mother was still unyielding. "Vincent, this ain't you. Please, stay and get your life right. God will work it out for you, baby," she cried.

"Jean, let him go," Aunt Linda yelled.

"No, he's not your son. He's my only child. I can't let him go and destroy himself."

"Ma, let me go. I'm good," I said.

"No, you're not. I want you to stay! Talk to me," she screamed.

Aunt Linda was pulling at my moms, trying to get her away from me while my mom kept pulling at me. I tried to make my way to the car. I saw some of the neighbors being nosey and I got upset.

"What the fuck y'all lookin' at…? Mind y'all fuckin' business!" They kept looking and shaking their heads.

Finally, I was free of my mother's strong grip and ran for the car. My mother tried to chase after me, but my aunt grabbed her and held onto her. I tossed the bag in the backseat.

"Vincent, don't go….don't leave me. God, please bring him back. Oh God don't let him leave, protect him, protect him," she cried.

"Jean, let him go. Can't you see that he's stubborn?"

My mother fell on the grass, her tear-stained eyes looking at me in despair. We gazed at each other briefly and I started to tear up. I was breaking her heart. It was the last thing I wanted to do. My life had changed dramatically and I didn't want to get my family caught up in the streets.

Aunt Linda held my moms and was consoling her, saying, "He'll come back and get his act right. He'll come back, Jean."

"I love y'all," I said.

I quickly jumped in the GS, started it and sped off the block as fast as I could. Racing down the street, my tears were streaming down my cheeks. The life I had with my mother and aunt was over.

Twenty

I was talking with Tyriq about the deal with Inf. He loved that I took the initiative setting up shop and trying to put more money in his organization. He looked at me like a proud father.

"We already have Tango up in north Philly." Spoon was against it.

Tango was Spoon's boy and he didn't want to be stepping on toes. Fuck stepping on toes! Philly was a big city and this was my connect. I was in the inner circle. I was an associate holding down my own. I proved that I could kill at will and moved drugs from state to state with no problems. I was a fast learner and caught on quickly.

Tyriq offered me the buildings between South Rd and 107th Avenue to run business. I had to get a crew and move the work. I had seven project buildings. He would front me keys from the Jamaicans and I had to bottle it up and stretch the work out to the crews.

I was trying to lock down respect and my name. There were still many that didn't know my name. In the long run, that meant problems.

Soul and Omega helped me run the spot. They were a few years younger than me to. Soul, I knew from the basketball courts back in the days when we used to go balling all the time. He was a cool dude who was musically gifted and a real hustler. Soul was known for having the baddest bitch. She was a ten, America was her name. He was ready to kill anyone who came at her sideways.

Omega came from a family of gangsters. Back in the eighties, his older brother was an enforcer for the Supreme team. Omega and I weren't cool like that. He was Soul's right hand man and he felt I didn't deserve to be running shit. He had been in the game since he was thirteen. I've been doing this shit for months and I was already locking shit down. Omega was ambitious and ruthless.

Tyriq gave me a south Philly pipeline. Thanks to Tyriq, I was officially Inf's connect.

"Vince, that's yours. You set it up, get the weight from me and supply that nigga down there. You ready for this right?"

"Yeah, I got this," I said real confident.

Tyriq smiled and said, "Ayyite, it's good to see you step up my nigga. Get this money and us right?"

"Us," I said, giving him dap and embracing him.

I was definitely becoming a legit player in this game. Bricks from Tyriq cost me twenty-one thousand dollars. I charged, thirty-thousand. They would take as many as twenty birds at a time. With the many spots Inf had controlled over he was flipping them making forty-five to fifty grand on each bird. The drug game in Philly was crazy.

In my spot we moved eight to ten birds. Inf was moving fifteen to twenty-five. But the money was good and abundant all over. We moved dope, coke, ecstasy and weed straight off the boat.

I adopted Tyriq's method in transporting the keys out of town. Young girls were dressed in cotton pregnant suits with the tight stitched lining for drug support. With my suits, each girl could carry up to six kilos. Anything over that we shipped in vehicles or trucks with large secret compartments and air shocks so that the car wouldn't fall to the ground. With cities like Memphis, we would ship one-hundred kilos at a time across state lines and in Okalahoma up to fifty kilos. In Gary, Indiana they were getting a hundred and fifty bricks. Gary was a straight slum. All the fiends got high. It was '02 and the drug game was still lucrative.

After 9/11, people were scared of there being another terrorist attack and they wanted to escape the fear, so they got high, and getting high cost money. I mean it was a good year for the game, because the government and the feds had their noses so far up Osama Ben Laden's ass hunting him down, that the drug game felt it got a free pass for the moment.

Jobs were lost and a few businesses closed down, leaving folks running to the unemployment line and worrying about a source of income. We provided relief for people. The fiends came to us like we had the answers.

I got Shae involved with my movement. Ever since our trip to Albany; I had developed a soft spot for her. I'd give her money to take care of her son and looked out for her when I could. We even went out a couple of times.

By November, I was making so much fucking money that I didn't know what to do with it. As my life flourished in the drug world, the relationship I had with my family was crumbling. I hadn't spoken to my mother in a month and it was even more of a strain with Chandra. I was seeing my son less and less, and when I wanted to scoop my little man up to chill with him, Chandra would be against it, saying to me, "I don't want our son around what you've become. You've become a dangerous man, Vincent."

"What the fuck you mean I'm dangerous to my son," I barked. "I'm a man, holding down my own and taking care of my business, Chandra, respect that."

I heard her snicker over the phone. "Uh huh, I can't respect that."

"Fuck you, Chandra. A year ago you was thirsty for me giving you that paper, now you wit' this all holy act and shit. You playing yourself," I shouted.

"See, there goes that attitude. I'm tryin' to talk to you in a civilized manner and you acting a fool over the phone," she said.

"Whateva…!"

"And you need to call your mother; she and your aunt are worried sick over you, Vincent?"

"Y'all been talking?" I asked.

"Yes, I call her and she calls me, asking if I heard from you. I tell her yes. You're breaking that poor woman's heart, Vincent. Why don't you just go back to her, let her know you're okay."

"I got my reasons," I explained matter-of-factly.

I heard her sigh. "I'm gonna pray for you Vincent, because your soul is heading in the wrong direction."

"What, you wit' religion," I said, chuckling.

"Yes, I got baptized three weeks ago," she informed.

I was shocked. "Fo' real…?"

"Yes, and Jamal goes to church with me."

Hearing her speak his name got me upset and I said, "Yeah, whateva, that nigga got you brainwashed."

"You're the one brainwashed, Vincent. Look at what you're becoming. The devil is in you, you just don't know. You think what you're doing is rich. Your life is not rich, it's blasphemy," she said.

"Chandra, please preach that somewhere else. I just wanna talk about my son," I said. "Can I talk to him at least?"

"He's sleeping right now, call back tomorrow."

"Whateva, you need money?"

"No, I got a promotion at my job. It's getting better for me. God is good," she proclaimed.

"That's what's up. Tell my son I love him. And you be safe," I said calmly.

"Can I pray for you Vincent?" she asked.

"Nah, I gotta go," I said and hung up.

I sat alone for a moment, thinking about my son and Chandra and my moms. I could no longer look that beautiful woman in the eye and not think about the pain I caused her. I didn't want my moms to see that I'd become a bonafide drug-dealer and killer. The further I was away from my peoples, the easier it was to continue doing what I had to do to stack papers.

Getting back with Chandra was no longer a reality for me. We both were going different ways, living different lives. I was still in love with her and the thought of her and Jamal becoming a family together hurt me. My family was this game and my crew. In order for me to survive this game, I had to let my domestic life be nothing but a memory. Constantly I reminded myself that the past was in the past. I was in too deep to stop.

Twenty-One

I loved the stares and awes that we got on Supthin Blvd as I cruised in the passenger seat of Tyriq's 2002 blue Aston Martin Vanquish. It was a hundred and thirty thousand dollar car with fine beige leather interior, rarely seen anywhere especially Jamaica, Queens. I was there when Tyriq purchased it in cash, from a high-end dealership in Great Neck, Long Island. I wanted one but had my eyes on a burgundy Bentley coup.

I was on the phone talking to a bitch, while Tyriq navigated through light traffic while puffing a Black & Mild. Business was great and the streets were our personal bank. I was pumping out over a hundred grand a week in some spots, pushing coke and weed to fiends. That Philly money from Inf was triple that.

I had diamonds, platinum and cars. I had money. And finally, I had respect. Tyriq continued supplying the product and my life felt like I was in the shoes of Tony Montana. I was slowly becoming Tyriq's right hand man and with Spoon, it felt like the Three Musketeers.

We pulled up to this club on Hillside Avenue called, Left Lane. There was a crowd of hundreds waiting outside to get in to see *50 Cent* perform. He was a hot, up-and-coming rapper from around the way that was doing his thang on the mix tapes. Dozens of cars jammed the avenue, with strong police presence in the vicinity.

Tyriq slowly drove by the barricade and parked in front of the club. All eyes were on us as we got out the car and made our way to the front, skipping the long lines that snaked around the corner. We went passed security without hassle. They knew who we were and gave us a head nod.

Inside, the club was jammed packed with revelers grinding and dancing it out on the floor, as the DJ provided hot mixes. The thunderous bass from the half dozen speakers in the club ripped through the crowd. A few bitches caught my eyes when I walked in. I watched them pull up their skirts a bit and back it up, looking like they were ready to fuck on the dance floor.

I followed Tyriq through the dense crowd that parted as we headed to VIP.

"Tyriq, what up?" some dude greeted, giving Tyriq dap.

"Tyriq, what's good?" a man greeted.

"Yo, T., I need to holler at you when you get that chance," a chubby nigga with a fat chain around his neck said to Tyriq.

"Hey Tyriq, hey Vince," a fine shortie in a tight black cat suit greeted us.

"Hey, Vince, we need to talk," this big booty shortie said hugging and kissing me.

Tyriq and I smiled and kept it moving to the back. We came to a remote black door, where a burly bouncer was keeping guard.

"He up in here…?" Tyriq asked.

The bouncer nodded his head and moved to the side. We both entered the room, and I was shocked to see a NYPD sergeant standing before us in uniform and all, with the three chevrons decorating his shoulders. He was tall and lean, clean-shaven, with sandy-blonde hair.

"Tyriq, what's good?" he greeted.

"Manny," Tyriq greeted back.

The cop looked at me and twisted his face and asked, "Yo, who the fuck is this?"

"Yo, chill, this is my boy, Vince. He's cool people. We grew up together," Tyriq informed the officer.

"You know how I am about having new faces around me, Tyriq, that's not good business. I deal with a selected few."

"Get used to him, ayyite Manny? He's gonna be around more often," Tyriq said.

Sgt Manny looked over at me, his face not looking too pleased. "If you say he's your boy and he's cool, then ok but no more faces, Tyriq. I fucking mean that."

"What, you threatening me, Manny?"

"This is my fuckin' Job, Tyriq. I'm risking a lot dealing with your black ass, you hear me. If it wasn't for the money, I'd have your black ass up in Rikers Island so fast, you'd think that your mother gave birth to your there."

Tyriq laughed, peering at Sgt Manny. "Money talks, right?"

"That's right, my nigga and don't ever forget that," Sgt Manny sarcastically replied. "And speaking of money, where's our cut?"

Tyriq reached into his jacket and pulled out a white envelope bulging with cash. Sgt Manny took it and counted the cash quickly.

"Fifty Gs' all there," Tyriq said.

Sgt. Manny smiled and stuffed the envelope in a bag.

"Do I still have a clean bill of health?" Tyriq asked.

"Everything's alright at the precinct. The Lieutenant will be happy. This little incentive keeps you off our shit list. My officers are gonna keep doing what they do, as long as you keep doing what you do and that includes dropping fifty grand a month."

Tyriq gave Sgt Manny a wicked smirk. "Don't worry about the money. That's not a problem. Money is gonna keep coming."

Sgt. Manny smiled, staring at Tyriq. Tyriq's stare let Manny knew he was not the one to be fuck with.

"I'll see you around, Tyriq."

"Use the backdoor. You don't want my peoples to see your white ass." Tyriq cautioned.

"Fuck you!"

The officer left and I asked. "What's up with that?"

"One hand washing the other," he said to me. "See the one thing you need to go far in this game here, is influence. A bulky envelope to the city's finest once a month is all the influence I need to keep my business going without problems from these crackers. Cops gonna be in your shit one way or the other, either locking you up, or getting a piece of the action—either way, you're gonna pay.

"You trust that cracker?" I asked.

"Nah," he admitted. "That's why I always have a back-up plan."

"And what's that?"

Tyriq chuckled. “C’mon, enough about business, let’s go get our party on,” he said putting his arm around me and leading me out the room. We went back into the main club.

“Soon, you’ll be a pro at this, Vince.”

Twenty-Two

Spoon...

Spoon walked out his three bed-room home in Brentwood feeling sick. He had to make another trip down the New Jersey Turnpike. It was three weeks since their last meeting. His stomach was in knots. *Fuck snitching*, he thought but his back was against a wall.

Spoon tossed his .9mm handgun onto the passenger seat and then quickly curved over facing the grass and vomit. He stayed in that position for a few moments, then wiped the corners of his mouth with the back of his hand and stood up, trying to regain his composure.

Life was getting risky and he wanted a way out. The safety of his kids and his two baby mammas were on his mind. The heat was on and the government was using him as their pawn for the meltdown. Spoon had been wired up for weeks taping. He had the recorder in his pocket and wanted to smash it but knew better. Tyriq was his brother. He hated the feeling of betrayal. His cell rang.

"Yo," he answered.

"You remember the location?"

"Yeah…"

"You have sound?" Agent Smith asked.

"Yeah…"

"Be there on time."

"I'll be there."

Spoon hung up. He had recorded Tyriq along with others in the crew. It wasn't concrete evidence but Spoon knew it was something.

He got behind the driver's seat, started the car and was ready to back out the driveway. His cell rang a second time.

"Yo..." Spoon answered.

"Where are you?" Tyriq asked.

"On my way out to take care of sump'n..."

"We need to meet. Sump'n came up."

"What...?"

"I don't talk business over the line. Meet me at the lounge, we'll talk," Tyriq said.

"I'm busy..."

"Busy doing what, my nigga? Shit's important, come holla at me..."

"I'll be there in a minute..."

Nervousness coursed through him. Tyriq was shrewd but Spoon was careful when he was around the crew. Tyriq had many inside paid moles in the streets, from law enforcement, to civil service workers and attorneys. Spoon didn't know who knew what. The Jamaicans had so much money to spread around for information they wanted on an individual that niggas would give up their own mothers for the power of a dollar.

Spoon had witnessed what the Jamaicans were capable of doing firsthand. They sometimes knew about informants, upcoming raids by police, or future warrants on certain spots before they were carried out. Payments to civil service workers, clerks, or court officers got them information.

The Jamaicans would take care of the informant ASAP.

Demetrius had came to Tyriq and asked for his help in locating Stipple, one of his drug runners who was about to turn states evidence against them. He had been hiding in Queens to escape death. In return, Demetrius promised to give Tyriq five extra bricks free.

"Just find dat blood-claat snitch and terminate him," Demetrius said.

Tyriq subtly put the word out about Stipple around town, turning to moles and paid officers for any information about Stipple. With enough money being spread around, word got back to Tyriq. Stipple family's whereabouts were discovered, and where Stipple would be testifying at a preliminary examination were also known. Demetrius put two of his most feared enforcers to handle the hunt—Rude Boy Rex, and Nappy Head Don. They both were callous, brutal, and skillful. These two men were ready to kill at will, even shoot someone in cold-blood in public.

With the information on Stipple's family, Spoon rode with Nappy Head Don and Rude Boy Rex to Astoria, Queens. It was Spoon's first time meeting the two Jamaican hit men. By their cold stare, Spoon knew these men were pedigree killers. They parked in front of the projects on 27th Av and calmly made their way into the belly of the projects to carry out the mission.

It was a chilly November morning and many residents busied themselves with the day's chores. No one noticed Nappy Head Don strolling through the streets in a long, leather trench coat, with his neatly cared for dreads falling down to his back and tied together with rubber-bands. Concealed under his coat were a machete and a fully loaded Glock 17. Rude Boy Rex had on the same style trench and wore his dreads out, looking like a lion's mane was around his face. He carried a long machete and a fully loaded Uzi. He sported red beads and wore a murderous stare that made him look crazy.

Spoon wore a dark brown North Face Parka and ski hat. He followed behind the homicidal duo the .380 concealed snuggly in his waistband. The men were unfazed by the cold. Nappy Head Don looked at Spoon.

"Bredren, mi gwan find dis batty-boy-snitch and cut off his bomba-claat head…yuh hear? Mi kills for fun."

Spoon went along and braced himself for anything that could go down. They made it to the building and took the elevator to the fifth floor and found the apartment. Nappy Head Don put his ear to the door and heard the television playing loudly. He knew someone was home. Nappy Head Don then looked at Rude Boy Rex and said in his thick Jamaican accent, "Rude Boy, we come n' silence."

Rude Boy nodded, knowing what he meant. While Spoon sat back and watched, Rude Boy Rex began picking the lock to the apartment door silently and skillfully with a small electric pick gun. Within a minute they had entrance to the apartment with the element of surprise to the residents.

All three men walked in. Spoon quietly closed the door behind him and removed his .380. Nappy Head Don and Rude Boy Rex pulled out their long machetes and examined the place. The TV was on in the living room. No one was watching. Soon they heard voices coming from the kitchen and the bedroom. The hallway was short and narrow, and cluttered with sneakers shoes and children's toys. Nappy Head Don was the first to slowly creep down the cluttered corridor with his machete gripped in his hand and heard a woman say, "Stipple, I'm scared baby. Where are you?"

Nappy stopped, listening to the conversation and then heard the woman say, "I got our shit packed. What about the police? I know baby. My sisters in the bedroom with Sheila…Do you gotta do this? I need you here…okay…yes…I hear you…"

Before she could say anything else, Nappy Head Don moved stealthily at the woman and put the sharp blade to her throat. She shrieked, and her eyes widened with fear. The phone had dropped from her hands and fell to the floor.

"Mi come fi yuh blood-claat husband," Nappy said. He had her in a stronghold position and pressed the machete deeper into her exposed throat, nicking her with the blade.

"Via, you there….Via, what's goin' on?" Nappy Head Don heard Stipple shouting through the phone receiver.

Rude Boy Rex rushed into the bedroom wielding the machete around like a mad man and soon Spoon heard screaming and panicking coming from the bedroom.

"Mi wan talk to Stipple, pick up the phone slowly," Nappy ordered.

She was in tears and shaken, but did what she was told, picking up the phone and holding it in her hand. She still heard Stipple's worried voice crackling over the phone line.

"Via, talk to me…Via, what's going on. Via! Via!" they all heard Stipple scream out.

It didn't make Stipple nerves any better when he heard his daughter and Via's sister screaming. Via put the phone to her ear again and in a traumatized voice said, "Baby…baby..."

"Via, what's wrong? You okay?" Stipple yelled.

Nappy Head Don snatched the phone from Via's hand and shouted into the phone, "Stipple…mi need fi talk to you right now."

Hearing Nappy Head Don's voice made Stipple's heart drop into his stomach. He knew everything he loved was fucked.

"Where's my wife!" Stipple exclaimed.

"In mi hands. Da machete is on her blood-claat throat."

"Oh fuck! Don't you dare touch her," Stipple yelled.

"Yuh think yuh can run from us…mi come fi ya, Stipple."

"What you want from me?"

"Bredren, yuh know what we want…meet us here, at dis place soon, and nah bring batty bwoy cops wit' ya, Stipple…mi want yuh alone, bredren… come alone for yuh wife and family's life," Nappy Head Don sternly said and hung up.

Nappy Head Don pushed Via to the floor and glared at her. Rude Boy Rex dragged her sister and the little girl from out the bedroom at knife point and they pushed the two down next to Via. The three were in tears, crying and panicking and huddling against each other in fear.

"You think he's gonna come?" Spoon asked.

"Bredren, Stipples gwan come, cuz he know di shotta reputation vicious…him not gwan want ti find his family butchered in trash bags."

Hearing that, Via and the others cried out louder and prayed.

An hour and a half later, there was a loud knock at the door. Spoon quickly stood up from the couch with the .380 in his hand and became alert. Nappy Head Don walked to the door and peered through the peephole, the blade still in his hand.

"Stipple…?" he asked.

"Let my family go," Stipple shouted.

Nappy opened the door, and Stipple charged in like a mad man with a .45 firing a shot at but missing. Stipple was desperate and knew the only reasoning done with the Jamaicans was through violence. He wanted his wife and family freed from this brute's hands by any means necessary.

He couldn't overpower the six-two Jamaican gangster in the corridor Spoon had his gun trained at the struggle but couldn't get off a shot. Nappy Head Don quickly reacted and grabbed Stipple by his arms, and tossed him against the wall. Rude Boy Rex was about to come to his friend's aid bu Nappy Head Don soon had the struggle under control.

He swung the machete downwards with monstrous force. It sliced through Stipple's arm, easily severing flesh and bone. Stipple screamed in horror, as his arm with the .45 in it fell in a pool of blood.

"Aaaaaahhh…fuck. Ah shit……Aaaaaahhh," Stipple screamed

collapsing to the floor.

"Bombo-claat!" Nappy shouted. He was upset and kicked Stipple in the stomach while he was down screaming in agony.

Nappy Head Don dragged Stipple into the kitchen, leaving a trail of blood. He saw his family gagged, tied and sprawled butt-ass naked on their stomachs. When the family witnessed Stipple being dragged into the kitchen screaming with half his arm cut off, they squirmed, cried, mumbling incoherently from under the duct-tape covering their mouths. There was horror in their eyes.

Spoon walked into the kitchen. He was about to observe the savage killing that was ready to go down. The door was locked and the next door neighbors weren't home. Stipple's fate was sealed.

Rude Boy Rex and Nappy Head Don towered over the helpless and whimpering Stipple as he lay curled up on the floor. He was bleeding and was turning pale. He pleaded with his attackers.

"Please, let my family go. They have nuthin' to do with this."

"Stipple, yuh fate is their fate," Nappy Head Don said.

"No…fuck you! Fuck you!" Stipple cried.

"Mi tired a the game, batty-bwoy," Nappy said.

He walked over to Stipple's wife and looked at her. Via's arms were tied behind her back. Her naked breasts and nipples pressed against the kitchen floor. Unbeknownst to Stipple, Rude Boy Rex had raped, tortured and sodomized his wife beforehand with a broomstick and then did the same to her sister.

"Mi boy, Rude Boy fucked yuh blood-claat wife's pussy hole real good…Stipple, why yuh runnin' yuh blood-claat mouth to da blood-claat police? Ya were family, Stipple. Why yuh wan gwan and vex a man like me…huh, Stipple? Now ya fucked," Nappy Head Don said.

"C'mon man, don't fuckin' do this," Stipple shouted.

He watched Nappy stand over his wife with the machete gripped tightly in his hand. Nappy crouched down over Via, grabbed her by the hair harshly, yanking her head back with force and put the machete to her throat.

Nappy glared at Stipple one last time and said, "Yuh get to watch ya Bombo-claat wife die in front of yuh, for betrayin' Shotta."

Nappy Head Don carved open Via's throat with the machete. Blood squirted everywhere like a sprinkler. Via's sister and the daughter squirmed frantically in fear witnessing Via dying slowly. She gurgled with her mouth still taped shut and began choking from blood.

"God no, no, no,Via!" Stipple cried out, trying to crawl to his wife.

Nappy carved open her throat so deep, that he nearly took her head off. Rude Boy Rex smiled at the heinous act done and wanted next. Spoon shook his head looking stunned.

Nappy then stood over Via's sister, and pulled her by her hair forcefully, snapping her neck back. She struggled but it was useless. Nappy put the blade to her throat and carved open the sister neck, spilling blood onto the white tiled floor, creating a crimson stain on the kitchen floor. She choked and died under his hands.

Stipple cried like a baby. His only concern was for his eight-year old daughter.

"She's just a child, don't do this to her. Please, I'm begging you!" Stipple exclaimed.

Nappy stared at Stipple with ice-cold eyes and smirked. He then reached down for Stipple's daughter and grabbed a handful of her hair. He pulled her head back relishing the agony and fear building in his victim's eyes.

Spoon's heart raced.

"Why the kid…?"

"Bredren, mi wan leave no livin' soul behind…mi spread dis room wit' fear….to let all know, man, woman, and child… Shotta is king of all! Shotta rules!" Nappy shouted then butchered the girl.

Spoon closed his eyes and turned his head, but he still heard the painful wailing of Stipple. It was a dreadful sound like a wild animal being eaten. The painful cries of Stipple echoed in Spoon's head. It was one he never wanted to hear again. Spoon thought of his own children and knew he would die protecting them before any savage muthafucka laid a hand on them.

With his hands red with blood, Nappy Head Don then walked over to Stipple. He looked at Rude Boy Rex and nodded. They both raised their machetes in the air and swung down with extreme force, hacking Stipple up and decapitating him like he was a lamb in the slaughter house. Nappy Head

Don then picked up Stipple's removed head and looked into the dead man's eyes—it was frozen with death and horror, just the way Nappy loved his victims.

"Y'all some sick-asses," Spoon said.

He watched Nappy placed the head over the sink and began draining the blood down into the kitchen sink. He then washed it off and placed it into a black plastic garbage bag.

"Da boss wanna see da head of a snitch," Nappy said raising the bag.

By noon, all three men were out of the apartment and back out into the cold bitter air. Nappy and Rude Boy showed no remorse for the atrocious acts they committed. It was business and a strong message needed to be sent.

A frantic neighbor would find the bodies a few hours later. It'd be the most horrible crime scene that the neighborhood would experience. The media ate it up especially the part about an eight-year old girl being murdered and the headless corpse found.

Spoon knew that his world and the Jamaicans were completely different—the Jamaicans took murder to a whole new level. He witnessed firsthand what would happen to someone if they ever crossed them. From that day Spoon never trusted the Jamaicans and knew to be extra cautious whenever he was around them.

◇◇◇◇◇◇◇◇◇◇◇◇◇◇◇◇◇◇◇◇◇◇◇◇◇◇◇◇◇◇◇◇◇◇◇◇

Spoon sat in his truck for awhile thinking about the meeting he had with the agents. Then mulling over about Tyriq calling him and why he wanted to meet. He was uneasy about the meeting and thought against going but didn't want to have anyone doubting his loyalty.

He got out his truck and rushed back into the crib. He went down into the basement, went over to where his discreet safe was stashed and began punching in the combination to get it open. He swung open the door and dropped stacks of money into a blue duffle bag. He dropped three-hundred thousand dollars into the bag and quickly zipped it up and rushed back to the Range Rover.

He backed out of his driveway like a bat out of hell and as soon as he hit the stop sign at the corner, he got on his phone and called Melissa, one of his baby-mothers.

"What you want, Spoon?" Melissa asked, sounding disturbed.

"Listen, I'll be at your place in fifteen minutes," he quickly said.

"You coming over?" she asked.

"I'll be there soon, just be up."

"Just ring me when you're near." Melissa sucked her teeth and hung up.

Spoon jumped on the Southern State Parkway hurrying to Queens. He had the duffle bag with the money right next to him on the passenger seat, and knew he was living on borrowed time. He did so much dirt in his lifetime that he knew one day karma would probably come back on him twice. He had this eerie feeling that something was about to go down.

Spoon pulled up to Melissa's home in Queens Village and got out of the truck carrying the duffle bag in his grip. He wanted Melissa to hold on to the money in case something happened to him. He wanted his kids to have an optimistic future for themselves—one that he never had growing up.

He knocked on Melissa's door, waiting impatiently for her to answer. Time was important for him. Melissa opened the door and snapped, "Nigga, I said call when you get near. I'm not even dressed."

There was no time for arguing. He gently pushed Melissa to the side and made his way inside. Melissa looked at him like he was crazy, but kept her cool and noticed the small duffle bag on her couch.

She walked over to Spoon wearing a white Terry cloth robe and looked at the bag and asked, "What's inside?"

Spoon looked at her and stated, "I need you to keep that for me. There's three-hundred thousand in that bag for you and my kids in case something happens to me."

Melissa suddenly became worried.

"What do you mean, Spoon? What's goin' on?"

"Just take the money and put it someplace safe," he instructed.

"Are you in trouble?" she asked worried.

"Just take the shit and keep it safe, Melissa," he barked.

Spoon was never the type to explain himself to anyone. He wanted to keep it moving without being interrogated. Melissa cared, but knew that jail and death could be around the corner for him.

Spoon made his way to the front door, but Melissa pulled at his shirt, slowing him down. She looked deep into his eyes. Spoon returned the gaze. "Baby, please be safe. I love you your kids love you, too, please come back to us."

Spoon smiled. This thang ain't for him anymore, he thought. He was having mixed feelings about killings, the trafficking and the drugs he pushed that made him millions. The game was really ugly. He had seen things that'd make any man crawl into a corner, freeze up and have nightmares.

He was thinking about his kid's safety and the real estate business he had started. Spoon wanted to get out the drug game and go legit. He wanted a new life, something the feds were promising him if he continued to cooperate. Spoon contemplated being a tax-paying civilian and raising his family like a regular father. The odds of that happening were stacked against him.

Spoon towered over Melissa's beautiful petite frame.

"I love you, baby, and the kids. "

It was the first time Melissa had ever heard him say "I love you." She had tears in her brown eyes when she leaned and their lips fervently locked. Spoon pulled himself away.

Melissa stood in her doorway, and watched Spoon get into his truck and tears flowed. She held herself with her arms folded across her chest, leaning against the doorway, watching. When the Range Rover was no longer visible, she closed the door and slowly made her way back into the living room. Melissa looked at the duffle bag and thought she might not see Spoon alive again. She fell to the floor and cried, knowing death was coming for him.

Twenty-Three

Spoon pulled up to the club, thought about his options, and cocked his weapon, securing a deadly round in the chamber. He concealed it in the waistband of his jeans and stepped out of the truck. Coolly, he walked to the entrance. Unsure, he was when greeted by security and his family, giving certain niggas dap navigating his way through the dense revelers that danced to the deafening sounds of Biggie Smalls, *Hypnotized.*

Spoon made his way upstairs and saw Tyriq lounging on the couch talking to an associate with stacks of money on a table in front of them. The only other person in the room was Tip. He was lounging around on a nearby couch and nodded when Spoon walked in.

"What's good, Tyriq?" Spoon hollered.

"Nigga, I called you what, an hour ago…? Fuck, you just coming now," Tyriq spat.

"I had to take care of some thangs," Spoon informed.

Tyriq looked at Spoon for a moment. He reached down to the floor and tossed a package to Spoon. A kilo of cocaine landed in Spoon's hand, and Spoon barked.

"Nigga, what the fuck is wrong? You know we don't keep drugs in here."

"Taste it," Tyriq said.

Spoon looked at Tyriq and then cut open the package with a small blade and tasted the kilo that was supposed to be pure uncut cocaine. It left a bitter taste of baby powder mixed with baking soda.

"What the fuck is this?" Spoon asked.

"You tell me, nigga...your peoples were supposed to deliver five bricks to Beng here, and all he got was three pure bricks. The rest was some bullshit. Niggas switched up," Tyriq informed.

"Tate...?" Spoon asked.

"Them your peoples, Spoon...you need to handle that," Tyriq said.

"Tate's sixteen year old, younglings..."

"Uh huh... and played you. He's stealing from us, Spoon. I mean an ounce or two, that's one thing, a nigga get beaten down, hospitalized and shit. The disrespect had our organization looking like we a muthafuckin joke—we out two bricks to Beng and a message needs to be sent. That's your peoples, you handle yours, ayyite!" Tyriq sternly stated.

It was a situation that Spoon didn't want to be in. Tate was Melissa's younger cousin. He put Tate onto the game a few months ago, to help put some money in the little nigga's pockets. He had Tate bagging up drugs and making deliveries. Tate was really smart. He was from a broken home like Spoon and needed a break. Tate was wilding before Spoon put him on, robbing people and shooting folks in the foot. The streets were swallowing him up. All Tate needed was guidance. Spoon offered him fifteen-hundred a week to work for him. Tate jumped at the opportunity.

Within three months, Tate had put together his own network and they started getting money with Spoon. They all hung out on Supthin and Foch and were given respect. They were all a young, fresh crew and some too smart for their own good.

Now hearing the news that Tate was stealing from them, upset Spoon. He had love for Tate who was like family. But stealing two keys was the death penalty.

"You gonna handle that, right Spoon?" Tyriq asked.

"I'm on my thang," Spoon replied nonchalantly.

Tyriq and Spoon locked eyes for a short moment. Tyriq then took a pull from his Black & Mild, and then said, "What's up wit' you nigga? You acting like you bothered by this shit. What, you bitching up on us, Spoon? You scared to kill now? Or are you stealing too, nigga?"

"Nigga don't go there...you know I've been doing my thang since day fucking one!" Spoon barked.

Tyriq smirked and nodded his head. "Ayyite, fucking around my nigga... You've been like distanced from us the past few weeks. Everything good…?"

"Everything's good."

"Alright, I like that, but Tate gotta go," Tyriq reiterated.

"I understand."

"Matter fact, take out his whole crew, clear that corner up…bitch asses probably all stealing."

"Why?"

"Cuz nigga, one message ain't strong enough. I want niggas out there to understand that if one nigga fucks up by stealing, everybody in the crew fucking pays. That's how you keep little niggas like that in check. I want everybody watching everybody!"

Spoon was against what Tyriq was saying. He was the one who brought Tate into the game and had to be the one to take him out. Tate trusted Spoon it'd be easy to kill the nigga since he was close.

"When will I get the two keys I paid for?" Beng asked.

"You'll get your shit, nigga. Let us handle this problem," Tyriq snapped at Beng.

"Time is money, Tyriq," Beng replied.

"You think I don't fucking know that. How long we been doing business, Beng?"

"Too fucking long," Beng replied.

"You'll get your shit, you just fucking chill," Tyriq barked.

Beng looked at Tyriq knowing not to push the issue. He sat back on the couch and took a deep pull from his cigar and went on to minding his business.

Tyriq stood up and walked over to Spoon. He then said to Spoon in a calm voice, "I know you're still a wild nigga on the inside, even though you ain't bust off your gun in a minute. But let's not let these niggas forget who we are and what we about. Remind them how we came up in this game, murdering niggas that fucked wit' us. Us, always…right Spoon?"

Spoon nodded and replied. "Us…"

Tyriq then embraced him a strong hug so close that if Spoon was wearing the wire, Tyriq would have felt it on him. Tyriq then broke away from Spoon and looked him in the eyes and alleged, "We get this money like brothers out here."

"Like brothers," Spoon returned.

Spoon then walked out the room feeling uneasy. Everything seemed all good and calm, but that was the problem, it was too calm. Spoon began to wonder why Tyriq hugged him so close, yeah it was love, but to Spoon it felt like Tyriq was searching for something when he hugged him.

Tip followed Spoon out of the room and they both got into his truck and drove off toward Supthin. Spoon glanced at the time. Five minutes passed ten. He was supposed to meet with the agents at eleven off the Turnpike. That meeting wasn't happening.

Spoon was behind the wheel, heading toward Foch and Supthin, knowing that his situation was getting tighter by the moment. It's been a year since he bodied anyone. The last was in Connecticut. The feds threatened to charge him if he didn't cooperate. Spoon had committed a dozen bodies and only been tried twice.

He was acquitted of both murders due to lack of evidence and witnesses not showing up. He felt his luck running out on the streets. The game was tightening like a noose, squeezing breath out of him.

His cell rang when he reached Supthin Blvd. He looked at the caller I.D. and it said, "Bitches…" It was the feds trying to reach him. Tip was riding shotgun, he had to be careful.

"What up, baby," Spoon answered.

"Where the fuck are you?" Smith barked.

"I'm kinda caught up doing my thang, right now," Spoon said.

"Spoon, we need you here with that audio ASAP. Stop fucking around."

"I know, baby…but I'm gonna be late."

"How late…?"

"In the morning, or tomorrow night sometime," Spoon said.

"Tomorrow night, the same location, no more games, Spoon. We need you to play ball with us all the way, or you'll find yourself striking out sooner than you think…"

"I'll see you soon, baby," Spoon said and hung up. His stress level zoomed upwards.

Never one with many words, Tip looked at him. He was about action and his gun did all the talking. He continued to look at Spoon.

"You got a new bitch on the phone?"

"Yeah, some ho I've been fuckin' for a minute now. Why you ask nigga?" Spoon asked, not fearing Tip.

"I'm just asking," Tip deadpanned.

"Then don't ask, I'm doing my thang with the bitch, not you," Spoon said.

"Ok, my nigga," Tip returned.

Tip took a pull from his Newport and turned his attention from Spoon. Tip had a feeling that something was up with Spoon. There was a vibe about him that wasn't good. Tip could stare a man down and knew if there was fear in him. Or he would know if that man was flaky and couldn't be trusted. Because of Tip's strong sixth sense about people Tyriq liked having him around. He told him who to trust and who not to.

Tip took a few more pulls from his cigarette and knew that wasn't a bitch Spoon was talking to on his phone. He wanted to take a look at Spoon's last call to confirm his suspicions.

Spoon rolled up on a few niggas chilling on Foch and Supthin Blvd, but none of them was Tate or his crew—just associates. The Range Rover came close to the curve and Spoon rolled his window down, staring at three young knuckleheads lingering in front of a bodega.

"Yo, anyone of y'all niggas seen Tate around?" Spoon shouted.

One of the young thugs recognized Spoon and approached the car with his pants sagging.

"Nah, he ain't been around all day, Spoon. He probably at his girl's..."

"You know where she stay?" Spoon asked.

"Yeah, in LI."

"You know where?"

"Nah, but Notch probably knows where, he be fucking her sister. I've been hitting these niggas all day. Ain't no one picking up. Everything alright, Spoon?"

"Yes, its okay," Spoon dryly answered.

The young thug peeped Tip and got nervous, fearing his murderous rep. To gain rep with the infamous duo he went on, “Yo, if y’all wanna know where Notch be, I can take y’all there.”

Spoon glanced and Tip and then turned his attention back to the youngling.

“What’s your name lil’ nigga?” Spoon asked.

“Ronny…”

“How old are you, Ronny?”

“Fifteen,” Ronny answered willingly.

“You sure you know where Notch is at right now?” Spoon asked.

“Yeah, he be shooting dice at this spot on Liberty, some back alley shit.”

“Get in nigga and show us,” Spoon said.

“Yo, hold it down, I’ll be right back,” Ronny said to his friends hanging with him. He jumped in the backseat and rode with gangsters he respected and heard much about.

Ten minutes later, the Range Rover pulled up to a back block off of Liberty, near 169th street. A few men were standing outside a dilapidated two story house smoking. They glared at the vehicle like it was trouble. Spoon moved his truck close. The back window slowly came down. The men had their hands near their weapons, preparing for anything. They chilled when Ronny stuck his head out.

“Yo Moe, is Notch back there?”

Moe took a pull from his cancer-stick and replied, “That nigga’s back there collecting paper.”

“I hear ya my nigga,” Ronny said and sat himself back in the seat. “Y’all want me to go get him?” Ronny asked.

“Yo, just tell that nigga to come to the truck,” Spoon said.

Ronny nodded and jumped out the truck and rushed to the back, not before giving Moe and his man, Left some dap. He then disappeared into the backyard leaving Spoon and Tip waiting. Moments later Ronny emerged with Notch by his side. Notch towered over Ronny by five inches. Notch was six-three, and lean, with nappy black hair. He came from the backyard smoking an L with a clump of money in his hand.

He knew the truck and approached it without a care. He stared at Tip and then noticed Spoon.

"What's good my niggas?" Notch asked puffing the burning L.

"You strap nigga?" Tip asked.

"Nah, shit's in my ride. Why, we got beef?" Notch asked. "Let me go get my gat."

"Nah, you good…just ride," Tip said.

Notch took one last pull from the L and flicked it into the street. He jumped into the truck. Ronny tried to follow.

"You stay here," Tip said handing Ronny a C-note

"Good looking."

The truck pulled off leaving Ronny smiling.

Notch sat quietly, wondering what this was about.

"Where's Tate? I've been looking for him." Spoon asked.

"He's been at his bitch's crib in LI for the past two days. He told me he was going out there to get his mind right."

"We just need to get up with him," Spoon said.

"I'll show y'all where it is," Notch said.

Spoon steered the truck toward the Southern State Parkway and pushed seventy to Brentwood. In no time, they were pulling up at the location.

"There's his ride right there," Notch said pointing at a white Porsche in the driveway.

Spoon got out the truck, followed by Tip and Notch. The three walked to the door covered by the thick shrubberies that lined the paved walkway and the cool air that blanketed the suburbs of Long Island. It was tranquil and the streets were lined with tall trees.

Spoon got to the wide oak door. He hoped that Tate was alone with his girlfriend. Notch was getting suspicious and wished he had brought his gat.

"The nigga in trouble?" he asked.

Tip didn't answer, in one rapid motion he held the 9mm to Notch's head.

"Get your boy outside to the door," Tip said.

Notch's eyes widened with fear. He had his arms spread out.

"What we do?" Notch asked panicking.

"Your boy fucked you," Spoon answered.

"I don't know what the fuck y'all are talking about," Notch said.

"Get him to the door or I'll blow your fuckin' head off," Tip threatened.

Notch knocked on the door, both men stay hidden. Tip's gun was trained on Notch.

Notch knocked on the door, acting like everything was good. Soon movement behind the door was heard.

"Who…?"

"Tammy its Notch, open up."

When she opened the door, Notch asked, "Tate here, right?"

"Yeah, he's in the bedroom. Why are you here so late? Sandy's at home," Tammy said.

Before Tammy could say anything else, Tip and Spoon quickly emerged from their hidden location. Tip grabbed Tammy and covered her mouth with the gat before she could shriek. Spoon pushed Notch inside closing the door.

Tip quickly pulled out the silencer to the .9mm and twisted it onto the gun. He pulled out white latex gloves from his pocket and tossed Spoon a pair.

Tammy was on the thick carpet clad in pink panties and a small T-shirt. She had an attractive slim figure with long blond hair and deep blue eyes.

"Bitch don't scream, yell or move," Tip warned with the gun aimed at her.

"How many in the house…?" Spoon asked.

"It's me and Tate," she answered in fear.

"You sure…?" Tip asked.

She nodded.

Tip then fired three shots into her scantily clad figure. Then he turned to Notch who had his back against the door and fired three times, dropping him. Tip didn't care if Notch was involved. There was a message to be sent to other crews.

Both men quietly made their way upstairs. They heard the television from the master bedroom. They walked down the corridor and pushed their way into the bedroom to find Tate sprawled out butt-naked on a king size bed.

When Tate saw Tip, he tried to jump out of bed and reach for his gun. Tip fired one shot into the back of his leg. Tate collapsed gripping his injured leg

"I ain't do it. Spoon. We boys, please..."

Spoon stood over him with the .45 in his hand.

"What you do with them two keys?"

"They gone man, but it wasn't on me. I wouldn't cross you like that. You fam."

Tip rushed up to Tate, grabbed him by his head and shouted, "Open up."

Tate tried to resist. A violent blow to his head with the gun ended that. Blood trickled from his mouth.

"Open up, nigga…!"

Tate slowly opened his jaws and felt the 9mm being stuffed down his throat, causing him to gag. Spoon looked down at Tate, staring into his pleading eyes.

"I'll make sure Melissa sees that you have a good home going service," Spoon said.

Poot-Poot!

The silent sound of death ripped through the back of Tate's throat. Tip stood up and looked down at his work. Gun smoke came out of Tate's wide opened mouth. There was a large crimson stain expanding in the back of Tate's head. They left Tate and Tammy's bodies for her parents to witness when they got home.

Leaving no prints behind, both went back to the truck and drove away with one problem solved.

◇◇◇◇◇◇◇◇◇◇◇◇◇◇◇◇◇◇◇◇◇◇◇◇◇◇◇◇◇◇◇◇◇◇◇◇

Miles away from the murder scene, Spoon pulled up to a local bodega for a drink and some cigarettes.

"You want anything?" Spoon asked, as he was about to exit his vehicle.

"Nah, but let me use your jack for a moment," Tip said.

"Where's your phone?" Spoon asked.

"Battery's dead," Tip answered showing Spoon his low battery signal.

Spoon looked reluctant, but didn't want to cause any suspicion. He removed his cell-phone from his hip and passed it to Tip.

"Don't call Tahiti," Spoon said. "I'll be right back."

Spoon ran into the store while Tip went searching incoming calls. He remembered the exact time of call. Surprisingly, the call Spoon got at eleven-fifty five was not there—*probably erased it*, Tip thought. He continued scrolling and saw Spoon had an unknown call at nine-forty five. Tip had reasons to believe that Spoon wasn't being straight-up.

Before Spoon came to the truck, Tip quickly called a bitch, talked for a short moment and hung up. Spoon came to the truck with a small bag in his hand. "You good…?"

"I'm good," Tip responded dryly.

He gave Spoon back his phone and knew they needed to dig deeper. He would tell Tyriq about his concerns. Spoon started the truck without knowing that the wheels of fate already began turning.

Twenty-Four

"To Vince, you always got love in Philly."

Inf raised his Moet bottle showing me love at his club on Board street.

He was celebrating his thirty-fifth birthday like a megastar. Inf had dozens of Cristal and Moet in the club. Numerous girls cluttered the club in their sexiest and skimpiest tight fitted attire. Diamonds and every fashion brand known were being flaunted by the fellows.

Because of me and the shit Tyriq was supplying, Inf and his goons made millions. I became richer. Inf and his crew had south Philly on lock with drugs and fear. The many cars, women, jewelry, violence and guns made them the epitome of ruthless drug dealers. The murder rate in South Philly was skyrocketing. Crime and drug use reached an all time high and the Tasker homes was one of the most feared projects in the city.

I felt like a superstar among Inf and his crew, they looked out for me and I did the same for them. Philly was becoming my town to party, fuck bitches, and get money. The food, lifestyle, and women had me spending more time there than anywhere else. Cashmere was my Philly bitch. We fucked like crazy but I had a wandering eye when it came to the sisters with the big booties and slim curvy waistlines. I had bitches scattered in every town for my enjoyment.

There was Meeka in Albany, Danielle in Connecticut there was this fine bitch in Baltimore named Shannon, I was fucking with. She was twelve years older than me and had two teenage kids in high school. In New York, I was getting with Shae. Out of all my hoes, Shae was wifey.

Despite Shae's occupation, she was more woman than the chickenheads I was fucking. She had goals and wasn't caught up in money, sex or bling. Shae was not up on a nigga because his pockets were fat like Starr Jones before surgery.

"I haven't been with someone in almost a year. Please be good to me." She told me the night I got with her.

She gently spread her legs for me. I slowly climbed on top of her. It was the best pussy I ever had. Her love making—wicked. I held her in my arms and we talked after.

"I want to control money, so money doesn't control me," she said to me.

She wanted to go to school for business investment. I was willing to put her through school and let her do her thing. She was my investment. Besides Chandra, Shae was the only girl that I loved. But that didn't stop me from slinging dick state to state. Money and pussy was becoming the root of all my evil.

◇◇◇◇◇◇◇◇◇◇◇◇◇◇◇◇◇◇◇◇◇◇◇◇◇◇◇◇◇◇◇◇◇◇◇◇◇

I was at the bar getting my drink on and chatting it up with this big titty, dark hair Dominican bitch. I was in a red velour suit and Sean John T-shirt, sporting new Jordan's. Diamond and platinum gleamed around my neck at Inf's party. I was a baller and bitches ate that shit up.

"You gonna buy me a drink?" she asked.

"Depends if you tell me your name," I replied.

She smiled, rubbed against my forearm and said, "Cherie."

"What you drinking, Cherie…?"

"Grand mariner and pineapple juice," she said perking her lips.

I ordered her drink, look at her from head to toe and smiled. She was wearing a short skirt, platform heels and a shirt so tight that it looked like her nipples were trying to escape.

My strong appetite for women grew the richer I got. Cherie sipped her drink and we talked. She wanted to do more.

"Your name ring bells," she said.

"What you heard?" I asked humorously.

"Good things," she smiled.

"Like what," I flirted.

"Que realmente sabes tomar cuidado de una mujer," she said with a thick Spanish accent.

I smiled, understanding her lingo.

"You looking for some maintenance?"

"Quiza…"

"We could do sump'n."

Cashmere stormed our way with a drink in her hand and a serious glare on her face. She threw a drink in Cherie's face and hit her with righ hook.

"Bitch, what da fuck you think you're doing with my man!"

Cherie quickly rebounded and went to attack Cashmere. I grabbed her and said, "Chill."

"Fuck that! Don't disrespect me like that. You stupid cunt," Cherie shouted.

"Bitch, do you know who the fuck I am?"

"Vete a la mierda, perra…I'll slice your fuckin' throat open," Cherie exclaimed.

"Let that bitch go!" Cashmere shouted trying to attack Cherie.

I continued to hold Cherie back from Cashmere.

"Vince, why you holding that bitch, huh…?"

There was a crowd around us. No one intervened because they didn't want it with Inf.

"Fucking chill wit' it, Cashmere," I shouted.

"Are you fucking the bitch?" Cashmere asked.

"Baby, let me go!" Cherie said enraging Cashmere.

"Who da fuck you calling baby?"

Cashmere went to the bar, picked up a beer bottle and smashed it against the counter top.

"Cashmere, fucking chill," I warned.

"Fuck you!"

Inf and his crew was coming our way. I didn't want the situation uglier but was ready for anything.

"Cashmere put the fuckin' bottle down. You trying to fuck up my party?" Inf asked his cousin.

"I'm bout ready to murder this bitch. Why she gotta be up on my man?"

"Vince, what's good?"

"Your cousin is wilding right now. It ain't even like that," I said.

"I ain't trying to have no drama on my birthday," Inf said. He looked at Cashmere. "Jake, take my cousin home."

"What…?"

"You ready to kill somebody and I can't be having no fucking bloodshed in my place on my birthday."

"Fuck y'all! I don't need this shit. I'll get that bitch on the rebound," Cashmere shouted.

She tossed the bottle, grabbed her purse and left with Jake following her. Inf came up to me and said, "Vince, let me holla at you for a sec."

I walked with him and he took a swig from the Moet.

"That's my cousin, right and I love her. You my nigga and I'd hate to see my cousin do something stupid because she's emotional off of you. That means I'm gonna have to get stupid and do what I gotta do. We don't need to get stupid up in here, you feel me?"

"Yeah, I feel you."

"We getting good money out here, so be good to her. I know you gonna do what you do…but don't fuck wit' her, cuz remember, she's family."

"It's all good. I'm gonna make it right wit' her."

"That's what I want to hear," he said giving me dap.

He then walked away. It was cool I definitely was gonna do me. I loved pussy too much to let it go, especially new pussy.

I strolled back into the party and went looking for Cherie. I caught the bitch coming out of the bathroom. She gave me a look I didn't like. We got to talking then took a stroll, ready to get it on and poppin.

◇◇◇◇◇◇◇◇◇◇◇◇◇◇◇◇◇◇◇◇◇◇◇◇◇◇◇◇◇◇◇◇◇◇◇◇◇◇

I had to pull over and quickly put the ride in park. Cherie's head game was serious. My dick was so far down her throat, it felt stuck there. She was sucking my dick so good she'd make a nigga crash.

"Oh shit," I moaned, with my hand tangled in her hair and my seat reclined. Cherie lips wrapped around my thick dick had me in bliss. *Yeah, this is how life should be—fucking bitches and getting paid.*

Cherie continued to deep-throat me, I stared out into the vast terrain of dilapidated row-houses stretching blocks down, abandon cars lining the streets, with fiends creeping through the cracks and alleys trying to score their next hit. I noticed a young teenager posted up on the corner, and his attire screamed hustler. He saw me getting a blowjob and he smiled. I smiled back.

Cherie was going to work on me down below; she began chewing on my nuts and jerked my long shaft with her soft delicate manicured fingers. Her lips and tongue coiled around every inch of my dick and I began finger-poppin' her. She had one leg propped against the dashboard and her panties were on the floor.

I looked at the young hustler again and knew he had to be about seventeen or eighteen. I remembered when I was his age, I was starting college—*look at me now*, I thought. I looked ahead and saw a young mother crossing the street with her daughter in her arms. It was three in the morning.

She dragged the young girl along, heading straight for the young hustler. Draped in long shabby looking coats and tattered shoes, she was a fiend going through hard times because of her addiction.

I watched the girl unwillingly going along with her mother. Her hair hadn't been comb in weeks, her expression showed tiredness. That little girl needed to be in bed.

The mother said something to the hustler but he wasn't having it. She was fidgeting like the monkey was riding her back.

After about a minute of negotiation, the young mother disappeared into the alley way with the hustler leaving her two year old daughter alone on the curve.

What the fuck. I gazed at this little girl waiting for her mother to come out the alley after giving the hustler a sexual favor. The child stood alone in the night, unfazed by the absence of her mother.

I was about to step out the car forgetting the blowjob. It was a cold dangerous area. This side of life reminded me of being thirteen. When my father took me driving in his sky blue Plymouth and showed me the good and the ugly side of life. He showed me what life was like on Park Avenue and Jamacia Estates, and then showed me what life was like in the slums of Brooklyn and Queens. He loved to drive and talk.

"Remember life is a gift, Vincent. How you live it, is your choice. I want to see you achieve and go far. I don't want you to waste your life on drugs, sex, and alcohol. You're better than that. I know you're my son."

I got emotional thinking about my father's words. I watched the girl standing alone on a cold street corner while her mother was in the alley, and thought, this is the ugly side of life. I had whips, cribs and money, but far from my father's standards.

"Ease up," I said no longer in the mood.

Cherie lifted her head from my lap, wiped her mouth, "What's wrong, baby?" she asked.

"Ain't nothing."

"I did sump'n wrong?"

"I'm gonna take you home," I said, starting up the car.

"You okay?"

Ignoring her, I watched the girl like I was her guardian angel. I was about to intervene when her mother emerged from the alley. The young hustler behind her was zipping up his pants. That bitch's crazy leaving her daughter alone on the streets like that. I thought driving slowly by her with a mean stare.

Who was I to be mad? Her addiction was making me a rich man. I dropped Cherie off and made it back home to my boo Cashmere.

It was four in the morning when I walked into the three bedroom apartment, with marble floors, and two bathrooms in Germantown. The place was dark. Cashmere was upset when she left the club hours ago. Here I was at four in the morning, quietly roaming the place, aware that Cashmere had a loaded .380 and knew how to use it to.

"Baby, where you at?" I asked cocking my gat.

"Where you at…?" I was looking from room to room.

I went into the master bedroom and noticed that the bathroom door was shut but the light was on. Slowly I crept to the bathroom.

"Cashmere, you okay?"

No answer.

I pushed open the bathroom door and braced myself for the worse.

With the door pushed completely opened, I saw Cashmere sitting on the toilet, scantily clad in a silk robe and in tears.

"Cashmere, what's goin' on?" I asked.

"I'm pregnant!" She said tossing me the home pregnancy test.

"Oh shit," I replied.

"And you wanna fuck that bitch!"

Twenty-Five

Spoon...

"Spoon, turn to channel nine news right now," John-John hollered over the phone.

"What happened?" Spoon questioned.

Spoon was on his way out the door when John-John called with some urgent news to tell him.

"That bitch Tip murdered in LI was the daughter of a DEA agent," John-John said forgetting how Feds could be listening.

"What the fuck is wrong with you?" Spoon snapped.

"My bad, Spoon," John-John said.

"Good night!" Spoon said.

In two hours he had to meet with the agents on the turnpike. Curiosity got the best of him. He walked into the living room, picked up the remote and turned on the 60" television. It was as clear as day, the home he and Tip had murdered three people.

Spoon had his eyes glued to the TV. He raised the volume.

"*Behind me in this home, the Nassau county police are investigating the murders of three people found shot to death late this evening. It was confirmed that one of the victims is the daughter of a DEA agent. His name is being kept confidential, as detectives comb the area talking to neighbors and looking for witnesses to this gruesome crime. Police are gathering information as I speak. Once again, three victims have been found shot execution style in this Nassau home, and police urge anyone with any information to call crime stoppers at..."*

Spoon turned off the TV and tossed the remote on the couch.

"Fuck," he uttered.

What were the chances of Tate fucking the daughter of a DEA agent? Spoon thought. In a way, Spoon was glad that he murdered the little nigga.

Spoon made his way outside and hit the remote to the Range Rover. He glanced at the time. It was after ten. He was in a rush and peeled out the driveway without any idea that he was being watched by two goons.

◇◇

Spoon was ten minutes on the Turnpike when his cell-phone went off. He looked at the caller I.D. and saw that it was Tyriq.

"This nigga," he uttered.

He answered the call and exclaimed, "What's good?"

"You heard, I assumed," Tyriq said.

"Yeah, I heard."

"We need to meet up," Tyriq said.

"Ain't no thing, when?"

"Tonight…? Where you at…?"

"Nah, tonight's no good. I got thangs to handle," Spoon said.

"You close by, I can meet you," Tyriq said.

"I got thangs to do, Tyriq," Spoon repeated.

"How long you gonna be?"

"Don't know…but I get at you when I'm through," Spoon said.

"You do that," Tyriq said suspiciously.

"One..."

"One…" Tyriq replied dryly.

Spoon hung up the call and felt mistrust between him and Tyriq. Shit was about to hit the fan. First, the murder of a DEA agent's daughter was gonna jump off crazy in the hoods. He was meeting with agent Smith and Pena to hand over audio recordings. It wasn't much evidence but it was something.

Spoon pulled up the rest stop, parked his truck next to the black Sedan, looked around then made the move from his truck into the backseat of the Sedan.

"You got sound?" Smith hastily asked.

"Yeah…" he said passing the recording device and leaned back in the seat.

"You okay?" Pena asked.

"Shit's fucked up," Spoon said. "We were fucking brothers, once. The three of us, now look at me…snitching on a nigga that's family."

"You're doing the right thing, Spoon. You're becoming a changed man," Pena said.

"It doesn't make me feel right!"

"Are you backing out, Spoon…huh? You know if you don't cooperate, then you got twenty-five to life and if I push it, the death penalty. Don't bitch up on us, now, Spoon…we like you. We wanna work with you, as long as you work with us," Smith said.

"I want my kids out of Queens and put somewhere far from NY," he said. "Y'all can do that for me?"

"We can work that out. You have to give us everything and be willing to testify against your associates. We want to know it all, murders, drug transactions… give us the Jamaicans, even if that means implicating yourself. We'll guarantee immunity from prosecution. It'll help with your case. You'll be home to see your kids grow," Smith said.

"This thang I'm doing is for my kids…"

"What's on the tape?" Pena asked.

"It's nothing hardcore. We don't talk about murders that already happen. It's a rule. I can put Tyriq in a place where he meets with the Jamaicans. I'll confess to the murders I've done under him. I'll give you Tip, his top enforcer. I'll give you locations, drug runs, and back up the shit that's said on that tape. You promise me the safety of my kids. I'll give you every fucking thang."

The agents smiled broadly, they finally had their main witness to bring down Tyriq and the Shotta's. The tape ran for twenty minutes and they listened to every detail.

"It ain't much but with you backing up everything. We'll bring them down," Smith said.

"Do you know anything about the murder of a DEA agent's daughter?"

Pena asked.

"I'll find out about that for y'all."

"That agent is a good friend, his daughter was only seventeen," Pena added.

Spoon got out of the Sedan and jumped back into his truck with an agenda. He called Melissa and asked about her and the kids relocating to a different city. He also asked the same of Wendy, his second baby mother.

Twenty-Six

Tyriq...

It was midnight when Soul and Omega approached Tyriq in Omega's pearl BMW rolling on 20" chrome rims. They carried disturbing news. Tyriq waited patiently with Tip near Tip's truck parked by Baisley Park. Tyriq stood tall in the shade of night, clad in a three quarter length black leather jacket and smoking a Black & Mild. Tip sported a black hoodie the .45 concealed underneath.

Tyriq watched Soul and Omega come forward. These two hoods were his best soldiers. They were loyal and ruthless. Their names rang loud and they were becoming a feared duo.

"What y'all got for me?" Tyriq asked.

"It ain't good, Tyriq," Omega said.

"Ayyite, just fucking say it, I'll decide," Tyriq barked.

"We followed that nigga to Jersey Turnpike. He went south. It looked like he was in a rush to be somewhere," Omega said.

"He was alone?"

"Yeah…"

"What about you?" Tyriq asked, looking at Soul.

"I went all through that nigga's crib. I ain't found shit to say that he's a snitch. His crib was clean," Soul reported.

"That don't mean he ain't snitching, Tyriq," Omega said.

Tyriq looked troubled by the news. He had called Spoon earlier, and he was definitely in a rush to be somewhere. Having doubts was upsetting Tyriq. He hated to think of Spoon as a snitch. They had twenty years of friendship between them.

"What you want us to do?" Omega asked.

"Y'all niggas did good," Tyriq said. He tossed them a small knot of money. Omega and Soul drove off.

"What you think?" Tyriq asked Tip.

"Why take a chance. I know he's your boy from back in da day. But that was back in da day. Times changed, people changed. Why chance it? We do him before he does us," Tip said.

"That's my nigga."

"You got doubts right now. That ain't good. He could bring us all down…even the DEA's daughter..."

"What you been hearing?" Tyriq asked.

"Feds are stepping in, knocking down doors, and putting pressure on the block, trying to get niggas to talk. They want sump'n and they want it quick. If Spoon talking ain't no telling what kinda shit he's giving them, Tyriq. We gotta handle that," Tip persuaded.

Tyriq puffed the Black & Mild in deep thought. Looking at Tip, he said, "Set it up. Let's make it clean. I don't want the whole world knowing."

Tip nodded.

"I want Vince on this too," Tyriq said.

"Why…?" Tip asked.

"Spoon will die by our hands, nobody else's," Tyriq said.

"I could take care of shit dolo, make it quick and everything disappear," Tip assured.

"You got enough heat with that other thing. I want Vince on this. I wanna see where his loyalty stands. I wanna see what dude made of," Tyriq said.

"You da boss," Tip nodded.

Tyriq took one last pull from the burning Black and tossed it. Knowing that he had to murder Spoon hurt him deep. Spoon was his ride-or-die man from jump-street. To think a hardcore nigga flipped and turned informant had Tyriq worried. You snitch, you die. You steal, you die. You fuck up, you die.

Tyriq got into the truck and sat quietly for a moment. Spoon wa weighing heavy on his mind.

"You ready?" Tip asked.

"Just drive," Tyriq said sounding irritated.

With Spoon out the way, Tip would be the man to run things. He had been patient and fearless, waiting for his time to shine. He drove off smiling.

Twenty-Seven

Late that evening it was all over the front page of every newspaper in the city when I arrived in Queens. The cops and feds were busting heads in Queens and Brooklyn searching for killers. The daughter of a DEA agent had been gunned down in her father's home with Tate and Notch, two small-time drug peddlers from around the way.

I laughed at the irony story and rolled up on the block. It was a fucking ghost town, mid-December and brick out. I saw the unmarked cop car posted near the corner bodega. The block was hot. I paid the pigs no mind, parked my ride and walked into the forty projects. I had to check on business.

My Philly connect was poppin. Since they murdered that young white bitch in LI and found out that the niggas was connected to a Queens' drug crew, business slowed. It wasn't affecting my pockets—moving product out of town was the move. I made my way down the hall to apartment 4b. I'd been out of town for two weeks and wanted to see what's been going on. I knocked on the door and Soul answered being shirtless, an expensive long chain dangling from around his neck.

"Vince, what's good my nigga," Soul greeted me with a dap.

"Fuck's been up…?" I asked walking into the apartment.

Soul closed the door behind me and said, "Yo, cops are gettin' crazy out here. I know you already heard what went down with Notch and Tate Them bitch-asses was fucking a DEA agent's daughter and got bodied out there. Shit's fucking bananas right now. Money is slow-mo."

"I heard. Where's Omega?"

"Tyriq got him handling some other shit."

Three keys of coke were on the coffee table along with bag full of ecstasy and a 9mm. A naked bitch was sleeping with her head faced down on the couch—dead to the world.

"What the fuck, Soul!" I barked pointing.

"Yo, don't mind that bitch."

"Who is she?" I asked.

"Some hood-rat I'm fucking. Da bitch stays more fucked up than sober."

"Get rid of her. We got enough problems."

"You talked to Tyriq?"

"Not yet. Why is there a reason why I need to get up wit' him?"

"Just asking…"

"Y'all niggas can't get sloppy around bitches."

"I'm on point, Vince. But I hear you."

He went over to the couch and began rousing the girl.

"Bitch…get the fuck up!"

Soul slapped her in the back of her head and began pulling her off the couch. "Bitch, you heard what the fuck I said, you gotta go…get your naked ass up and bounce."

"It's like dat… Soul," the hood-rat replied drowsily.

"I got business to take care of," Soul barked pulling shorty by her arm to the door.

She sucked her teeth as Soul pushed her out into the hallway butt-naked and tossed her clothes out right behind her.

"You're wild," I said.

"I don't give a fuck. She ain't wifey."

"I'm gonna get up wit' y'all niggas, later," I said giving Soul dap.

"Watch your back out there."

I left the apartment and went to the third floor to see Shae. Getting some of her good loving right now would do me good. I paid the rent and provided her with whatever she needed. I loved her and was taking care of her son like he was my own.

It was after eleven. I walked into the apartment, and saw Shae wrapped in a blanket on the couch watching TV. I didn't want to disturb her.

Slowly, I tiptoed behind her and threw my arms around her, pulling her close to me and kissing her on the neck. I loved the way she felt, smelled in my arms and talked to me. When I was with her, I stopped thinking about my life in the streets. I forgot about my problems with Chandra. I forgot my worries.

"I missed you."

Shae's sweet voice was warm.

"I missed you too, baby," I replied squeezing her gently. "Jonathan's sleep…?"

"I put him to bed an hour ago. How was Philly?"

"Business as usual..."

"Business, huh?" she teased.

"Baby, you're the most important thing in my life," I said kissing her on the neck.

"And you better not forget that," she smiled.

I got under the blanket and embraced her lovingly. She was watching Sex and The city, one of her favorite shows. Under the blanket my hands began slowly feeling across her tender breasts down to her hips. I sucked on the back of her neck while sliding my hands under her T-shirt, cupping her breasts.

She moaned, leaning back and her long stylish hair getting tangled in my face. I continued kissing her neck, while I slid my hands into her sweats and grabbed her shaven mound. I tunneled two fingers into her tight wet pussy and heard the blissful sounds of thrill escape her sweet lips.

"You miss me," I whispered affectionately in her ear.

"Yes," she cried out.

I was so fuckin' horny with Shae in my arms. Shae reached her arm around me, turning to face me, our lips a breath away. I still was gradually finger fucking her. Her juices poured over my fingers. I squeezed her tit and then we touched lips. Our tongues entwined, kissing feverishly like it was our last. I began fondling her, exploring places that I already discovered, pulling her shirt over her head and having her facing me, with her tits pressed against me. I cupped her ass and removed her sweats.

I was tired of the foreplay. My dick was so hard that it hurt. I pushed Shae down on her back and admired her curvy nude figure for a moment. Then I climbed between her long defined legs, fucking her. Shae indicated that she wanted it from the back. I quickly flipped her over, had her face down, her ass in an arch, her legs spread. I began slowly until she screamed.

I was deep in her, fucking her doggy-style and playing with her clit. She went crazy, gripping the armrest and throwing that ass back at me.

"Aaaaaahhh….shit," I exclaimed, enjoying good pussy, her juices all over my dick.

"Fuck me, Vince," she cried out sliding pussy on me.

I cupped her tit and pushed her down onto her stomach. I had her pressed against me and the couch looking like a sex sandwich. I continued to thrust my erection into her, my dick swollen and ready to nut.

We panted and were sweaty against each other—grinding it out on the leather couch making stains.

"I'm comin'!" I shrieked.

Shae gyrated her ass against me with force. I pulled her close, my chest pressed against her sweaty back, my hands in hers. I thrust, feeling her pussy tightening.

"Fuck me! Oooh…. Fuck me! Oooh…fuck me!" she chanted.

I erupted in her quivering ass. She climaxed with joy. I fell on my back on the floor, dick hard, peering up at the ceiling.

Shae fell down on top of me, and nestled against me. I held her clammy soft figure in my arms and found myself drifting off to sleep.

Next morning I awoke up to Shae massaging my chest. I wasn't complaining that she was feeling horny again. I was with the program. We were still naked and she straddled me, riding with her hands pressed against my chest. I gripped her ass and threw my head back, feeling her pussy tightening. There was a loud knock at the door.

"What the fuck!"

I ignored it but the knocking continued. Shae jumped off. I found my pants. The loud knocking continued.

"I'm fucking coming!" I hollered.

I glanced through the peephole and saw Lil' Goon standing in the hallway. I opened my door.

"It's eight in the fucking morning. Why the fuck you knocking at my door, Lil' Goon…?"

"Five-o ran up on Soul and the work upstairs," he answered.

"What the fuck…?"

"They got task force and everything outside," Lil Goon said.

"Stay right here," I instructed.

I ran into the bedroom, snatched up whatever clothing I could reach the fastest and ran back out into the hallway with Lil' Goon. Shae was looking at me dumbfounded. I had no time to explain.

I ran down the stairs with Lil' Goon right behind me and darted outside into the December cold. The fucking block was shutdown. It looked like a zoo on the block, with the dozen marked blue and white cop cars flooding the block. ESU was out in their full body gear, blue flight vest, tactical weapons and the dogs. A helicopter hovered, giving police a bird's eye view of the projects from above. Sgt. Manny, the crooked cop Tyriq was paying off walking around with ESU. He saw me and winked.

"Be careful," he mouthed at me.

I was shocked and also nervous. *Were they coming for me too?* I asked myself. The residents were out in bathrobes, slippers, and coats, being nosey.

"Lil' Goon what happened?" I asked.

"They got Soul and some bitch when they ran up in the apartment with a warrant. I heard they're looking for Omega. They say he shot at a cop."

"Fuck!" I shouted.

Business was fucking slow, now this shit. I retreated to the apartment and informed Shae what went down. She had a nervous look on her face. I told her that they weren't coming for me.

"How you know? I can't go through this, Vince," she stated. "I don't want any cops charging up in here and scaring my son."

"Everything gonna be okay, Shae," I assured her.

"You don't fucking know that," she hissed.

"I'm careful, Shae. Don't fucking beef."

She looked upset. What happened this morning was out of my hands. I started to get my things together when my cell rang. I looked at the caller I.D. It was Tyriq.

"Yo," I answered.

"Meet me down at the club in an hour," he instructed and hung up.

I got dressed and rushed out the apartment without giving Shae a proper goodbye. I was at the club in thirty minutes. Hurrying out my truck, I banged on the entrance. It was early morning and the place was barren. Tip opened the door.

"Go downstairs."

I moved toward the basement and headed to one of Tyriq's back offices. I walked in and saw Tyriq sitting in a leather reclining chair staring at some papers. He looked irritated. Tip walked in behind me closing the door. I got nervous but kept my composure.

"I know you heard about this morning," I said.

"How long we've been boys, Vince?" he asked, ignoring what I had said.

"Damn near since we were what…seven, eight years old. Why?"

"Open up your shirt," Tyriq said harshly, staring at me.

"Fuck is wrong wit' you?" I asked.

"Open up your fuckin shirt, ayyite Vince," Tyriq instructed sternly again. This time Tip stood closely behind me in an intimidating posture.

"Yo, Tyriq, what's good…what the fuck is up wit' you?"

"Vince, you're a brother to me, but I'm not gonna repeat myself again," Tyriq warned.

"You crazy, nigga...?"

I began unbuttoning my shirt, taking it off and tossing it at his feet. I then pulled my wife-beater over my head, showing him that I was clean. And to take it even further, I began unbuckling my belt and was ready to drop my pants to show him that I wasn't wired up. "You good, nigga!" I barked.

He didn't answer. I began getting dressed. Tyriq stared at the papers in his hands and I started to wonder what the fuck was up.

"You gonna tell me what this all about," I said.

Tip took a few steps back from me and I glanced at him over my shoulder. His demeanor was unusually eerie and I hated the way he looked at me.

"What we gonna do about Soul?"

"Soul is the least of our problems."

"What you mean?"

He passed me the papers and said, "Now is the time to show where your loyalty truly stands."

I looked at the papers. They were federal documents of a CI that the feds were consulting with for information into the organization. They were trying to put indictments together against Tyriq, his crew and the Jamaicans.

"Where you get these?" I asked.

"Keep reading," he said.

I read on, looking to see if my name was in the investigation or indictments. My heart began to race, because I knew it was nothing good. I got to the end and saw the name of the CI that the feds were consulting to—with his name at the bottom—Timothy Grant, aka Spoon.

"Get the fuck outta here," I exclaimed, tossing the document to the floor. "How the fuck you get that info?"

"You pay enough money to the right people and the info falls out," Tyriq stated.

"Spoon ain't no snitch, man," I said.

"Nigga, wake the fuck up. His name is on the fucking papers, right? They flipped him when he got locked up in Connecticut. We don't know what the fuck he been telling 'em crackers."

I couldn't believe it. It wasn't happening. Tyriq walked up to me and put his hands on my shoulders and looked me in the eyes.

"I need to know, where you stand on this with us, Vince. Where your head is at?" he asked.

I stared back, teary eyed. The three of us all went back since the days of Krush Groove, when we used to emulate Run-DMC and danced our asses off at neighborhood block parties.

"You know what we gotta do, Vince, right?" Tyriq said gravely.

"Spoon's fam man…"

"He ain't family no more. He's a fucking snitch, ready to bring down his own brothers so he can save his own ass."

"You sure that's the shit's real?" I asked.

"Muthafucka, I got it straight out the hands from the clerk of the D that's tryin' to indict us. We move first, cuz they don't know we fuckin' know yet. Are you with us, Vince?"

It was hard to answer. Spoon had my back since we first met. He at that charge for me in '95 so I could attend school. Tyriq was asking me to do the unthinkable—kill a friend, a brother to me. Shit, I was the Godfather of two of his kids.

It had to be done. If the indictments were carried out, that would be the end of everything. There was a possibility of a lengthy sentence for my involvement.

"Vince, You know it's gotta be done. You with us on this…? I'm shutting everything down. Nothing gets moved unless I say so."

"What you mean?"

"Business is shut the fuck down. No transactions, no pick ups, no phone use….nada," he exclaimed.

"What about my Philly connect?"

"Them niggas gonna have a short drought."

"That's money lost, Tyriq."

"I don't give a fuck…tell your peoples to chill the fuck out and let 'em know we going through some things for a moment. And if they got a problem with that…then fuck them niggas!" Tyriq shouted.

It was going to be hard to go to tell Inf and his crew that product could be put on hold for a while.

The feds and DEA were hot about the agent's daughter, Soul was locked up this morning and finding out that Spoon was a fucking snitch. My head was spinning. Christmas was one week away. It looked like things wasn't about to get very merry for me.

Twenty-Eight

Christmas Eve came and business in the streets was on pause until shit got dealt with. I tried not to be stressed, but knowing that my best friend was a snitch and the feds were watching us, had me feeling like shit.

I had to meet with Inf in Philly and told him what was going on. He didn't take the news lightly.

"Fuck you mean, a drought," Inf barked glaring at me, his crew standing behind him.

"Shit's fucked up in New York, Inf. We ain't moving shit right now until the heat dies," I said sternly.

"So y'all niggas fucked up, kill a DEA agent's daughter, got bitch-ass-niggas running around in N.Y…and you telling me I can't get any weight next week. I got blocks to supply, nigga."

"It is what it is, Inf. We ain't taking any chances."

"I ain't trying to fucking hear that ying, Vince. You my connect. Money's good out here and y'all trying to fuck my shit up!" Inf shouted.

"Calm down, nigga…"

"Don't tell me to fucking calm down when you feeding me bullshit 'bout some fucking drought."

"What you want me to do, Inf?"

"Make it right, nigga."

"I will…I promise you that."

"Fuck a promise. You gonna make it right. I trusted you to do business. I trusted you with my cousin. She's having your fucking seed, nigga. You fucked her. Don't fuck me, Vince."

"I ain't…"

"I know you won't…but check this, follow me my nigga," he said walking off.

I had followed him into another room. It was big and dark. Inf turned on the lights and I saw two males bonded to a chair, butt-naked and beaten. This is how they resolved situations. Niggas in Philly were beasts.

I knew what was about to happen. Both men had duct-tape over their mouths with their arms tied behind the chairs. They squirmed and mumbled. I wasn't trying to listen.

Inf walked up to one of the men and said, "You see these niggas right here. They tried to fuck me. This nigga here, stupid muthafucka tried to rob a stash house with his peoples. And this other nigga here, part of a crew that's trying to move on me. I got enemies, Vince. They waiting for me to fuck up. But I'm gonna show you how I really get down, nigga," he said.

One of his boys walked up to him and handed Inf a power drill with a long tip. Inf turned it on, while staring at me and said, "We murder niggas out here, in case you forgotten."

He thrust the power drill deep into one of the man's knees and drilled through flesh and bones. He pulled it out and began drilling into his other knee. He pulled it out and began drilling into both of his feet. He drilled into the nigga's thighs, worked his way up to the chest area and finally shoved the drill into the man's ear. The second victim helplessly watched, awaiting his fate.

There was blood everywhere, but I wasn't queasy. I just looked on. Inf kicked over the dead man in his chair, and the body dropped heavily to the floor. Inf's hands were covered with blood and his expression showed wickedness.

Inf stood over his second victim, switched on the power drill again and began torturing his next victim. When he was done torturing and killing the next victim, he kicked the body over and it fell to the floor with a thud.

With the bloody drill still gripped in his hand he walked over to me.

"You see that…I don't give a fuck. Now Vince, you make it right. I need a shipment soon, cuz I wanna continue to do business with you. You cool peoples, and I don't want things to get messy. Just because you're my connect, don't mean you're in control."

"You'll get your shit nigga…don't even worry."

"That's what I want to hear."

Inf was a fucking lunatic. It was my bed and no matter how messy it got I would have to continue laying in it.

◇◇◇◇◇◇◇◇◇◇◇◇◇◇◇◇◇◇◇◇◇◇◇◇◇◇◇◇◇◇◇◇◇◇◇◇

Christmas Eve was about spreading joy and giving. But we were ready to murder, spreading grief. Tyriq put together a little party that evening with strippers and his goons to have a fun time. Spoon came through to show his support and wished everyone a merry Christmas.

I spoke to my son earlier in the day and was excited about seeing him tomorrow. I had bought many gifts for him. Chandra was cool with me stopping by. She mentioned that she had some news to tell me. I kind of blew it off.

Half-hour before midnight, soon it'd be Christmas day and the party was on fire. Bitches got butt naked and were fucking and sucking niggas in every room. Knowing Spoon was a fucking snitch and knowing his fate made it difficult to look at him. He had a drink in one hand and was feeling on tits and ass with the other, seemingly unfazed.

Tyriq pulled me to the side and told me the hit was going down.

"Tonight…?" I questioned. "You can't be serious."

"Nigga, if we wait around, there might not be another chance. Spoon ain't stupid, he's gonna catch on, and with it being Christmas Eve, shit's gonna be less hectic for us cleaning up."

I felt sick to my stomach. Tyriq was talking about Spoon like he was a stranger to us. I understood the situation clearly.

"Keep him here, until everyone leaves," Tyriq said walking away.

I went to the bar and got a shot of Hennessy. I downed that quickly and got me another.

"Damn, Vince, take it easy on 'em drinks. You good…?" Spoon said leaning on the bar.

"Yeah…I'm good."

"Merry Christmas, Vince…"

"Same to you," I said halfheartedly.

Spoon stayed by my side. We continued downing Hennessy and cranberry, talked about our kids and reminisced about past Christmases w had together. It was hard for me to look in his eyes and laughed. I hugged him, knowing that it would be our last time together.

The night carried on, the crowd of strippers and the rowdy men dwindled by the hour. Soon there were a handful of people. Spoon was at the bar, tipsy but cognizant of what was going on. Tip was eyeing Spoon from a distance, ready to strike like a cobra. Tyriq was busy with couple bitches in the back. Everything seemed normal.

Spoon raised his glass in my direction.

"A toast to my nigga, Vince, to us our prosperity, our strength, friendship and trust. We been doing our thang for a long time. Let us continue to journey a long way," he said.

He then handed me some keys and said, "Happy holidays, my nigga."

"What's this?"

He smiled and said, "It's a brownstone in Brooklyn. My gift to you…"

"You serious…?"

"We gotta be smart with money. We gotta start somewhere. It's an investment for our kids when they grow," he smiled.

"Spoon, you ain't had to do all of this. I would have been happy wit' a fucking card." I joked feeling sick.

"I told you, ownership in real estate is the thang. You can never go wrong with owning property. Vince, you okay?" Spoon asked.

"I gotta use the bathroom." I did a beeline straight for the nearest bathroom and threw up in the toilet. I dried heave a few more times and thought…*it ain't suppose to be like this…not Spoon. I'm the fuckin' godfather to his kids*.

There was a knock on the door.

"What…?"

"You good, Vince…?" Spoon asked.

"Yeah, give me a minute."

"Fucking with Hennessy straight will do that." He laughed.

I collected myself, washed my face and walked to the bar. It was three-thirty in the morning, and the bar was empty accept for the bartender. Tyriq nodded to him and he disappeared. The three of us were alone with

Spoon.

This is a man's world, by James Brown played from the jukebox in the corner. It was about to get crazy. Time seemed to slow down. I stared at my image in the mirror behind the bar and tried to control my mood.

Spoon downed his umpteenth drink for the night and then placed the glass down on the countertop. Tip locked the door. He and Tyriq strategically moved in closely behind Spoon. I raised myself off the barstool, preparing for what was to come.

"So, y'all niggas gonna murder me on Christmas Eve?" Spoon said, raising himself off the barstool.

He looked at each of us in the eyes. There was no fear in his eyes.

"You was family," Tyriq said.

"Twenty-years, right Tyriq…down the line, a man gets tired o' shit… gotta move on and do your thang," Spoon said.

"So you sell-out your fucking brothers to save your own ass?" Tyriq asked removing a large blade from his jacket.

"I do this thang for my kids, not y'all," Spoon said.

"Ayyite, do your kids know that their daddy's a fucking snitch? Why the fuck you couldn't keep your fucking mouth shut?" Tyriq shouted.

"Like I said, I'm tired of this thang," Spoon said calmly.

"Y'all niggas do what you do. Cuz in the end, it's always tragic," he added.

Tip abruptly rushed at Spoon, throwing a phone cord around his neck and grabbing him up in a violent stronghold. Spoon tried to resist, kicking over bottles and chairs, struggling to get free.

"Ayyite, do it," Tyriq said passing me the blade.

"What…you must fucking crazy," I spat.

"Vince, I rather leave this bar with one body instead of two. Show me you got heart for this shit," he exclaimed placing the blade in my hand.

"He dies by your hands or Tip's. Take our friend out of his misery."

I gripped the large blade and approached the scuffle with tears of hur and pain streaming down my face. Tip still held Spoon in a choke hold with the phone wire digging into his neck. Spoon's eyes was bulging from the sockets and the veins in his neck looked like they were about to explode.

I moved in closer, nearing the tip of the blade close to Spoon's gut. I was hard to look at him.

"Just do it...muthafucka!" Spoon shouted.

I lunged forward and thrust the knife deep into his stomach, having him jolt in shock in my arms. He was free from Tip's violent grip and fell into my arms with the knife shoved deep into his stomach.

He coughed and I stabbed him again, crying as I felt the sharp blade rip through his flesh. I continued to hold him up in my arms and whispered in his ear as he was dying, "I always got love for you…my nigga, don't worry about your kids. I'll look after them. I'm sorry."

I pulled the blade out and plunged it deep into his chest, stabbing him a total of three times. I felt him die painfully in my arms. There wasn't shit I could do about it. I held him that way for a moment. Tip and Tyriq looked on. He was slumped in my arms, getting heavy but I held him, tears flowing down my face. He did so much for me and I was the one to take his life. I felt selfish. He was the one betraying us, so why did it feel like I had betrayed him?

I removed the knife from his chest, tossed it to the floor and gently laid Spoon's lifeless body to the ground. His blood was on my hands. No matter how many times I washed them, his blood would stain my hands forever.

"You done nigga?" Tyriq asked looking down at me with a smirk.

Coldhearted bastard, I thought. He was a fucking coward. Tip and I did the dirty work, while this nigga sat back and watched me murder a friend. I remembered Spoon once saying…. *This shit here; will change a man.*

I stood up and walked away, leaving the dead behind. What was done, was done, there was no changing it. I went into the bathroom, slammed the door shut and cried over a friend. I didn't care if Tyriq saw. I didn't give a fuck anymore. That day my friend's death changed me. Before we left the bar, we wrapped Spoon's body in sheets and threw it in the trunk of a car parked in the back. We had to make him disappear. He was a dead federal informant.

Twenty-Nine

Christmas day I couldn't eat or sleep. Spoon's death was in my head, fucking with me. Tyriq made arrangements to move the body the day after Christmas. He had some peoples in LI that helped us with the disposal. But all Christmas day, we left Spoon rotting in the trunk of a car out in the cold.

By noon, I was knocking on Chandra's apartment door with a bag filled with gifts for my son. I needed to relax and was hoping her man wasn't around. I wasn't in the mood for him.

Chandra opened the door and said to me with a half way smile, "Merry Christmas."

"Hey, merry Christmas," I replied nonchalantly.

She allowed me into her apartment. I felt better when my son came running up to me shouting, "Daddy….merry Christmas, daddy."

He jumped into my arms and I hugged him so tight "Merry Christmas, lil' man," I said in a cheerful tone.

"I missed you so much," I said.

It was a month since I last saw him. He was growing up.

"What you got me, daddy?" Vinny asked a board smile across his face.

"Plenty of things," I smiled.

I handed him the bag of toys and games. He tore into the neatly wrapped packages and bags like a happy child on Christmas day.

He unwrapped the presents and I looked around Chandra's apartment and saw that she was definitely into the Christmas spirit. There was a tall sheared green Christmas tree almost touching the ceiling. It was decorated with colorful ornaments, candy-canes, colorful lights, and many wrapped gifts under the tree. She had an assortment of Christmas cards lining the walls and Christmas carols was playing soothingly in the background.

Her apartment made me think of home and the past Christmas we had. I missed those times. I glanced at Chandra and she looked good in some tight black shorts, wearing pink fuzzy slippers and a decorated green shirt that showed a picture of Vinny and her talking to Santa Clause.

"Cute," I muttered.

"How've you been, Vincent?" she asked.

"Could be better," I said shrugging.

My son was going crazy over the gifts I brought him. Wrapping paper was spread all over the floor and his new toys were out in all directions. It made me smile. My son's happiness made me feel good about the holidays.

"Where's homeboy?" I asked not caring.

"He's working and won't be home until five."

"So he does have a job."

"Are you hungry, thirsty?"

"I'm good," I said, taking off my jacket.

She looked at me and asked, "Vincent, are you sure you're okay? What's wrong with you?"

"I'm just here to spend some time with my son on Christmas day."

"You called your mother?"

"Nah…"

"Why not…? She's worried sick about you, Vincent. Give her a call and let her know that you're okay."

I hesitated before saying, "I will."

"Ooh, thank you daddy…thank you," Vinny shouted, going crazy over the X-men I bought him.

They seemed so happy and joyful. I was still mulling over Spoon's body rotting away in a trunk. It was my burden, not my family's. While I was out in the trenches getting paid, Jamal was taking over things on the home front. Chandra had more bling on her hands. There was hot meal cooking in the kitchen and extra toys my son was enjoying before I came.

Her apartment looked like a home. My son was being taking care of. The more I hustled, the more I was absent from his life. It was too late for me to turn back now. I was in deep and it was hard to grasp the fact that I fucked up my life.

I remembered that Chandra had something to tell me. Before I asked, Vinny smiled and said, "Daddy, guess what?"

"What?"

"I'm gonna have a new step daddy," he blurted out.

"What?"

"Mommy getting married…"

My heart suddenly dropped. I didn't show my disappointment. I let out a weary smiled and said, "Oh word...?"

I looked over and saw Chandra coming out of the kitchen with a nervous smile.

"I guess you heard…"

I looked at her left hand and saw the diamond engagement ring on her finger.

"He asked me last night, and I said yes."

"I'm happy for you," I lied.

"You okay with this?"

"Hey, it's your life, not mines. You doing your thang."

She smiled and said, "Thanks, I'm glad you're so understanding, Vincent."

"I'm gonna have two daddies," Vinny said.

I smiled to hide the anger. I was angry with myself for letting her go easily. A piece of me still loved her. That was the small piece of me that thought I could get my life back with her. All that went out the door with her marrying that fucking Jamaican.

I needed to get out before I got upset in front of my son and ruin his Christmas day. I threw on my leather coat and said, "I'm out. I got things to take care of."

"So soon, it's Christmas. I thought you wanted to spend time with Vinny," Chandra said walking over to me.

"Y'all are good. I'm gonna let y'all be."

"Daddy, are you coming back?"

"I am."

Chandra locked eyes with me and asked again, "Are you sure you're okay? What's wrong, talk to me, Vincent?"

"I'm good, Chandra. I gotta run."

She looked at me in disbelief. I kept it moving not wanting to explain myself.

"Before you go, take your gift with you," she said moving to the tree and getting a wrapped present.

"Merry Christmas, Vincent…"

"You shouldn't have. I mean, I'm good," I said, not wanting to take the gift.

"Take it, Vincent. It's Christmas, it's from your son and me."

Reluctantly, I took the gift, looked down at my son and said, "C'mere lil' man, give daddy a hug bye."

He jumped up and ran towards me, leaping into my arms. I hugged him close to my heart and felt like crying. I kept my composure, whispered in his ear, "I'll always protect and love you," and released him.

"Daddy, you gonna cry?" my son asked.

"I'm good lil' man…"

Chandra seemed even more beautiful than I remembered. She had her hair in a short medium curled-out bob, her dark skin flawless.

"Give me a hug," she said.

I hugged her holding her tight against me. I remembered how soft her body was. She was becoming a married woman. I pulled myself away from her and said, "I'll catch y'all later. Merry Christmas." I bounced out the apartment like it was on fire.

Eight blocks away, I pulled over to think. Spoon was dead, Chandra was getting married and I haven't spoken to my mother in three months. I picked up my cell-phone thinking of my mother. I began dialing her number, feeling my heart race because it's been a while since I talked to her. I hesitated pushing in the last digit. Finally, I did and her phone began to ring.

The phone was pressed to my ear, I listened to it ringing for a moment and thought, *she probably ain't home*. I was about to hang up, I heard my mother quickly answer, saying, "Hello…merry Christmas."

There was still air over the phone as I hesitated to speak.

"Hello," she repeated.

I wanted to hang up, not knowing what to say. But it was like my mother had a sixth sense. I heard her say, "If it's you, baby please say something to me."

My heart pounded like a jack-hammer. I opened my mouth but remained mute.

"Vincent, talk to me," she said, like she definitely knew it was me.

I began tearing up, because it was good hearing her voice again. I held the phone tightly and stated, "I love you mama."

"I know you do, baby. I love you too," she warmly returned.

"How've you been?" I asked.

"I'm fine. Why don't you come home, Vincent? I missed you…"

"I can't. I did things, ma…not so good things," I admitted to her.

"Oh Vincent, please come home and we can talk. I'm here for you, baby. Aunt Linda and I want you back home with us. Let's be a family again."

Tears came knowing that couldn't be. "How's Aunt Linda?"

"She's good, working and missing her favorite nephew," moms said.

It made me laugh.

"Where are you?" she asked.

"In New York…"

I heard her let out a dry cough and I became concerned.

"Ma, you okay?" I asked.

"Yes, baby…I just been a little under the weather lately," she replied.

"You need money for a doctor?"

"No, I need my son home with me. I need my son out of trouble. I need to see my son, that's what I need," she stated steadfastly.

It made me feel bad.

"I'm taking care of myself, Ma. I'm doing great," I lied.

She let out another dry cough and it sounded like she was short of breath.

"Ma, you sure you're okay?" I repeated.

"Baby, don't worry about me. If you're so concern about me, come home and talk to me."

"I will, ma…I promise."

"When, Vincent? I want to see you. I want to talk to you. It's Christmas day."

"I love you, ma…I gotta go," I said.

"Vincent, I want to say a prayer for you."

"Ma, c'mon…I mean, you ain't got to."

"No…you're out there on them streets doing God knows what and I pray for you every single night. I pray for you to come home. I pray for God to touch your heart. I pray for you to change your ways. Now I wanna pray for you with you listening," she said.

I sighed, knowing that my mother could be relentless. "Okay ma, go ahead, I'm listening."

"Our Father…our blessed Father in heaven, watch over my son, please. Talk to him, Father. You are his way, our Father. You're always there guiding us, protecting us, steer my son in the right direction. Let him know that You are the only way on this earth, steer him from these worldly temptations. Let us surrender to You. Give us our all and have him understand You are love and understanding our blessed Father. Despite what he's done in the streets, You are forgiving towards him. Let him not fall, oh Lord. I'm crying out to you dear Lord. Show him how to do things Your way, please Lord, our Father…lead us not into temptation, but deliver us from evil, for thine is the kingdom, the power, and the glory, forever and ever…amen."

"Amen, thanks ma," I said after the long prayer.

"Believe in God and He will deliver you out of whatever trouble you're into…just believe in him, Vincent," she said.

"Ma, I gotta go…merry Christmas."

"Merry Christmas, baby," she replied in her loving tone.

I hung up and was in full blown tears while sitting in the driver's seat. I had family that loved me so much and was out here doing me. My mother was praying for me every night. I loved her with all my heart, but was ashamed to go home and look her in the eyes after the sin I committed. I had become addicted to the life.

◇◇◇◇◇◇◇◇◇◇◇◇◇◇◇◇◇◇◇◇◇◇◇◇◇◇◇◇◇◇◇◇◇◇◇◇

Early the next morning, Tyriq, Tip and I rode out to the shores of Long Island with Spoon's body stinking in the trunk. We lined the trunk with heavy plastic, put a garbage bag over his head, taped his legs together and tied him up in the sheets with duct-tape and rope.

It was four in the morning. I was tired as fuck barely able to sleep in the past two days. I was in the backseat, peering out the window feeling fucked up. I was nervous traveling with a body in the trunk, thinking about state troopers pulling over three niggas in a car. But traffic was very light on the Southern State parkway. We didn't see any cops around on our way to the fishing pier, an hour away from Queens.

I just wanted to get things over with, go home to take a much needed shower and catch some z's. Tip was driving and Tyriq looked asleep in the front seat.

Around five, we arrived at the pier and surprisingly it was the same fishing pier that my father used to take me fishing on the boats when I was a kid. It had been years since I was out here. Pulling into it brought back fond memories of my father. I got seasick on my first fishing trip.

"Yo, Vince, remember your father took us out here one time when we were like thirteen," Tyriq said, it was like he read my mind.

"Yeah, I'm surprised you still remember where it was," I replied.

"I didn't forget. I got peoples out here that look out for me."

Tip parked the car in the empty parking lot, and we all stepped out, stretching and yawning. All the fishing boats on the pier seemed to be closed down for the winter. One appeared to be still doing business.

A grey beard, pale and wrinkled old man was on the pier. He was in a heavy brown snorkel, with thick rubbery boots and smoking a cigarette.

"Chester, my dude, what's good?" Tyriq greeted, shaking the man's hand.

"You got the money?" Chester asked.

Tyriq handed him a thick white bulky envelope and Chester opened it and went through the hundred dollar bills quickly counting them.

"All there…?" Tyriq asked.

"Yeah, all here… we need to hurry. Low tide should be coming in a few hours. I wanna be docked here by afternoon," Chester said.

"Let's get it poppin' then," Tyriq said, moving toward the car.

We all followed. Tyriq popped the trunk and we moved the heavy carcass to the boat in the early morning cold. Tip had him by the feet while Tyriq carried him by the shoulders. I followed them onto the boat and they dropped the body onto the deck.

"Damn, this muthafucka got heavier," Tyriq complained.

"We ready?" I heard another voice say from behind me.

There was another man on the boat with us. He was Chester's nephew and had a grizzly beard sporting a snorkel that was similar to his uncle's.

"Let's get the fuck outta here," Tyriq said.

It was cold like ice outside and my fingers were frozen even though I was wearing gloves. I took a seat and slowly felt the boat push off the pier as we began coasting.

About an hour from shore they would dump the body. While we sailed, Tip went to work on Spoon's corpse. He punctured Spoon's lungs with a long thick ice-pick. The body would sink and not float. He poured acid on identifying tattoos and cut off fingertips. It was sickening to watch this process.

We sailed into the Atlantic Ocean. I peered at the sea and the sunrise. I gripped the railing trying to control motion sickness.

Before the sun was at its peek, the body was ready to be dropped. It was covered in plastic, bonded with chains, weights and rope to make it sink faster, and looked inhuman.

"Y'all ready?" Tyriq asked.

I nodded.

Chester brought the boat to a complete stop and we were miles away from land. I couldn't even see the shorelines anymore. The three of us picked up the body and heaved it over the railing. Spoon's body hit the water with a thud and splash. We peered down as it sank. *What the fuck am I going to tell his kids, and Melissa?* I kept thinking. We just made a friend disappear forever. There would be no home going service, just a watery grave for Spoon.

"Fuck him!" Tyriq said.

"So this is what it's come to?" I said.

"We don't give a fuck about snitches," Tyriq said.

Chester turned the boat around and we coasted back to the shorelines of Long Island. I stared quietly at the vast deep blue sea, thinking of Spoon. I wished myself a Happy Birthday and what a fucked up way to begin my twenty-sixth birthday.

Thirty

New Year's Eve came and Tyriq had this big shindig at one of his clubs on Merrick Blvd. I attended the New Year's party with Shae under my arm planning to have a good time. I wasn't going to worry about Inf, the DA or the murders.

Everybody that was everybody showed up—Tip, John-John, Red, Malik, Killer Ty, Bones, and Omega, unfortunately Soul was still on Riker's Island facing charges.

It felt awkward seeing the entire crew partying together and knowing Spoon wasn't around. I tried not to let it fuck with me but it did.

Melissa, his baby mother been stressing me about Spoon's sudden disappearance. She called everyday, inquiring about his whereabouts.

"He didn't see his kids on, Christmas. He always sees his kids on Christmas. It's been a whole week," she had whined.

I felt awful lying to her.

"Spoon's good. He probably left town to take care of some business As soon as he calls I let you know."

"But Spoon wouldn't leave town and not tell me. I know we weren't together but I loved him and he trusted me. The other night he came by and left me three-hundred thousand dollars. Like he knew sump'n bad was about to happen," she mentioned.

"Melissa, don't worry. I'm gonna look into it. I know Spoon, he's good. He probably needed to just get away," I had lied again.

"Vincent, don't lie to me. Something happened to Spoon. I can feel it. He wouldn't leave without seeing his kids. I know…especially not around

Christmas. It's something to do with Tyriq, right?"

"Melissa, calm down…there ain't no need for you to get upset."

"Don't tell me to calm down. Where's Spoon, Vincent? Where's the father of my kids," she had shouted.

"I promise…I'll find out."

"Just tell me the truth, is he alive?" she asked frantically.

"Melissa…."

"Vincent, you're his friend, the godfather of our kids. He had much love for you. Please, just tell me the truth. Is he still alive?" she asked, persistent to know the truth.

I couldn't tell her that Spoon was murdered by my hands and dumped into the sea. She was crying over the phone when she was talking. My heart cried with her. I couldn't incriminate myself. Spoon used tell me—you kill a man and you never speak on it again. I was doing just that.

"Vincent, if I don't hear from Spoon within the week, I'm going to the police," she had threatened.

"Melissa, look, you ain't gotta involve them."

I heard dial tone. She hung up. I got nervous. Melissa going to the police would open up a can of worms.

I kept her threats to myself for a few days. She was wilding out. I had to understand her pain. I was going through it also.

I stood by the bar nursing a shot of Hennessy in my hand. The party was jumping all around me. I couldn't be a part of it. I was in a different zone. Shae was dancing with a few of the girls she knew. She looked magnificent in the red Ruched dress that I got for her with the chain back detail, complemented by red pumps.

For a short moment, I admired her from the bar loving the way she moved and looked. She wasn't Chandra but she was a beautiful, arm-candy and wifey.

Tyriq was drinking a bottle of Moet, his arm around Iris. She stood tall and lovely in a metallic cowl neck dress. Her long graceful hair flowing down to her shoulders—her big tits and slim figure made that dress fit her perfectly. She sought my eye and threw me a smile.

I nodded, turning my attention away from them, finally tossing back the Hennessy. The deejay was playing old school, Big Daddy Kane's, *Ain't*

No Half-Stepping. It was forty minutes from the New Year's countdown and the crowd was definitely ready for '03 to come.

"I see you're having a good time," Iris said.

She stood next to me and ordered an Absolut Peach.

"I'm having a ball," I replied sarcasm dripping.

I glanced around for wifey and heard Iris say, "She's still on the dance floor having a good time. Tyriq went to talk to some friends outside. Are you nervous?"

A chuckle escaped my quivering lips.

"Have a drink with me," she said grabbing her drink.

"What's good?" I asked.

"You tell me," she replied.

"Look, I got a lot of shit on my mind right now, and being seen alone wit' you, is only goin' to make my situation worse," I admitted.

"Talk to me, maybe we can help each other out."

I chuckled again. "How can you help me?"

"You'll be surprised about the things I can do." She flashed me a flirtatious smile and took a sip.

"You're just Tyriq's bitch…nothing personal"

"Boo, don't get it twisted, I've been on these streets for a long time and I know who to fuck to get what I want," she said.

Iris was a bad bitch but I knew she was trouble. There was a mystique about her that had me a curious. I knew she was from the streets, looking at her and talking to her, I knew she wasn't as naive as I thought. She was young but had that same bad-ass bitch attitude as Cashmere.

"I like your swagger, Vince. To be honest, I had my eyes on you the first time we met," she admitted.

"And…?"

"We need to talk. I know about the drought Tyriq got y'all niggas on. I know about your Philly connections. You tired of being on that nigga's leash?"

"I ain't on no one's fucking leash," I spat.

"We'll see," she smiled staring at me with unbelieving eyes. "I watched you step up within months. You getting it and I know you got what it takes to run an organization."

"And…?"

"Listen, we can talk later but if you want meet me downstairs in five minutes. You know where…we can finish this talk in private," she said then sashaying away.

My eyes followed her backside and her strut through the crowd. I loved her sex appeal and realized it came with smarts. My dick got hard just looking at her. Knowing and loving that it was new pussy. And New pussy could be trouble, especially when it belongs to Tyriq. Temptation stirred my heart. It was risky. Sometimes it felt like I love risks.

I glanced around, searching for Shae or Tyriq. Shae was getting her groove on, dancing with her home girls and I thought, damn, she can dance. I didn't see Tyriq.

The thought of fucking this bitch replaced Spoon on my mind. I downed another shot of Hennessy and skated away from the bar, disappearing into the crowd and making my way downstairs. It was easy access. The bouncers knew me and they didn't say anything as I moved passed them. I walked down the stairs to my own private party.

Downstairs was a smaller club, unused for the night. The lights were dimmed. My heart rate increased as I moved toward the back office. The lights were on and the door ajar. I made my way into the office and saw Iris seated on top of the desk with her dress pulled up slightly. Her legs were partly opened.

"I knew you wouldn't disappoint," she smiled.

"We gotta make this quick," I said. It was twenty minutes to midnight and I needed to be with wifey.

"Don't worry…It'll be pleasure before business," she said approaching me.

I threw my arms around her and shoved my tongue down her throat. I reached down and squeezed her phat round ass like a piece of juicy fruit in my hands. I then slid my hands under her dress only to discover, she wasn't wearing any panties.

Iris began sucking and biting on my neck like she was a fucking vampire. I had to pull her off of me, not wanting any marks for wifey to see and said, "Chill, I don't want no fuck marks on me."

She flashed a devilish smile and started undoing my pants. I didn't resist. I felt her hand digging into my jeans and allowed her soft manicured hand to grip around my growing erection.

"Umm…you're big," she whispered.

I moaned, loving the way she was handling my member. She slowly jerked me off and then when I was hard like stone, she pulled down my pants and with my dick fully out and ready for action. She walked away from me.

My eyes followed her every move and she went over to the desk, pulled up her metallic dress to her hips, giving me a full view of that ass. Then she slowly curved her back over, gripped the desk and said, "Now fuck me!"

Her pussy was phat and nice like a Biggie rhyme. I stepped out my jeans and boxers and walked to her. I gripped her hip, with my fist around my dick and slowly slid into her pussy raw like meat. I was wilding, but the only thing I cared about was fucking new pussy.

"Oooh," she cried throwing pussy back at me.

Her shit was wet and tight and we went at it—fucking our brains out with the New Year only eighteen minutes away. I needed to hurry so I moved like a jack hammer. I had that bitch hollering and screaming so loud, you thought that she was getting murdered. The loud, thunderous and deafening music coming from upstairs drowned our actions.

I continued to thrust into her, and was constantly keeping check of the time.

"Fuck me!" Iris screamed.

I did, gripping her hips cupping her huge tits and throwing everything I had in her. I was smacking her ass and pounding out the pussy. I needed to hurry it up. I pushed my dick deep into her and Iris jumped, loving how long my dick stretched her.

"I'm cumming!" I exclaimed, glancing at the time. I had ten minutes.

"Do that shit….Oooh, do that shit," she shrieked, with her head against the desk and her ass in the air.

I felt that pussy getting wetter and tightening up. She had an orgasm and after a few more thrusts, I exploded into her without pulling out. Her pussy was so good, I felt my knees buckling. Now was not the time to be vulnerable.

I pulled out and got dressed as fast as I could. I then dashed into the bathroom to wash my face and wash the scent of new pussy from my dick.

It was five minute to midnight. I checked myself in the mirror. I was satisfied and darted back upstairs to look for Shae. The crowd was crazy but I navigated my way keeping an eye out for wifey. I spotted her by the bar, holding two glasses filled with champagne.

"Hey boo," I greeted, rushing up to her.

"Vincent, where were you? I was looking all over for you," she said.

"Outside getting some air," I lied.

"Here…" She passed me a glass of champagne.

I held her close in my arms and was getting ready for the countdown. I saw Tyriq up on the stage gripping another bottle of Moet and standing with his peoples and bitches. I looked over and saw Iris making her way toward the crowded stage. She was trying not to appear like she had just been fucked crazy. She moved up on stage and nestled against Tyriq. They looked like the perfect thug couple.

"Ayyite …y'all ready for 2003?" Tyriq shouted over the mic.

The crowd got loud and shouted, "Hells Yeah."

The deejay was playing Biggie and P. Diddy, *All about the Benjamin's*, the crowd was hyped, everyone dancing and waiting for the New Year.

"We gettin' money … Ayyite we get that money…we gettin' that money," Tyriq sang out.

I looked up at him and smirked, knowing I fucked his woman, and it felt good doing it.

"Here we go…everybody make sure them glasses are filled. We about to go hard for 03, y'all ready?" the deejay shouted.

The music was blaring and the crowd was going berserk. Soon the countdown to 2003 began. I held Shae in my arms. Our drinks clutched in our hands and prepared myself for the blowout.

"…7-6-5-4-3-2-1—HAPPY NEW YEAR!"

The crowd shouted. Bottles popped and everyone started downing champagne and the revelry was on in the club.

The music got louder and the deejay played hot mixes. I downed my champagne and hugged Shae close to me and said to her, "Happy New Year, baby."

"Happy New Year," she returned. We kissed and I hugged her.

I looked over at the stage and saw Iris looking at me with a smirk on her face. Tyriq then turned and looked at me and then he raised his bottle in my direction and shouted out, "Happy New Year, my nigga."

I gave a head nod acting like it was all good, "Happy New Year," I shouted.

The New Year wouldn't be the same without Spoon around. Here I was in a crowded club with friends and my girl but without my homey it didn't feel right.

I remember last year I spent the New Year with Chandra, my son, my moms, and Aunt Linda at the crib. We drank wine, watched movies, talked and laughed. I had a good time without going to the club and getting drunk. Spoon came by to see the family New Years day, and it was great having him around. My family loved him.

Now, there would be no more of those happy times with family and friends. Everything had changed dramatically. I've changed considerably. I probably have committed every sin known to man.

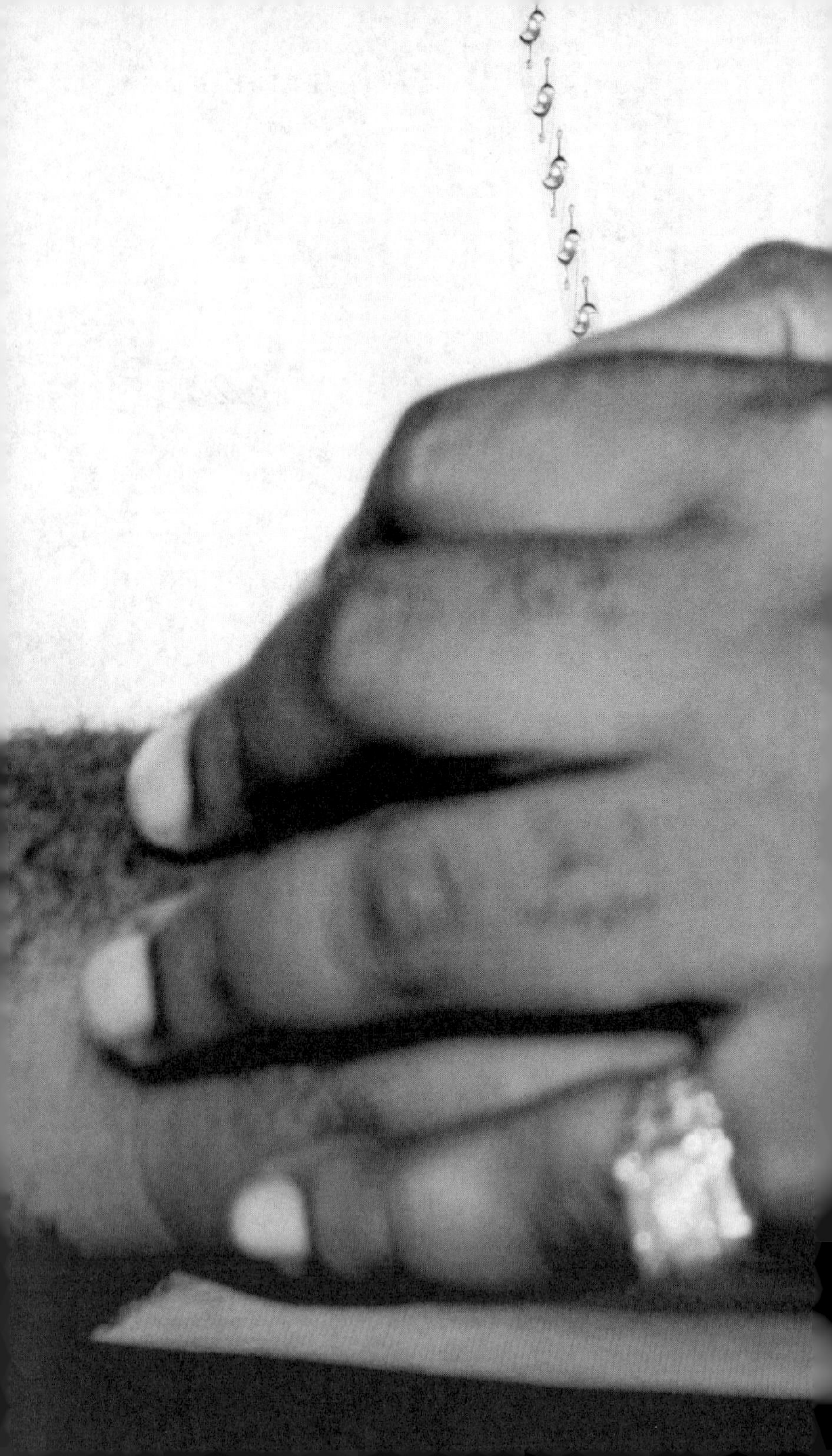

Part Three

Hope for the best.. prepare for the worse...

Last year's drama was carried forward to the New Year. Two days after the New Year '03. Melissa was running her mouth about Spoon being murdered and was positive that Tyriq had something to do with it. I was his lackey to help cover it up. She even put up a fifty-thousand dollar reward on the streets for information about Spoon's sudden disappearance.

The murder of the daughter of the DEA agent wasn't going away. The feds and cops were still on niggas asses trying to find the culprits. They raided drug spots pressuring informants to give them something. I had my speculations about Tip's involvement in the murder.

Inf was becoming a pain in my ass. Philly was a hot market and he couldn't afford to let his product run dry. He was getting desperate—shit, I was desperate. Since finding out that Spoon was snitching to the feds, Tyriq had become paranoid. The nigga was acting like everybody was turning against him. I was starting to think that he was getting crazy. He wanted to kill a few more people just to make sure niggas weren't setting him up.

I got an unexpected visit from two federal agents. Pena and Smith wanted to ask me questions about Spoon's whereabouts. I knew nothing. They tried to pressure me into giving them something. I wasn't in the game long enough for them to suspect anything. Spoon's disappearance had the streets talking. Foul play was suspected by our hands or rivals.

Tyriq blamed Law for Spoon's death, possibly as payback for PR's murder. I murdered PR and that was kept on hush. Tyriq needed a scapegoat and pointed fingers at Law, a rival dealer from Hollis who had a grudge against us since forever.

Law was a big money playa from Hollis Queens who moved dope and coke and been a rich man since the late nineties. Tyriq and him never liked each other but respected each other's position in the game until PR's death. PR was kin to Law and Law was the type of nigga who believed that revenge was best served cold.

One situation after another was bubbling and getting ready to explode. I didn't want to get caught up in it, but already was.

I was in the empty bar drinking Vodka, trying to drink my troubles away, watching the Knicks lose to the Rockets. Jake kept my company from behind the bar. Tyriq walked into the bar with Tip behind.

I sighed and paid no attention to them. I sipped my drink and continue to watch the TV mounted above the bar. Jake was acting nervous when Tyriq came close to me.

"Jake, go take a walk for a minute," Tyriq ordered.

Jake stopped what he was doing and moved out the bar like he was being timed. Tyriq sat on the stool next to me and asked, "You good, playa?"

"Yeah," I dryly responded.

I got edgy thinking that Iris told about us fucking. Now Tyriq was here to get revenge against me. I was a changed man and was ready for anything that came. I remained calm and collected, my eyes focused on the Knicks game and holding my drink.

"Yo, what da fuck is up with, Melissa?" Tyriq asked bluntly.

"She's just talking crazy," I said.

"Ayyite but she's making too much noise out there, putting up fifty grand. I ain't feeling that shit, Vince."

"What you gonna do wit' her? Shut her up?" I asked in mockery.

He just looked at me and his expression told me the nigga was serious.

"I know you're fucking kidding me, right?"

"Yo, we need to handle that bitch; I don't like my name coming out her fucking mouth. And where the fuck she gets fifty large to put up? Spoon had to pass that bitch some serious cash."

"Tyriq, this is Spoon's baby mother, she ain't no threat."

"She is. I want you and your crew to handle that bitch, ASAP," he ordered.

"Nigga what…?"

"Handle it, Vince."

"Nah, you wilding, I ain't touching her," I let him know sternly.

Tyriq and Tip glared at me when I shook my head.

"Nigga what…?" Tyriq spat.

"I ain't touching her," I repeated eyeing Tyriq and Tip.

Tyriq sized me up and said, "Oh, so you big dawg now, huh, Vince. Nigga, don't forget who put you on to the game. Don't bite the hand that fucking feeds you."

"Spoon's gone, why you gotta fuck wit' his family for?"

"How 'bout, the bitch gotta big mouth, and I'm gonna shut it for her," he snapped at me.

"Let her be, Tyriq. What's done is done."

"Nigga, you gonna do this or what?" he dared asking again.

I stood up from the barstool and boldly said to him, "Nah, if you want her dead, that's on you nigga…not me."

"Ayyite, it's like that, huh…? After all we've been through, after everything I done for you, you gonna just turn your back on me?"

I ignored him and continued out the bar, exchanging hard glances with Tip, he wanted to strike at me. I realized the twenty years of friendship I had with Tyriq meant nothing when it came to the game. Tyriq would be willing to have me killed any day to keep what belonged to him and his black ass out of prison.

I had to either strike first or watch my back on these streets. After turning my back on him and disagreeing on a murder, it would be much sooner than later.

Thirty- Two

Tyriq

Tyriq wasted no time trying to kill Melissa. She was a threat to him and his business. He had set up a meeting with Omega the same night after he saw Vincent. The two met in the cold in St. Albans, not too far from Omega girl's crib.

Omega stepped out of his pearl BMW and approached Tyriq sitting in his polished black Infiniti M, with the buffed up chrome rims. Omega approached the car with a cool swagger. A thick leather coat protected him from the cold. He wore an orange Coogi sweater underneath, beige timberlands on his feet and his 9mm tucked snuggly in his waistband. He was ambitious and ready to prove loyalty to Tyriq.

"Tyriq, what's good, playa?" Omega greeted, giving Tyriq dap.

Tyriq was sitting alone in his whip. Omega looked around for Tip, but he was absent.

"I need a job done ASAP," Tyriq said, getting straight to the point. "I know you're the man for this."

"Who is it?"

"Spoon's baby mother…"

Omega seemed unfazed. He knew of her but cared nothing for her. He was more ruthless than his partner in crime, Soul. Omega saw this as opportunity to let Tyriq and others know how far he was willing to go. He wanted to climb up in the game and spread his fierce rep.

Omega was on the run for shooting at the cops when they raided a stash house a few weeks back in forty projects. He was there but escaped before the raid and didn't shoot at any cops. The streets spread lies. That was what they expected from him. Omega's reputation for violence was growing.

"You got an address for the bitch?"

"Do what you do best, my niggah…make it go away." Tyriq smiled and gave him the location.

Omega nodded.

"Oh, and the bitch probably got some serious loot hidden up in there…maybe a few hundred thousands. You find it, it's yours. It's a late Christmas gift," Tyriq said.

"I got it."

"Ayyite, my nigga," Tyriq said giving Omega dap, rolling up his window and driving off.

Omega looked at the address, memorized it and ripped the paper up. He made a phone call. It was payday, he was definitely going to make it happen and fuck shit up.

◇◇

Melissa pulled the Lexus into the dark paved driveway. She had a long day dealing with her three kids, taking them shopping at Green Acres mall, then to a movie. Finally dropping them off at her mother's house for the weekend she needed a breather. Spoon's disappearance was tearing her apart, not knowing if her children's father was alive or dead. Among her friends, she displayed strength and confidence alone, she often broke down crying. She was very aware that the way he lived was possibly the way he died.

She put up the reward to call out Tyriq and put him on blast. Melissa never liked him. She always warned Spoon about trusting Tyriq. She knew that he was a snake and a grimy dude. Spoon would shush her saying they'd been friends since forever.

Melissa was unaware that she was being watched from a short distance. She began to gather up her belongings from the car and slowly got out. She was digging in her purse for the house keys, walking to the back entrance of her Queens Village home. Melissa was exhausted and wanted to get some sleep. Her three-inch heels clicked loudly against the pavement and the cold January wind nipped at her open face.

Finally, she located her keys and began to enter her home. But a creepy chill overcame her when she heard movement. Her hands were sweaty as she quickly tried to insert the keys into the lock, hurrying to get inside.

The second door was unlocked but it was a little too late. Three masked men with guns rushed her from behind and forced their way into her home.

Melissa screamed running but one of the men caught up with her, hitting her in the forehead with the butt of the gun and violently dropped her to the kitchen floor.

"Shut da fuck up, bitch," the masked gunmen cursed, training his Glock 17 at Melissa.

"Lock that door," the second masked gunmen told the third one.

With the door locked, they dragged Melissa to the living room and asked, "Where the fuck is the dough?"

"What money?" she replied.

The first gunmen swung and bashed Melissa in the face with the Glock, damn near broke her jaw. Teeth, blood and spit spewed out staining the thick carpet.

"Don't fuck around, bitch!" the first gunmen shouted.

Melissa was in severe pain and was crying out hysterically, as she laid face down on the stained carpet, still coughing up blood and spit and holding her bruised jaw.

"Where the fuck is the money?" the same gunman asked, showing no remorse of his actions against her.

Melissa slowly turned herself over and looked at the gunman with her tear stained eyes, blood trickling from her mouth and her beautiful face bruised from the brutal assault.

"You gonna kill me like you did, Spoon?" she said, staring into the eyes of the first gunmen.

"Bitch, I done told you, stop fucking around!"

"Fuck you!"

All three men didn't expect her to be this bold.

"You killed Spoon, right…? Now you want his money? Go to fucking hell!" She angrily spat, no longer in fear.

"You know what bitch…you first," the first gunmen said. He quickly moved toward her, snatched up a cushion from the couch, pressed it to her face, and then fired into it the thick cushion twice.

"We'll find it ourselves," he then said, staring down at the body and blood with a scowl on his face.

"Damn," the third gunmen said, shaking his head.

All three then began tossing the place and pulling shit out of closets, drawers, even pulling up the carpet searching for the money. They ransacked Melissa's entire home from floor to floor to no avail.

"Fuck!" the first gunmen shouted.

"Let's be out then," the second gunmen said.

They began fleeing back to their ride, knowing they fucked up. The hit was carried out and that was the thing the gunmen cared about. She was going to die anyway.

Once they were all in the car, the first gunmen, Omega sighed, pulling the ski-mask from over his head and said, "Fuck that bitch…shoulda shot her four more times!"

Thirty-Three

I was fucking furious when I got the news about Melissa. Tyriq had to kill her. I wasn't naïve I knew something was going to happen. I just didn't want to believe it. I thought about the three kids not having a mother or a father. Despite the shit I did, I had a heart and concern for my Godchildren.

They were staying with their grandmother while detectives were investigating their mother's brutal death. Someone shot her twice in the face and my first thought was Tip. He was wicked and would carry out a hit like that.

I knew things were changing around me. My life was turning into one crime scene after another. I needed to make moves with the quickness.

I hooked up with Iris again. She aroused my curiosity. I was relying on Tyriq for the bricks I needed to supply Inf. I couldn't trust Tyriq anymore. I had to get a new connect and was ready to go behind Tyriq's back. I had a hundred-thousand dollars saved and was ready to get my shipment from somewhere else.

I met up with Iris in an upstate N.Y motel, off Interstate 87. We had talked and she had some peoples she wanted me to meet. But I had a big trust issue.

"Who are these people?" I asked over the phone.

"They good and can give you what you need," she said.

"I don't fucking know them."

"I know them."

"I don't really know you like that," I said.

"Vince, you're in trouble. Tyriq's putting word out on the streets that you had something to do with PR's death and that you also had something to do with Spoon's disappearance."

"How the fuck do you know this?" I barked.

"I'm fucking the nigga. I hear things and I see things, even when he thinks I'm not listening. I know what's goin' on. I know I'm not the only bitch he's fucking…its all good, cuz I'm gonna get mines."

Hearing this, I was displeased with that fucking coward. Dry snitching on a nigga, violating the one code Spoon taught me to uphold. *You kill a man and never speak on it again*—you shut your fucking mouth. He was trying to set me up. When I murdered PR, I had no idea who the nigga's kin was.

Law and his boys were looking to spill blood over his nephew's murder. Tyriq pointing the finger at me made me furious. He was fucking devious. I knew his motive—Spoon was loved in the streets, and PR was well known in Hollis. If I'm blamed for their bodies, I'm the bad guy. I'm the one niggahs will be gunning for cause of this bitch ass nigga.

In Spoon's case there was no body— no crime. The cops had nothing but in the streets, niggas were blood thirsty like vampires and were ready to suck you dry. The streets didn't care about a body.

Tyriq was making his move against me subtly. I had to react.

"Iris, do not fuck wit' me," I warned her.

"Vince, you're the only nigga I trust to do me right."

◇◇◇◇◇◇◇◇◇◇◇◇◇◇◇◇◇◇◇◇◇◇◇◇◇◇◇◇◇◇◇◇◇◇◇◇

I pulled up into the motel parking lot in upstate, New York and approached the ground floor room, with a .380 tucked in my waistband and fifty-thousand dollars in the back of my truck.

I knocked on her room door and Iris came to the door wrapped in a white towel.

"You alone…?" I asked. My hand was near my weapon.

"Yeah…"

I walked in slowly and observed the room; it was small. A single made bed, a badly maintained television and cheap carpet, with a small wooden desk near the door.

Iris was freshly out the shower and was looking good. I took a seat on the bed and said, "What time do we meet?"

"Around ten, tonight..."

It was only five in the evening and getting dark. I sighed laying back. The drive to Connecticut was about two hours away.

We had time to spare. Iris dropped her towel to the floor and approached me in the nude. She slowly straddled me, while unfastening my jeans gripping my hard-on and guided it inside her. I moaned, getting in rhythm with her and held her in my arms thrusting.

We rode silently to Connecticut to meet up with a Colombian named Grotto. How did Iris link up with these Colombians, no idea—but the bitch was very resourceful when it came to the streets.

Around nine-thirty, we arrived in Westport, Connecticut, a few miles south of Bridgeport. The area was dense with many trees. The back roads were dark and winding.

In Compo Mill Cove, we drove up to a sensational and customized home. The driveway was lit with tiny lights engraved in the pavement. It was part of a gated community.

"We here," Iris said, getting out the truck.

I made sure the strap was in the right place before getting out.

"You trust these peoples?" I asked.

She smiled, and headed for the entrance.

From what I knew, her connect was from Miami—Columbians. I was nervous going into a situation I knew nothing about.

It was stupid of me. I armed myself. They could ask me to check my weapon at the door.

I followed Iris to the house. Two men dressed in dark suits stood guard at the front door. I didn't see any artillery on them. They stood at ease and were alerted by the sight of Iris and me. I didn't want to say the wrong thing and have these muthafuckas cap me.

"Estamos Aqui' a Se, Grotto," Iris spoke in Spanish as we approached the men.

I was shocked, not knowing that she spoke any Spanish. But people always thought the same thing of me.

She told them *we were here to see Grotto*.

“Espera aqua’,” one of the guards replied.

Pulling out a small, two-way radio, confirming our arrival, the guard told us we had to be searched before we were let in.

Shit! I thought.

“I tell you right now, dawg, I’m already armed,” I enlightened him.

I was intensely stared down and quickly relieved me of my weapon. It was then that I noticed the bulge under his jacket, he was packing heavy.

I felt helpless and hated going into the situation unarmed. This was their turf, therefore their rules.

One of the guards led the way into the place. Iris entered first and I followed behind. Inside, there was a three-story atrium living room, with beamed ceilings, a fireplace and handsomely finished white oak floors. We passed a large, open dining room with French doors. The guard guided us to the great room. I noticed the large size projection television and expensive stereo equipment.

There were three men in the room, two dressed in dark suit. One clad in a dark color velour sweat suit, seated by the doors that open to the deck. His leg was propped up on the armrest of a big La-Z boy leather chair. He slouched, playing with the remote to the stereo. Classical music played and the man in the sweat suit seemed to be enjoying the composition.

He looked early forties, with a gray goatee, aging light brown skin, dark eyes and salt and pepper crimped hair. He seemed low-key in fashion, showing no bling, the only piece of jewelry I spotted on him, was a thin gold chain around his neck and a small cross for a pendant.

“Iris…?

He was a tall and handsome man. He looked calm approaching Iris greeting her with a hug and kiss on the cheek.

“Grotto…éste es el hombre que te decía alrededor, Vincent,” Iris said.

I nonchalantly pretended I didn’t understand what they were saying. She was talking about me.

Grotto didn’t say anything for a short moment, but I could feel his powerful presence sizing me up.

“I hear you’re coming up in Queens,” he said to me in a cool manner.

"I try," I replied.

"Iris, come over here," Grotto said.

Iris went to him without any hesitation. He put his arms around her and said, "I used to fuck her since she was fifteen…when she used to dance her tight little ass off at my club in Miami. She's a good and sweet woman… literally." He smiled eying me.

I listened unemotionally to him.

"You fucked her too?" he asked me.

"I thought we were here to do business," I said.

He chuckled then turned to look at his men and said, "Papi aqui no puede incluso conseguir probablemente a su dick blando para arriba para la perra."

His men laughed at my expense. I knew what he said about me, he practically called me a limp dick and said I probably couldn't fuck the bitch right. I kept my composure and continued to look like I didn't understand.

Iris nestled in his arms and looking flawless in a bustle wrap sweater dress. I watched Grotto slowly moving his hands up her thighs and under her dress. His eyes were focused on me. Iris looked hypnotized by his touch.

"You like to watch?" he teased, whispering.

I smiled.

Grotto continued to fondle Iris like they were the only ones in the room. He cupped her breasts and I knew he was finger fuckin' her with his hand under her dress. Iris let out a blissful cry and looked lost in his arms.

Grotto then looked at me and asked, "She feels this way for you too?"

"It's your world," I said wishing he'd end the show.

Grotto smiled releasing Iris from his fondling grip and said, "I like you already…a man that doesn't get emotional over a bitch."

"I'm here for business," I said.

He nodded and walked over to the bar.

"You want a drink?" he asked.

"I'm good."

Grotto poured himself a drink from the bar and then said, "So, you're ready to do business with me. How do I know you're not the police?"

"How do I know you're not a cop?" I asked.

He smiled and returned, "True."

I suddenly noticed the gun in his hand, it looked like a Glock. I got extremely nervous. I thought that I was fucked but he turned the gun on to Iris. Her eyes widened.

"Grotto…no!" she exclaimed.

Bang! The gun went off. Iris dropped dead with a bullet to her head.

My mouth dropped opened and I was frozen to the floor, wondering, *was I next?*

"Like I said, I used to fuck her since she was fifteen. I loved that little bitch and warned her, that if she ever fucked another man, I'd kill her," he stated. "I never forget, my friend. Love is a very dangerous emotion…I'd rather hate a woman than to be in love with one. That should prove I'm not a cop."

"Do I need to be worried?" I asked calmly but my heart felt like it was about to rip my chest.

"No…it was between us. You, on the other hand, have a fresh start with me. Let's talk some business," he said, walking from behind the bar with his drink in one hand and the smoking gun in the other.

I looked down at Iris sprawled out dead on the polished oak floors with a hole in her forehead and blood escaping from the back of her head, staining the oak floors.

"Don't worry, my men will clean up the mess….come, let's talk," Grotto said, walking away from the body.

I sighed and thought, *damn, what a waste of some fine piece of ass.*

I walked with Grotto into the den area, where he shut the door.

"Have a seat, my friend, mi casa, your casa."

I took a seat on a plush burgundy leather couch. Grotto took a sip from his glass and sat behind his polished cherry wood desk.

"You came for business, let's talk business," he said. "I got fifty kilos of heroin that needs to be moved. There's another fifty keys of cocaine and ecstasy just sitting around in the cold. I want it all gone. Are you the man?"

I thought about it for a short moment and said, "Yes. I have a connect in Philly that's waiting for a re-up and I can move product in Queens too."

"Good," he said.

"I have one problem," I said.

"And…?"

"I got some peoples in Queens that's going to make it hard for me to move your weight."

"I see…the competition. Do I need to deal with them?"

"I need muscle to back me. They're both well known men. I kill them and their peoples will put a bullet in my ass. I need you to have my back on this. I'm fucking wit' their money."

"My friend, don't worry. I have power everywhere, you understand? Okay, the price is eighteen thousand a key, can you do?"

I smiled—could I? Shit, that was three thousand less than what Tyriq was charging me.

"Yes," I answered.

"Good."

"I can give you fifty thousand in cash up front…if you can front me everything else on consignment," I said.

"A man that comes prepared, I like that. We have a deal," he said.

I smiled.

I had an easy hundred keys of coke, dope and ecstasy to distribute. I had a new connect and acquired some muscle in the process. My climb to the top was moving rapidly and my head was spinning. I went through so many bumps in the fucking road.

We shook hands. Grotto pulled me close to him, fixed his eyes on me. "You fuck me over, and it'll take them years to find all of you. Remember Iris as an example. I loved her," he said in a grim tone.

"I'm no bitch."

"Let's hope not," he smiled.

Grotto got the money from the back of my truck. I left with fifty keys of coke and dope in the back of my truck. It was after midnight when I left Connecticut. I was tired and thought about poor Iris, she trusted Grotto and was the one who ended up dead. I watched two men in black cleaned up the body. They replaced the furniture like it never happened. God bless her soul. I had to thank Iris for the hook-up. It was time for me to show Tyriq that I was no longer under him.

Thirty-Four

Two months later....Tyriq

"Ayyite! This nigga, thinks he can fuck with me? Fuck that, nigga! I'll put that punk muthafucka in the fucking dirt. He thinks cuz we grew up together that he can fuck me over? I'm gonna get at this nigga!" Tyriq exclaimed from the passenger seat of the pearl white Benz that drove down Hillside Avenue.

They were on their way to meet with the Jamaicans and Bones was behind the wheel. Vincent was on the rise, making major moves and word quickly got out that Vincent was moving weight across state lines. He had gotten a strong crew together, including Lil' Goon and a few others. Soon, his reputation was spreading like the virus.

Vincent growing business was cutting into Tyriq's profits, and Tyriq and the Jamaicans were clearly upset about this. Money was power and power was influence. Next came greed, egos and violence always follows, flooding the streets with blood.

"Yo, fuck him and the Columbians. He wanna be a gangsta. I'm gonna show this nigga how. Fucking backstabbing muthafucka! I brought this nigga in! I wanna murder this nigga!" Tyriq shouted.

"It's a done deal," Bones assured.

"Ayyite, he want a war? I'll give this nigga a war. He ain't got enough soldiers to fuck with me," Tyriq screamed.

"It's a spit in your face, my nigga…very disrespectful," Bones instigated.

Tyriq was ready to break windows and crack skulls. There were no more friendship and bond. I was now his foe and a bitter rival.

Tyriq created a monster. With the Columbians supplying and backing Vincent for protection, he was making kingpin moves—distributing weight in Philly, Delaware and B-more.

Murders started happening and Tyriq began questioning the disappearance of Iris. It was two months since he last saw her.

Tyriq had other important things to deal with than worrying about Iris. He had to meet with the Jamaicans about issues. He hated meeting with the Jamaicans, they were unpredictable at times. He didn't know if he was walking into a meeting that would bring about his demise or someone else's.

The Benz pulled up to a Jamaican restaurant on Hillside Avenue, near the Cross Island Expressway. Two lavish looking Escalades were parked outside the restaurant, indicating that the major players were already inside.

Tyriq got out, followed by Bones and made their way to the front entrance. They were bothered by what the Jamaicans would do about the escalating feud.

Vince had the pipeline to Philly, that made Tyriq look bad. The situation flipped on him. Vince was eating lovely and putting a minor dent into Tyriq's organization.

The *Jerk –n- Stuff* Jamaican restaurant was a quaint eatery that catered mostly to a West Indian crowd. It was able to seat a crowd of twelve, but was also takeout. Pictures of the scenic island of Jamaica lined the walls of the restaurant with the colorful green, black, and yellow flag representing the island displayed throughout the place. The aroma of Jerk chicken and patties lingered through the dining area.

Tyriq walked into the dining area with a screw face. The staff was busy in the kitchen quarters. Bones was behind Tyriq, a .9mm tucked in his waistband. He was a young nigga under Tip's guidance and was willing to continue killing because he did that best.

A dread-lock Rasta with thick long knotted hair crawling down to his back emerged from the kitchen, eyeing Tyriq and Bones. He was in a blue and white sweat-suit, dark shades covering his eyes.

"Demetrius downstairs," the Rasta informed them.

Tyriq nodded and the Rasta approached him and said, "Ya must get searched."

"Whateva man," Tyriq said raising his arms.

He quickly patted Tyriq down, finding no weapons on him. He then looked over at Bones and Bones lifted his shirt, revealing the .9mm he was carrying.

"Yo, you already know," Bones said, far from being intimidated by the Shotta's.

"Him stay…you go," the Rasta said.

"Hold it down, Bones," Tyriq said, and then made his way toward the back.

He hated being alone and unarmed, never knowing the outcome of any meeting. He's been in bed with the Jamaicans for three years and made plenty of money. There were minor problems but none so major until now. The Columbians were moving in on their turf. Tyriq felt the guilt of it bringing in a friend who turned around and betrayed him. A war was brewing between the groups.

Tyriq went down the rickety wooden steps and made his way to a room where he heard commotion. Two more Jamaican bodyguards stood outside the door with a scowl on their faces. They glared at Tyriq like he had done wrong.

"Where's Demetrius?" Tyriq asked.

"Wait here," one said and walked into a private location.

He soon came back out and said to Tyriq, "Come."

Tyriq walked into the room where Demetrius and his followings were engaged in a game of dominos. Four men sat at a small square table enthralled by the game.

The room was filled with many Jamaican gangsters drinking, smoking, gambling and playing dominos. It was like a different world underneath the restaurant—Bob Marley's, *Is this love,* playing in the backdrop. It was an underground social gathering for Shotta, where they held important meetings, prepped drugs for street distribution and on occasions they dismembered foes.

Tyriq stood among the fearful Shotta and held his own. He looked into the eyes of Demetrius, "We need to talk."

Demetrius was six-five, a strapping physique and long locks down to his back said, "Bredren, how ya let di blood-claat Columbians cut into me money. Ya losing control, Tyriq?"

"I ain't losing control of shit," Tyriq hissed.

A few of Demetrius men glared at Tyriq.

"Watch ya tone, bredren…ya in me place of business…me takes no disrespect from no man," Demetrius warned.

Demetrius was iced out in platinum and diamonds. He sported a black tank-top and had tattoos running up and down his arms. He had an intimidating, powerful presence and was willing to murder any men or women who disrespected him or his organization.

"No disrespect to you, Demetrius. I got things under control. I just gotta deal with this one muthafucka then it'll be all good, ayyite," Tyriq said.

"Me hear, Vince used ti be a close friend, I see trouble," Demetrius said.

"He ain't trouble…just headache. I brought him in and I will take him out," Tyriq assured.

Demetrius stared at Tyriq, unsmiling. He then continued with his game of dominos taking his attention away from Tyriq a bit.

"Bredren, yuh think its safe ti do business?" Jagged asked.

He was Demetrius right hand man and was as deadly as a venomous snake.

"Ya bringin' ti much heat, Tyriq…yuh got di bumba-claat feds investigating us…yuh bring trouble," Jagged continued.

"Like I said, I can handle things…now I made this organization plenty of money over the years, and I'm gonna continue to do that. This is only one bump in the road. I fucked up and I'll fix it," Tyriq sternly stated.

"Me don't like problems, bredren…we wan yuh ti gwan and find dis blood-claat Vince and deal wit' him and da blood-claat Columbians…mi gwan and send Rude Boy Rex and Nappy Head Don ti help yuh handle ya rassclaat problem," Demetrius said.

"I don't need help, I just need product. I just want to get back on the streets and let muthafuckas know we still in control," Tyriq said.

"Mi only deal wit' a blood-claat problem fi so long, me have no patient fi trouble," Demetrius warned.

Tyriq hated threats, but he had to listen to the Jamaicans. He knew he wasn't in the position to go against them—they were his life support. He ate the insult and lived to see another day.

"I'll handle it, I promise you Demetrius," Tyriq assured.

"Dat's what me want ti hear, now leave me," Demetrius said, and then went back to his game of dominos.

Tyriq turned and walked out the room—biting his tongue. The Jamaicans were very disrespectful, but he let the shit slide for now. He had his hands full without having to worry about Shotta as enemy.

Tyriq saw Bones seated at one of the booths. "We out," Tyriq said, walking toward the exit.

Bones got up and followed his boss outside, sensing that Tyriq was upset. Both men got into the Benz and drove off, unaware they were being followed.

"Yo, I want y'all to get brutal on anything that moves against us, Bones. The Jamaicans think that we're losing control."

"Fuck them Jamaicans," Bones cursed.

"Not yet, we still need them for the shipments. But when the time comes, we gonna run every fucking thing out here."

"That's what the fuck I'm talkin' about. I'm ready to lay any one out," Bones said enthusiastically.

"You will my nigga."

The Benz moved westbound down Hillside. Both men were oblivious that, a dark four-door Impala with heavy tinted windows was two cars behind.

Bones stopped at a red light and took a drag of his Newport. He bobbed his head to a Biggie track. Tyriq was thinking about his foes and how to deal with every last one of them. He wanted them to suffer by his hands.

While they waited for the light to change, the Impala moved along beside the passenger side, and the back window quickly came down. Bones quickly took notice and when he saw the tip of the Heckler and Koch Mp5k unexpectedly emerging from the back window. He yelled, "Tyriq, get down!"

A loud burst of heavy gunfire shredded the pearl white Benz, ripping through doors, seats and shattering glass.

"Aaaaaahhh shit, I'm hit!" Tyriq screamed, as he ducked into his seat to protect himself from the intense gunfire riddling the car.

Bones floored the accelerator and blew through the red light, barely missing an oncoming car. The Impala drove after them, firing heavy artillery, shattering the back windows to the Benz.

It was sudden chaos on the streets. Bystanders ran for cover as the gunfire caused confusion on Hillside Avenue. Many ran for shelter behind cars, trees or ducking into nearby stores to avoid getting hit.

Bones sped down two blocks. A few rounds ripped through the driver's seat, hitting him twice in the back. He lost control of the car and slammed into a parked car.

The men in the Impala were relentless. They sped to the crashed Benz and two men jumped out from the backseat, gripping the powerful guns and continued to squeeze rounds into the car.

Bones was killed. Bullets continued to rip through him and the car. Tyriq took cover and was shot in the leg. He wanted to bolt from the car but it was impossible for him to run without getting hit again. He was panting and bleeding heavily from the wound in his leg. He reached under the seat to grab Bones' .9mm.

Tyriq could feel the bullets still penetrating the car, missing him by mere inches. He remained crouched on the floor, gripping the gun.

As the two men fired into the Benz, they didn't notice the beige mini van speeding towards them. One of the gunmen turned around but was hit by the speeding mini van.

Nappy Head Don came leaping out from the passenger side of the van. A .50 Cal was in his hands and fired like a crazed madman at the last gunman and the Impala.

"Pussy-claat, batty-bwoy! Me come fi yuh, ya hear? Anything moving is dead!" Nappy Head Don screamed, firing.

They rushed to Tyriq, pulling him out of the riddled Benz and tossed him into the backseat of the mini van. Nappy Head Don covering them with gunfire.

The intense shoot-out on the Queens street lasted a minute and a half.

Soon police sirens could be heard blocks away. The Impala and the surviving gunmen sped off. The mini van sped off in the opposite direction with Tyriq clenching his right leg and cursing.

Cops swarmed the area within minutes, coming from every direction and drawing closer to the brutal crime scene, finding one man lying dead in the street and the second victim slouched down in the riddled Benz. Blood was everywhere.

The cops shut down blocks and began investigating the murders, collecting evidence and searching for the culprits responsible. Every news channel in the city was on the scene reporting live and showing the city the handy work of a vicious crime syndicate brewing.

Dangerous men were at war with each other and Queens would be paved with blood for men who craved control, letting greed persist in their hearts, and having money controlling them.

Thirty-Five

Two months in, and I was supplying Inf in south Philly, and Nikki Friday in West Philly. Money was coming in abundance and the bloodshed was on the rise. I was in Philly for two weeks, escaping the chaos that was happening in Queens and handling business. The violence happening in Philly was extreme.

My climb to the top was subtle but far from peaceful. It became more violent once I cut out the middle man.

I had money, women and cars. I had a house in Penn Valley, the outskirts of Philly. A second in upstate New York and I had power. I would wake up and say to myself, *how the fuck does a baggage handler from JFK become a drug kingpin in almost a year*. I knew I was smart but never thought that I would reach this status. I didn't ask for this, it just fell into my lap and I ran with it, losing myself on the way.

One friend was dead and another close friend was now a foe, gunning for each other. I had to watch my back. Queens became a hostile place but I had family out there. As long as Tyriq and the Jamaicans were alive and in power, my family would be endangered. I had to move against them—and going against the Jamaican mafia was suicidal.

I sat with Lil' Goon, Inf, and a few other hoodlums in this private strip club on City Ave, in West Philly. We were popping bottles of Cristal and Moet got high, fucking naked bitches that were entertaining. Money was spread all around. It was as if a bank vault exploded littering the place with hundreds, fifties and twenties. We were rich men and enjoyed the fruits of our labor. My lifestyle was like a rock star, mixed with a bit of Hugh Hefner and some Tony Montana.

Cashmere was three months pregnant and I had my wifey, Shae living in a lavish and well furnished three-bedroom apartment in Rochdale, Queens. I was fucking around on the both of them. It was like a fucking disease. I had so much lust in my heart that I began to yearn for it and in time I started to kill for it.

Lil' Goon was only five-seven, but stocky and a heartless muthafucka. He was getting paid through me and had my back. He was cool but ruthless nigga. We became closer in the two months of my ascension. His crew knew how to put in work on the streets. He became my number one guy after Soul got locked up.

"Vince, you good, man…?" Lil' Goon asked, as he drank beer and threw money at bitches.

"I'm okay," I lied.

I should be having a good time but my heart and mind wasn't in it. Tyriq knew everything about me. He knew where my mother lived, where Chandra was staying. I knew Shae was in danger if she remained in Queens. If anything happened to my family because of my actions and choices in life, I'd be devastated.

"Yo, we head back to Queens tomorrow," I told Lil' Goon.

"Everything alright…?"

"I gotta make sure my peoples are safe," I said to him.

"I got you," he said.

The party continued with me thinking about removing my family from Queens. Philadelphia's murder rate was high and the drugs were prevalent. I knew I played a major role in that—distributing kilos to the dealers who ran the streets. I wanted to continue to get rich and ignore the downward spiral of the black communities. Every night, I watched the news and read the newspaper daily trying to keep up with current affairs. I wanted to know what was going on. I hated to be in the dark with things. The other morning, a five year old boy was killed on his way to school, walking with his mother in West Philly. Two blocks away from his school, rival drugs crews got into hostility and the crews released a barrage of bullets at each other in the cold early morning. The boy, Nathaniel Walker, was hit once in the neck. He died in his mother's arms. City hall was relentless in arresting the men responsible. I was saddened by this, because he was my son's age.

The mayor addressed the senseless murder in public and vowed to uphold justice.

A week after Nathaniel Walker was killed; a family of four was burned to death in their own home on Spruce Street. They captured the killers two days later and it was discovered that one of the victims owed a local dealer twenty-dollars, and the victim has been ducking his debt for weeks.

The dealer and friends broke into the home while the family slept, bounding everyone with duct-tape at gunpoint. They dowsed the victims with gasoline setting them on fire.

The city was appalled by this action, and they were even more disgusted by the ages—the three offenders were only fifteen and sixteen years old. They were getting younger and the crimes more heinous.

But I was eating lovely off the drug trade and worried about violence and troubles of my own. Sitting back in a chair, watching the Knicks play against the Heats, my thoughts were doing laps. I kept the .45 on me and eyes in the back of my head. I had five-thousand dollars cash on me and had a polished black Escalade sitting on 24" chromed rims parked outside.

Ari was coming my way. I had my eyes on him. He was from Queens but lived in Philly working the blocks, getting my money.

Ari looked serious as he came closer. He leaned and whispered in my ear, "Yo, Vince, they tried to hit Tyriq a few hours ago. But they missed him and killed Bones."

"You serious…?"

"I heard some Jamaicans pulled him out of the car and sped off."

"Good looking out," I said.

"No doubt," he replied walking off.

The news had me thinking. Tyriq being alive was bad for me. But who set up the hit, I wondered. It wasn't me. Someone beat me to it. I wasn't complaining. It was inevitable that the bubble would pop soon and spill over. I wasn't the only enemy Tyriq had.

I knew that I had to get back to Queens right away—Philly was becoming a war zone, but the drama and violence in Queens was just as bad.

Lil' Goon did eighty on the Jersey Turnpike. I was in the passenger seat trying to call Shae for the past hour or so. She wasn't picking up and that had my stomach doing cartwheels.

"She ain't picking up?" Lil' Goon asked.

"Nah…fuck is wrong wit' this bitch," I cursed, speed dialing her number.

I had enough problems with Cashmere. The bitch was wilding the fuck out. Before I left, she had screamed on me, shouting, "What bitch you fucking in New York?"

"Yo, you need to chill wit' that jealousy shit, Cashmere," I said.

"Fuck you, Vince! I know you fuckin' some bitch! Why can't I come to New York with you? Huh? You leave me here, carrying your fuckin' seed in me, why you in New York sticking your dick in other bitches! I hate you!"

She started throwing shit at me. "I'm gonna get you fucked up, nigga! Don't play me, Vince!"

"I ain't fucking wit' you," I had yelled.

"I ain't stupid. You think I don't know you fucking that bitch, Cherie and the next bitch, and the next bitch," she continued in a jealous rage. "You think I can't go to the police and tell them everything about you? Keep playing me!"

I pushed her against the wall with my hand clenched around her neck. My patience was exhausted. Every time I'm in Philly, it was the same shit with her. Her insecurities were really starting to bother me.

"You gonna do what, bitch? You keep your fucking mouth shut about my business. I don't give a fuck if Inf's your cousin. I'll crush you and that nigga like that…I ain't the one to fuck wit!" I screamed.

"Fuck you!" she cursed spitting in my face.

I lost control of myself and punched her. She shrieked and fell to the floor, crying. I glared down at her, ready to murder her. She held onto her stomach and screamed up at me, "You dead nigga! Nobody ever puts their fucking hands on me!"

"Yo whateva!" I replied walking away.

It was a mistake striking her, but her mouth had pushed me over the limit. I left her there lying on the floor, crying and cursing at me. I thought to myself, *why did I get this fuckin' bitch pregnant?* I was caught up in good pussy and she hooked me up with a high-quality connect in the city. In the long run, she was a fucking headache and I couldn't deal with her attitude and mouth anymore. I had enough problems.

We got to exit ten on the turnpike and Shae was not picking up. Maybe she was pissed off because I hadn't returned any of her phone calls in the past three days.

"Yo, this bitch better be dead, cuz if she ain't, I'm gonna fucking kill her myself," I barked.

"Yo, she's just probably upset, Vince. Give her time," Lil' Goon said.

I tossed my phone on the floor and sat back in my seat, peering out the window. After exit twelve on the turnpike, my cell rang. I quickly picked it up and saw that it was Chandra calling my phone.

"What the fuck this bitch want, now?" I said out loudly.

Lil' Goon glanced at me and kept the Escalade moving

"Hey, what you calling for…? Everything good…?" I asked.

"Vincent, where are you?" Chandra asked, but her voice seemed somber.

"Philly, why…?"

"Your mother had a stroke last night."

"What…?"

"She's at Marry Immaculate hospital."

"Why the fuck didn't anybody call me last night!"

"Yo, everything good, dawg…?" Lil' Goon asked. I ignored him and continued with my conversation.

"We tried, but for some reason, we couldn't get through to you," Chandra said.

"Is she okay? I mean, she's alive right?"

"She's in bad shape, Vincent. You need to go see her," Chandra said. "Your aunt Linda is at her bedside. You need to be there."

"I'll call you when I get into Queens," I said and hung up.

"Yo, Vince, what's goin' on?" Lil' Goon asked again.

"My mother had a stroke last night."

"Oh shit, I'm sorry, my dude. How is she?"

"I don't fucking know!" I snapped.

"Don't worry, I'll get you there in no time," Lil' Goon said. My mind was elsewhere.

I stared out into the turnpike and couldn't help but worry about my mother. I haven't seen her in months. The last time we talked was on Christmas day. I tried to hide my grief from Lil' Goon with my head turned from him thinking, what kind of son abandons his mother. I should've been there for her instead I was sucked in by the streets. The sudden guilt overwhelmed me.

I was ready to put my hand through the glass and explode. Lil' Goon was doing eighty down the strip. For me, it wasn't fast enough.

"Yo, hurry this shit up!" I shouted.

"I don't wanna get pulled over," he replied.

"I don't give a fuck! Drive nigga!" I shouted.

He shrugged and accelerated to a hundred miles per hour, flying. I got to Mary Immaculate hospital late that evening and dashed from the truck. Running into the hospital, I passed security to see my moms.

"Sir…sir, you need to stop at the front desk first," security instructed, chasing behind me.

"What the fuck you say?"

"If you're here to visit someone you need to see the receptionist first."

"Yo, my mother just had a stroke," I told him.

"I understand your concern…but its protocol. You need a pass before you can go up. Just see the young lady in the front," he said calmly.

I didn't say a word. I walked to the front desk, gave them the information they needed, got my pass and headed to the sixth floor.

I stepped out on the sixth floor with my heart beating with so many worries. I clutched the pass in my hand and made my way down the hallway looking for room 606. I screamed hustler in my butter soft leather coat, diamond and platinum chain swinging around my neck, diamond earrings in my ears, designer jeans and fresh timberlands on my feet. I left my gun in the car with Lil' Goon.

At room 606, I hesitated in going inside and took a deep breath. I glanced around and hated hospitals. It was full of death, sickness and the weak. I hated to see my mother in such a weakened condition. I'd known her as a strong, vibrant and confident woman who kept a positive attitude. She believed in God.

I slowly made my way into the room and heard the soft humming of the machines plugged into her. The room was silent and eerie, it made my skin itch. I moved further into the hospital room and saw my mother lying still in the bed with her eyes closed. It looked like she was resting instead of sick.

I tried to fight back the tears. But it was useless. I stared at her and hated seeing her like this. It looked like she aged a bit over the months. Her long stylish gray hair was thinning out. She looked like a vegetable lying there.

"I'm here, mamma," I said holding her hand.

I looked at her, wishing she'd wake up giving me her words of encouragements like *everything's going to be alright*. I took her for granted and wished I never did. Now I wanted to be there for her.

Tears trickled down my cheeks, as I held her hand gently. I thought about my father and wished I had his strength. He knew how to handle a tough situation and was there for the family when my grandmother died.

I felt helpless, looking at my mother lying there and I didn't know what to say or do. For once, I wished I knew how to say a prayer for her, my mother was always praying for me.

"Mamma, I'm sorry that I've been away for so long. But you and pops always knew the right words to say and knew how to handle things. I can't lose you too, mamma. I love you and I know I fu… I mean, messed up. I wanna make things right. I missed you and you need to fight this. I need you in my life. Your grandson needs you," I sadly proclaimed.

I continued to talk to her, hoping she would wake up. I needed a second chance and my mother in my life.

"Vincent," I heard my name being called from behind.

I turned around and saw Aunt Linda standing in the doorway. She had a cup of coffee in her hand and was surprised to see me.

"Aunt Linda," I said.

"It's been months…did Chandra call you?" she asked.

"Yeah, I got word today. How's she coming along?" I asked.

My aunt sized me up. Her eyes stayed focused on the bling. She walked up to me and said, "So, you finally take time out from the streets and come see your mother. It's been months, and we've been worried sick about you. You don't come by and now you're showing some concern?"

"Aunt Linda, please…not here," I said.

"Then when, boy…when are you goin' to get some sense into you? You're mother is dying in that bed because of you," she spat.

"What?"

"Since you left, all she did was worry about you and pray for you. You were her only son, and you walked out on her to give yourself to sin and the streets. Look at you, dapper down in that devil's jewelry and living in the devil's way. I understand that it was hard, not working and raising a son…but not only did you give up on her and your son, but you gave up on yourself. Why do you wanna be out there poisoning our community and abandoning hope for yourself, Vincent?"

I was in tears and the burden that was fucking me up. Aunt Linda chastised me like I was some small boy being caught with his hand in the cookie jar. I was sorry but my words were muted in the room. Aunt Linda walked over to my mother's bedside and placed a bible near her.

The doctor walked into the room and said to us, "Hello, I'm Doctor Fermat."

"What's wrong wit' her?" I asked horridly.

"Vincent, let the man talk," my aunt chimed.

"She had what we call a hemorrhagic stroke. It's a result from a weakened vessel that ruptures and bleeds into the surrounding brain. The blood accumulates and compressed the surrounding tissue. We're prepping her for surgery, but her chances of survival… are bleak," Dr. Fermat grimly informed us.

I wanted to cry. I looked over at my aunt and her expression indicated she wasn't ready for this.

Dr. Fermat continued to talk, but I wasn't listening. I was too upset and needed some air—death was something that was becoming far too familiar with me—my father, Spoon, now possibly my mother. Without saying a word to anyone, I just walked out the hospital room in a hurry.

"Vincent," I heard my aunt calling out. "Vincent…Vincent!"

I ignored her calls and kept it moving. I skipped pass the elevators and went for the stairs. I rushed down the steps two at a time, reaching the front lobby in no time.

I jumped in the Escalade. Lil' Goon was waiting out front of the hospital.

"How is your mom?" he asked with concern.

"Just fucking drive," I said. "Take me to Rochdale. I gotta go see Shae," I said.

Thirty-Six

I got off the tenth floor and made my way to the apartment. I felt my life spiraling out of control and didn't know how to put it back together.

I wanted to move Shae someplace safe from the war zone. I couldn't handle losing someone else that I loved.

It was after nine when I walked into the apartment. The place was dark and silent. I pulled out my gat and moved to the bedroom looking for Shae. I cocked the .45 and called out, "Shae, where you at?"

"Shae," I called out again.

My heart began to race. I gripped the gun tightly and slowly entered the master bedroom. It was empty—no Shae and none of her clothing were in the closet.

"This bitch left!" I uttered incredulously.

I looked around the entire apartment and it indicated that she definitely packed up her shit and bounce on a nigga. I got upset. I wanted her to leave, but not like this. I walked back into the bedroom and tossed my gun on the bed. I went over to the mini bar and poured myself a drink. I walked out to the terrace. It was late March and cold still lingered in the air. I peered out at the vast Queens from ten stories up and couldn't help but miss Shae. She was gone from my life, giving me no hint that she was leaving. I felt that I had nobody—the richer I became, the more people I started losing from my life I had no friends left, and barely saw my son. Chandra was a married woman My mother dying was the straw.

I looked down at the ground from ten floors up and thought how easy it would be to just jump—end it all right now. I was sucked into a world tha was draining me.

Reminiscing about the past brought a few tears. More money caused more problems. Biggie wasn't lying about that. I became a powerful and respected figure in the drug world but my climb to the top was very costly. I won some and lost many.

I took a sip from the Hennessy watching dusk engulfed the neighborhood. *How would I die?* I asked myself. I wondered if my end would be violent by the hands of a one-time friend. My end wasn't going to be pretty. I remember my father used to say to me*, you live by the sword and you'll die by the sword.*

I heard someone at the front door unexpectedly. I got nervous and dropped the glass, running for my gun. Is this it, I thought.

I pointed it at the bedroom door and heard movement in the living room. The person was getting closer. I felt my body getting on edge. I was not going out without a fight. My finger against the trigger I was ready to squeeze.

My gun was trained at the bedroom entrance and waited. Time was moving slow. The door opened and Shae walked in. She saw me with the gun aimed at her head she gasped and jumped back, her hand over her chest.

"Vincent…Ohmygod," she cried out. "I thought you were still out of town."

"Shae, what the fuck," I barked. I was about to take her life, but it was a good thing that I wasn't trigger-happy.

"Can you please put that gun away," she said nervously.

I tossed the gun on the bed and asked, "Baby, I thought you left me… where are your clothes?"

She looked at me with uncertainty and then took a deep breath. "I can't do this with you anymore, Vince."

"Do what?"

"This life you live….I tried to love you, but I can't continue to put myself and my son in danger. You're constantly gone, leaving me here alone. And your ass don't know how to return phone calls."

"Then why you come back?" I asked.

"I forgot my son's medication in the bathroom cabinet."

"So this is it….after everything I've done for you, you just gonna walk out on me," I said.

"I thought you were different. I thought this life was only temporary for you. But you're like my son's father. You're just like the rest of them. You're letting the money control you. I can't be around a person like that," she proclaimed.

"Shae…you tell me this shit after my mother had a stroke," I informed.

"I'm sorry about your mother, my heart goes out to her, but I gotta go," she said.

"Where are you staying?"

"At a friend's place, I only came by to get a few things and leave your keys here. But since you're here," she said. She began removing the apartment keys from her other keys and handed them to me.

"It ain't gotta be like this, Shae, you know I love you," I said.

"I can't be coming home to guns pointed at me, Vince."

"I thought you were someone else," I said.

"And what if I was…you'd be ready to kill them, wouldn't you? Look at you, you're paranoid. What if I was home alone with my son and your enemies decide to pay you a visit. I can't risk our lives. I've been through this shit before with Jonathan's father. It doesn't get better. I need to think about my safety and my future, Vince. Please respect that."

"There's no more chances wit' you?" I asked.

"I told you in the beginning…please be good to me. But you and your disappearing acts for days and weeks at a time in the streets, I can't. Me not being able to reach you, having a gun pointed at me is not being good to me," she said.

"Will I see you again?" I asked.

She sighed, embracing me. I wrapped her petite figure in my arms always loving the way she felt. I didn't want to let her go, but I had to.

She pulled away from me and said, "You be safe out here, Vince. Remember this; we cannot always afford to be materially rich and spiritually poor."

Shae was smart and goal-oriented. She was definitely all woman and wifey. I let her go reluctantly. I was able to give her anything she wanted money was no thang. But what I couldn't give her—was a change in me.

Unwillingly, I watched Shae walk out from my life and knew I fucked up letting her go. It was for the best. I chose the streets instead of love. I sighed flopping down on the bed, thinking about the women in my life. I was letting the good ones go so easily—Chandra, Shae, moms dying.

An hour after Shae left, I followed needing to go for a drive. It was cold out when I emerged from the lobby. I zipped up my leather coat and made my way over to the car. I had my keys in my hand and was about to hit the alarm when I saw blue flashing lights racing up to me. It was po-po, I thought. I stood frozen near my car waiting for them to come at me.

I wasn't going to run and I wasn't going to fight them. I was going to accept my fate like a man and eat whatever they were gonna throw at me.

It was a single unmarked car with two detectives inside. They hurried out their ride.

"Mr. Grey," one shouted loudly.

"Yeah…what the fuck y'all want!" I asked with sarcasm dripping from my voice.

"Federal agent Pena. You need to come with us," agent Pena said showing me identification.

"I know who you are. What's this about?" I asked.

"Get in the car," Smith instructed steadfastly.

I reluctantly got into the car with them and they quickly drove off, with me in the backseat.

Within no time, I was sitting in a concrete room with no windows, a long bared table in front of me and a few shaky chairs. I wasn't handcuffed. I sat and waited. Pena came into the room first, followed by Smith. They kept their eyes on me while taking a seat across from me. Then they sat in their dark tailored fitted suits with their identification tags displayed outside of their suit jackets.

I remained quiet and blew air out of my mouth.

Smith looked at me and said, "Mr. Grey, you've been a busy man in the past year…trafficking, murder, drugs…I'm curious, how does a hardworking tax payer like yourself, becomes a major part of our investigation within a year's time?" he asked rhetorically.

"You tell me," I replied dryly.

"I ain't got no time for you to be a smart ass…I'm here to be a friend to you, Vincent," Smith continued.

"Friend…I don't have those anymore," I said.

"Look, we ain't here to play games with you. We know you're not a hard ass, so lose the fucking act," Pena added. "You're deep into some shit, and you're going to continue to stink unless you come clean with us."

"Become a snitch? Are y'all charging me?"

"We're planning on carrying out over a dozen federal indictments within the month, and guess what; you're on our list for conspiracy to run a criminal empire, trafficking, murder, racketeering and whatever else we throw at you. You and your peoples have been under surveillance for a long while and here's where the real fun begins. I already got half a dozen CI's willing to testify against you and your organization. So you can play ball with us, or take your chances on a losing team."

I sat there holding on to my composure. I appeared calm and collected on the outside but on the inside, my heart was beating like African drums.

"Quiet now, are we," agent Smith said.

"Look, either way you look at it, Vincent, you're fucked. Two of our CI's have informed us that there's two contracts out on your head. One confirmed by the Jamaicans, and the next coming from Law. Word on the streets is that you popped his nephew a few months back, now he wants to return the favor. You step out this door and you won't last a week out there without our protection," Pena stated. "You'll be either dead or charged with the indictments coming to you soon."

"Let's not forget about your friend, Spoon. I haven't seen him around lately, any word on where we might find him?" Smith asked.

"You know, just because there is no body, that doesn't mean there's no crime," Pena stated.

"Yo whateva…Spoon, I don't know where he at," I lied.

"Let's cut the bullshit, Vincent. We know you had a role in his disappearance. We found his truck stripped and burnt in New Jersey. And the mother of his kids, Melissa, shot to death in her own home early this year. know they both were friends. They trusted you so much they made you the godfather of their kids. Now they're murdered and you don't want to see justice done for the family, for his kids at least?" Smith asked.

"Look, we're coming for y'all, Vincent. You can become one of many caught standing on the tracks when the trains comes speeding through or you can come aboard and make it easier for yourself. It's your choice. We want Tyriq and the Jamaicans? You're just some post 9/11 victim caught up in the system and did what you had to do out there to survive after the layoffs. You give us them and we can give you your life back," Pena proclaimed.

"Think about your son. He's a cute and a very smart kid. You can still be a father to him. It's your choice," Smith said.

Give me back my life, I thought. I laughed at the statement. What life?

"You know what, we'll let you sit here and think about things. We'll give you a minute to decide," Pena said.

They both got up and left the room, leaving me alone to contemplate about my life.

Thirty-Seven

The following evening I was at my family's home. I had time alone for myself while my aunt was at the hospital. The house was quiet. I was surprised that my key still fit the lock. But my mother always wanted me to come home and be a son to her again.

I pulled out the photo book and started looking at old photos of the family from ten to twenty years ago. I sat on the couch with a bottle of Jack Daniels next to me, smiling at the crazy pictures I took with family and friends. It seemed so long ago and in some pictures it looked like I had no worries at all. I was surrounded by many loving memories, happy occasions.

Each photo made me want to jump back in time and breathe a happy life again. There was no such thing. No more happy days in my future.

One particular photo caught my attention and I stared at it for a long time. It was of Spoon, Tyriq and me. We all were twelve or thirteen years old in the picture. It was taken in the park. We had just won the PSAL basketball tournament and were hugged closely together holding up trophies and smiling. My father took the picture of us and he was so proud of us.

That was many years ago, and times have definitely changed. I continued to stare at the photo for a long moment and then slowly began to tear it up, as I did with a few other pictures. I went through the entire photo album and tore up many pictures that made me emotional to look at.

I took a swig from the bottle and drenched myself in memories and sorrow. The world around me now flourished with many enemies coming against me. I had two contracts out on my head and the feds were soon going to indict me. They promised me a second chance of life and freedom, if only cooperate and turn state's witness against the world around me. I was trapped between a rock and a hard place, knowing any road I traveled would lead me to the same dead end street.

I took another swig from the bottle and heard my cell ringing on the glass table. I answered the call.

"Speak to me," I said.

"You put your fucking hands on my cousin and beat her like you her pimp," Inf barked.

"Inf, now is not the time," I said.

"Fuck you, nigga! I told you don't get fucking stupid. I don't give a fuck!" he shouted.

"Yo, fuck you Beanie Segal lookin' muthafucka! You don't control me, nigga. I fucking run y'all niggas out there. And fuck that ho bitch! The baby probably ain't even mines anyway," I retorted.

"I'm gonna see you, Vince. You disrespect me and my family…I'm gonna see you nigga, everything on that," he said harshly hanging up.

"Fuck him!" I said, tossing away my cell.

Let him come, I thought. That bitch, Cashmere was grimy and I should've seen through her snake-ass. Now she wanted to have her cousin come at me and start a war. The bitch was emotional and didn't think about the consequences.

I couldn't worry about that nigga, he was hundred of miles away in Philly and I had my own issues to deal with. But my list of enemies was slowly growing.

"Fuck this," I uttered.

I got up and wanted to go see my moms at the hospital. I needed to be at her bedside. I tossed the bottle in the sink and got my head right. I left everything the way it was in the house and walked out the door with dusk soon settling over my hood.

I got to my truck and opened the back latch. I went digging through a few items in the back, looking for a few things. I came across the Christmas gift Chandra had giving me a few months back, still wrapped neatly. I never bothered to open it.

Curiosity got the best of me and I opened the gift. It was a huge bible. I chuckled. I began going through it and two pictures fell out. I picked them up and one was of Chandra and my son, smiling with them hugging each other. It was recent. I smiled and then turned it over and noticed Chandra had written something on the back of it.

"Trust in the Lord with all your heart and lean not on your own understanding; in all your ways acknowledge Him, and he will make your paths straight...Proverbs 3:5,6."

I picked up the second photo and it was one taken a while back with all three of us in it this time. It was our first family picture. Vinny was one years old at the time. I turned it over and there was more writing.

"Do not conform any longer to the pattern of this world, but be transformed by the renewing of your mind...Romans 12:2".

I stared at both pictures remembering a time when I was truly happy—before the money, the cars and the rep. I had a family that loved and cared for me so much. I asked myself, *what happened?*

I stood next to my seventy-thousand dollar truck and wanted to pray for a change in me and my life. I was scared and needed some help. I had people out to kill me.

I stood out on the streets and cried some. I held both pictures in my hand and knew my end was soon. I haven't been the father to my son the way I needed to be in months.

It wasn't supposed to be like this—change was supposed to be for the better, not worse. I was losing more of me in ways that I couldn't have imagined.

"God, please help me," I exclaimed.

A voice inside of me said, *turn around and move.* I turned in time to see the barrel of a Glock 19 trained at me and coming my way quickly. My eyes got wide and my heart raced, and then I heard the dreadful sound.

Blam!

I jumped, trying to move, but a bullet quickly ripped through my shoulder. I dropped everything I had in my hands and fell to the floor. There were two masked gunmen coming my way, firing rapidly at me.

I grabbed my injured shoulder scurrying for safety. The shooters were relentless. I ran down the block hearing shots shattering back windows to cars and bullets whizzing by my ears.

They were close. I zigzagged my way into someone's backyard and jumped a fence. My adrenaline took over. The shots continued and I felt two more in my back.

"Aaghh!" I grunted.

My right arm became numb and my back was on fire. I collapsed to the ground. It was hard for me to move but I kept trying. My clothes were drenched with blood and I was becoming disoriented. The gunmen were near and I was helpless.

I fell against a high fence and remained there. My breathing was sparse and my hope for life dimming. They were close, nearing the kill. I didn't know who sent them. It could've been the Jamaicans or Tyriq. They could be part of Law's crew. Maybe Inf found a way to get at me early. It was fucked up not knowing.

"*Hold on, Vince,*" I said to myself, feeling my conscious slowly slipping away.

My body was leaking blood, and aching with pain that I never felt before. I heard someone in the yard creeping and then I heard police sirens blaring blocks away. I hid behind a tool shed and the tall fence I propped myself against. I heard footsteps nearing closer and knew I was a dead man. My vision was blurry. I was helpless and bloody on the grass covered yard. I asked God to forgive me, it was my end.

The footsteps came from behind the tool shed and I wished it was someone to aid me. It was my attacker, standing tall in front of me, masked up and gripping the Glock.

He was looking unfazed by the sirens. He was a hardcore criminal. I stared into his eyes and they were filled with rage and hate.

"Just do it, muthafucka!" I shouted, repeating the same words that Spoon said to me when his life was about to end—*karma's a muthafucka*, I thought.

It felt like the gunman was toying with me.

"Why you do it, Vince?" the masked gunman asked.

"Fuck you talking about?" I asked, feeling my body ache with pain as I tried to speak.

He then pulled the mask off his head and it was S.S. Spoon's cousin. He came home a few weeks ago. I was in Philly taking care of business. He did some time at Riker's.

"Why you kill my cousin? Y'all were like brothers," S.S. asked.

We locked eyes for a very short moment and then I heard a neighbor say, "Who's back there? The cops are coming, leave from out my backyard."

The lights came on in the backyard and that's when S.S fired two shots into me hurriedly and ran off. It felt like my chest exploded and was being ripped open.

Thirty-Eight

Game Over

Game Over.....Tyriq

Tyriq stayed in a Brooklyn loft near the Navy Yard. He moved around on crutches and was trying to heal from the brutal attempt on his life that killed his man, Bones. He assumed that it was Vincent who had planned the attack on him. He trusted no one and carried a loaded .9mm wherever he went.

His relationship with the Jamaicans was sinking. He didn't know if they were the ones trying to kill him. But why save his life. The unanswered questions left Tyriq a nervous wreck. His life was in danger. He kept a low profile until everything was in order.

Tip and Omega watched his back, with the company of a beautiful female to keep him warm and satisfied at nights.

Omega was on the phone talking, when he heard Tyriq ask "What's goin on, my nigga?"

Omega hung up from the call, walked over to Tyriq and said, "Vince just got hit up by his crib a few hours ago…shot five times."

"Word… He dead…?" Tyriq asked.

Omega shook his head, "Nah…he still alive, but in critical condition. Nigga comatose…"

Tyriq didn't know what to think and he didn't know who got Vince. There was so much chaos and violence in the streets no one knew who was shooting who anymore.

"Fuck that nigga!" Tyriq uttered and rested himself against Peaches on the plush couch.

"What about the Jamaicans, you trust them?" Tip asked.

"Nah, I know we gotta move first, something ain't right," Tyriq said.

"For us to war with Demetrius we gonna need heavy artillery," Omega informed.

"Ayyite, I'll make a few calls and get things in order. We gonna get back on our feet and run this shit. These fuckin' Jamaicans ain't seen the end of me," Tyriq proclaimed.

Omega and Tip nodded. They both were ready for anything. But one was more ambitious and cut throat than the next and was ready to betray Tyriq so he could be the man.

"Yo, y'all niggas bounce and give me some alone time," Tyriq said.

"C'mere baby," his big-titty bitch said, pulling Tyriq closer to her.

Omega and Tip left the room, leaving Tyriq in the arms of Peaches.

1:35 am

Giant and a female companion he met that night laughed it up in a local quaint bar on State Street, in Albany New York. They downed Coronas, smoked, and mingled with each other. Giant was flirting with a friend, Jessica—touching her sexually, laying down the foundation for pussy.

"Yo, let me get another round of beers over here," Giant instructed the bartender.

He then focused his attention on Jessica again. "So, luv, what's good for the night, I'm trying to do some things with you."

"Oh really," Jessica replied teasingly.

She smiled and her soft manicured hand touched the side of Giant's bearded face.

They had immediately locked eyes when she walked into the bar an hour ago. Clad in some tight denim jeans that hugged her curvy hips and a tight snug shirt that accentuated her tits, Jessica was eye candy. Giant wasted no time.

"So, you ready to get out of here, and go somewhere private for the night?" Giant asked, pulling out a wad of bills.

"You tell me?" she asked seductively, with her hand reaching up his thigh and touching him someplace nice.

"My car's parked out back, and it's nice and quiet where I'm parked..

dark too."

"That sounds cool."

Giant began putting on his coat and took another swig from his beer. He was ready for some pussy and wanted to fuck Jessica.

She walked ahead of him. Giant stared at her lovely round ass wearing a grin. This older man on his right watched his moves. It bothered Giant. The tall stranger was dressed in dark clothing, had a bushy goatee, and a mysterious look. Other patrons in the bar paid no mind to the stranger. Giant coolly walked up to the man, eyeing him with the ice grill. His solid stout frame towered over the seated stranger and he locked eyes with the man and asked in an unfriendly tone, "Nigga, your eyes have been on me all fucking night!"

The man was not intimidated by Giant and replied calmly, "Respect, mon…me ain't got no problem wit' ya. Me just here ti drink and relax mi self."

Giant continued to ice-grill him and said in a bullying tone, "Then turn your old ass back around and mind your fucking business."

The stranger showed a cool smile and took a sip of his beer. His eyes followed Giant out the front door.

"You manly, man, I wanna fuck you," Jessica said pulling Giant's coat.

"I like your style. You a true freak," Giant said smiling and ready to handle his business in his ride.

They walked toward his car and Giant was unaware that he was being closely followed.

Giant reclined comfortably in the driver's seat of his burgundy Cadillac Deville and allowed for Jessica to do her thang—giving him a hand-job.

Giant moaned, enjoying her warm touch and then said, "Go ahead start sucking my dick and do me right."

He grabbed the back of her head and gently tried to force Jessica's head down into his lap.

"You ready for me, baby?" Jessica said, having her slender fingers massaging his thickness and her precious glossy lips inches from his long shaft. Giant closed his eyes, enjoying the hand-job and was ready for bliss.

Jessica quickly glanced out the back window, and noticed a tall figure dressed in black coming their way, but she bothered not to warn Giant.

"Ummm, I wanna fuck you, luv," Giant said with zeal.

"It's going to happen, be patient baby….you'll get yours," she replied.

Jessica continued to stroke his nine inch erection and played with the tip of his dick with her coiled tongue. Giant was so pleased with her action that he didn't notice danger ten feet away. With a six inch sharp blade clutched in his hand, the Jamaican stranger loomed closer to his victim. His eyes fixated on killing. The alleyway was covered in darkness and the night was quiet except for the soft moans from Giant.

"Hmm-m-m-m…shit, baby, you're gonna make me cum if you keep doing that."

Giant felt Jessica's thick lips wrapped around his cock. Without warning, the Jamaican stranger quickly swung open the driver side door, startling Giant and in one rapid motion, the knife was placed to Giant's open throat and his jugular was carved open like a Thanksgiving turkey.

Giant jerked and squirmed under his attacker's strong grip. His eyes were bulging with death as he struggled to breathe, gurgling with life viciously being snatched from him. His sight began to fade, while Jessica just stared at him. No ounce of remorse in her.

"Bumba-claat, batty-bwoy respect shotta," the Jamaican gangster proclaimed.

He moved away from the body and watched as Giant collapsed to the cold hard ground, his hands gripping his throat. A large amount of blood coated his neck.

Jessica stepped out of the car and stood over Giant, sneering watching Giant in the throes of death. When twitching ceased, the tall Jamaican crouched down near his victim and wiped the blood that stained the knife on Giant's clothing. He removed the latex gloves and disposed of them in a dumpster.

Giant's gruesome murder was only the first of many. Contracts of death were going to be carried out. The Jamaican mafia planned on cleaning house. The feds made their moves against Tyriq and his crew. No one would be left to connect the dots.

2:10 am

Two men exit the white Yukon parked on Farmers blvd. They walked into a two-story apartment complex, carrying Mac-10's with the silencers at the tip under heavy winter coats. On reaching the second floor, they skillfully picked open the lock.

Inside the place, the Mac-10's were out. They searched the apartment. Both quietly moved toward the bedroom.

Malik was lying under green silk sheets with a butt-naked bitch in his arms next to him. He was sound asleep not knowing that he had unwanted company.

The gunmen moved in closer to the bed, gazing at their victims with their weapons trained. One of the gunmen let off a loud whistle that slightly awakened Malik. He turned in bed and opened his eyes, only to see two Mac-10's pointed directly at him. His eyes widened, and he uttered, "Yo…what the fuck!"

Without hesitating, the men open fire on Malik and his sleeping beauty, shredding them.

Tat-tat-tat-tat-tat-tat—the gunfire was quiet but deadly as rounds pierced into both victims, ripping up sheets and flesh, causing them to jerk, slumping over each other.

The scene was chaotic and messy; blood drenching the carpeted floor underneath the bed and stillness filled the bedroom. Both men left out as quickly and quietly as they came, leaving behind a gruesome crime scene.

3:25 am

Loc was pressed up on some young bitch in a Brooklyn night club. He didn't notice the eyes focused on him the entire time. The club was packed, hot mixes from the deejay kept the party hyped.

Loc was wearing an expensive silk shirt, a pair of black slacks, polished wingtip shoes, and his hair styled into two thick braids. He had been doing his thang all night, feeling up shorties.

"What's your name?" Loc asked.

"Danielle," she screamed over the blaring music.

"You're cute," he complimented.

"Thank you."

"Who you here with…?"

"My girlfriends…"

"Leaving with them tonight?"

"You wanna take me home?"

"Yeah, I wanna fuck."

"Let's roll," the young chicken-head with an affable smile replied. "Can I get a drink first?"

"What you drinking?"

"Alize..."

"I got you."

Loc began moving through the dense crowd of sweaty club goers, bumping into a few. At the bar, he ordered Danielle's Alize and Rum and Coke for himself. He gave the bartender a twenty and moved on.

With his young gullible jump-off in his sight, he moved back through the crowd carefully carrying both drinks. Loc worked his way through the crowd again, cradling the drinks tightly in his hands, making sure they didn't spill. Suddenly he was bumped hard from an approaching stranger and the drinks spilled onto his silk shirt.

"What da fuck, yo!" Loc shouted.

He looked around to beef, but the culprit quickly disappeared into the large crowd.

"Muthafucka!" Loc cursed, knowing liquor and silk didn't mix. He was ready to fight, but instead retreated to the nearest bathroom.

Loc stood by the sink with the water running. He cursed and was ready to fuck somebody up. The bathroom was empty, with music blaring outside. Loc tried to clean his shirt, when a man walked in and went straight for the urinals. What Loc didn't know was that his partner was watching the bathroom entrance.

"Why niggas gotta be so fucking clumsy," Loc was heard cursing He stared at himself in the mirror and then went over to the urinals to take a piss.

Two urinals down, the troubling stranger subtly removed a .9mm and the silencer. He quickly put the weapon together and flushed.

Loc was peeing, wanting to hurry back to Danielle. He peeped the stranger making his way to the exit. The gun was discreetly down at his side. Loc was about to flush and the man quickly moved forward pointing at the back of Loc's head and squeezed off—Poot-Poot!

Loc dropped dead at the stranger's feet and the man fired three more shots into him. The kill was quick and quiet, and didn't catch the attention of revelers in the jammed club.

The night went on, John-John and Red also caught cruel and untimely deaths. John-John was shot in the face six times in his car and Red was strangled and left for dead in the woods of Long Island. All over the city, Tyriq's men were turning up dead and the authorities and the feds knew that they had a problem. The feds were bearing in mind that the men they were about to indict with federal charges were meeting a different kind of fate. That displeased the agency. The crew was dropping like dominos and suspected the Jamaicans orchestrated the murders.

9:25 am.

The constant ringing of the phone infuriated Tyriq. He was naked and in the arms of Peaches. His gun wasn't far from his reach, on a nightstand, fully loaded and cocked. The ringing disturbed Tyriq. He reached over and snatched it up, "This shit better be really fucking important for a nigga to be calling me so fucking early."

"We need to talk," Sgt Manny said.

"About what…?"

"Your whole crew was wiped out last night," Sgt Manny informed.

"The fuck you talking 'bout…?"

"Giant, Red, Loc, Malik….all dead."

"What? By who…?" Tyriq barked.

"It was a hit against y'all, professionally done…"

"Them Jamaicans…?" Tyriq asked.

"We don't know. It's being investigated now. But you're in danger. We need to link up," Sgt. Manny said.

"Fuck!" Tyriq shouted. "Ayyite, where at…?"

Sgt. Manny gave Tyriq the location and he then hung up. Tyriq was furious but concerned for his life. His mind was racing—Malik, Red, all of them. He picked up his gun from off the nightstand and then shouted to

Peaches, "Bitch, get the fuck up!"

Peaches slowly awoke, looked over at Tyriq with droopy eyes and asked, "What the fuck happened?"

"We're leaving outta here, get your ass dressed," Tyriq said.

"Baby, why you so paranoid, don't nobody know you're here," Peaches said rubbing her eyes.

"Bitch, I said get the fuck up and let's go!" Tyriq shouted.

Peaches sighed and slowly dragged her ass out of bed. Tyriq got on the horn, calling Tip and Omega to let them know what had happened.

Late that evening, Tyriq, Omega and Tip drove into an isolated and discreet location to meet with Sgt. Manny about the murders and the Jamaicans.

The four-door grey Maxima slowly drove behind the desolate warehouse in New Jersey, the outskirts of Newark. The area was surrounded with high grass that stretched for a few miles. It was the perfect place to meet.

Tyriq felt a bit comfortable meeting outside of the city. He sat in the front seat of the Maxima with a walking cane in his hand observing his surrounding.

Tip was the driver and Omega sat behind Tyriq with a .380 in his grip. They all were waiting on Sgt. Manny to show up and inform them of the situation and give them details.

"I don't trust this dude, Tyriq," Omega let known. "Why here?"

"The city is too dangerous and Sgt. Manny, he knows not to cross me. I got too much dirt on that muthafucka. I own that cracker cop," Tyriq said.

"Well, if he try to fuck us, I got sump'n for his ass," Omega said raising the .380.

Fifteen minutes later and the three knew they were living dangerous. Demetrius was a powerful and very resourceful man. He had enough muscle, connection and reach, that to war with him, would be suicidal. Demetrius proved how deadly and ruthless he can be by murdering majority of Tyriq's crew in a twenty-four hour time span.

Omega looked at the time. It was near seven.

"Yo, I gotta go take a piss," he said.

"Hurry the fuck up," Tyriq hissed.

Omega stepped out of the car and moved himself near the high-grass to pee. He had his .380 tucked in his waistband and looked around the area while draining his unwanted fluids.

Tyriq perked up when he noticed a pair of headlights approaching the car.

"That's him," Tyriq said.

Tip removed his gun and kept a keen eye on the car—knowing that a war was brewing and anything can happen. The dark Impala came to a stop a few feet from the Maxima and it appeared to look as Sgt. Manny came alone.

"Let's go talk to this muthafucka and see what he got for us," Tyriq said getting ready to step out of the car.

Tip nodded.

But Tyriq caught an eerie feel that crawled up his skin. Something didn't seem right. He looked around for Omega and saw him a great distance from the car. A nigga ain't gotta go that far to take a leak, Tyriq thought. Everything seemed to be too orchestrated—the location, Omega happened to pee when the meeting was near. He glanced at the time and saw that it was nearing seven.

Tyriq turned to look at the high-grass and saw some movement in the shadows. He knew he fucked up. He shouted to Tip, "It's a set up!"

Before they could react, three Jamaican men gripping Mac-11's hurriedly emerged from the high-grass and began letting off intense barrage of bullets into the parked Maxima. Dozens of hot rounds tore into Tyriq and Tip as they sat like sitting ducks in the car. Bullets ripped through flesh, tore through their skulls and blood and brain matter splattered everywhere inside of the car.

It was a massacre. Omega watched from a safe distance as his one time friends were torn to shreds by the heavy gunfire that engulfed the car.

When it was finally over, the Maxima looked like Swiss cheese, with the windows shattered and the two bodies riddled with bullets, lying slump in their seats, their blood and flesh decorating the interior.

It was that time for new management—too much shit was pointing back to Tyriq and his crew. Tyriq instead of being a profit to the organization was now high risk. They had the dead daughter of a DEA agent hanging over their heads. The many informants that were coming out that crew, Spoon turning snitch on them, and allowing Vince to bring Columbians on their turf, cutting into their lucrative drug market. Too many problems instead of layoff and cutbacks, the Jamaicans killed-off their problems.

Omega walked over to the car and peered inside, witnessing the gruesome death of his former bosses. Their bodies were bloody and contorted, and their eyes forever closed. He grinned knowing it was his time to shine. He would be the Jamaicans next man in line to control the drugs and other illegal activities that overwhelmed Queens and in other states.

Sgt. Manny walked up to Omega.

"You happy…?"

"Copasetic," Omega replied with a wayward smile raising the .380 to Sgt. Manny's head and fired.

Sgt. Manny dropped dead in front of Omega. It was to be done, strict orders from Demetrius to kill the cop too. Afterwards, they stuffed the cop's body into the backseat and set the entire car ablaze—burning everything around them.

In one night, Tyriq's entire drug crew met with ghastly deaths. They were distorted with greed, lust for power and influence. There was an intense craving for self gratifications. They murdered for control and poisoned others with drugs to feel like demigods.

In the end, the results remain the same.

Thirty-Nine

Five weeks later, I regained consciousness in Jamaica Hospital. I had been shot five times by a former friend. I was lucky to be alive. God had spared my life and allowed me to have more time on this earth.

The doctors told me that it was a miracle, no arteries were hit and one bullet missed my heart by half a centimeter. I had a collapsed-lung, and swelling of the brain and a few other areas. I was in critical condition for a long time. I had over a dozen surgeries performed on me. They said it would be a long time before I'd be able to walk. I needed months of physical therapy and a good aide after my release.

My life was spared but a few weeks ago, my mother had passed away. She hung on as long as she could. There was nothing else the doctors could do. God spared my life but took my mothers'. I cried so hard.

I needed to hear her prayer one more time. I wanted guidance. In the end, all I had were good memories and regrets.

I woke up feeling like I was in a nightmare. I was alive but my freedom was still in jeopardy. Being shot five times and put into a brief coma didn't mean the feds forgot about me. I still had criminal charges pending and they were still persistent in carrying out the indictments. I was handcuffed to the bed, while in the process of healing.

I found out that I was one of few still alive from Tyriq's old crew. Everyone was murdered or incarcerated. They found Tyriq and Tips charred and riddled bodies a few miles outside of Newark. Sgt. Manny was also burned to death and found in the car with them.

Tyriq died the way he lived. Part of me was saddened when I heard the news. We never could rekindle our friendship. His bitterness towards went with him to his grave. And that was a ending that I didn't want for myself. But I didn't know what the future held for me.

I also got the news on SS, after he gunned me down. He got into a gun battle with the cops and was shot six times. He died on the streets a block away.

Within a year, many friends and family were dead because of me, that thought made me numb. I lost my ability to walk and needed some intense physical therapy. I lost everything and gained nothing in the end. The moncy and car were seized. Girlfriends gone and my health was fucked. Freedom looked bleak.

I started to ask God why He left me on this earth to suffer and took my moms. I had done so much dirt, I didn't deserve to live. Lying in bed, I kept thinking about living right.

I tried not to think about death but couldn't help it. My life changed considerably. I stared up at the ceiling and even though I was grateful to be alive—I kept asking, why?

Thinking of the many mistakes I'd made brought tears to my eyes. I sighed heavily and wished I could start over. My reality—I craved all and lost it all.

I closed my eyes and whispered, "God please help me and give me some meaning why I'm still here."

"Daddy," my son shouted.

I opened my eyes and saw my lil' man coming my way with a huge smile on his face and his arms open. I cried and let out a smile. There was still hope, but who would be my son's heroes? Thoughts of my father telling me about Dr. King emerged: *The ultimate measure of a man is not where he stands in moments of comfort and convenience, but where he stands at times of challenge and controversy...*

To be continued

BOOK II

Love and a Gangster

Prologue 2002...

Soul laid comfortable on the green tattered couch with Keisha nestled against him, being in his arms clad only in a blue thong and a skimpy white T-shirt that barely covered her tits. He had just finished fuckin' her and now had his thoughts on America, his wifey going on five years now. Soul looked at the time and saw that it was five in the morning. He was still tired but knew he had to finish packing up the work that was sprawled out on the coffee table.

Three keys of uncut cocaine, three keys of Ecstasy, and a loaded *.9mm* laid on the cluttered table in front of Soul. This has been Soul's world since he was young. He sold his first vial of crack when he was ten and got his first piece of pussy when he was eleven. And it was all he knew and loved, besides America, who's been by his side since he was seventeen.

Soul glanced at the time again and saw that it was five-thirty. He closed his eyes and told himself, *another half-hour and I'll get back to work.*

With Keisha nestled against him, he suddenly felt her tugging at his jeans, with her hand reaching into his zipper.

"You don't get enough dick," he said lightly.

"You go ahead and sleep and let me do me, baby," Keisha replied, pulling at his thick piece of meat and stroking herself up a hard-on again.

But Soul didn't resist. He positioned his hands behind his head and allowed for Keisha to do what she did best—suck dick. He felt her thick sweet lips wrap around his member and moaned when she began deep-throating him.

"Mmmmmm....shit, *uh*...damn," Soul moaned.

He began running his fingers through her thick and rich weave and pushed her face further down into his lap. He was put in bliss and was ready to cum in her mouth when they suddenly heard an abrupt and loud sound bang against the apartment door.

Reacting quickly, knowing it was police, Soul pushed Keisha off him, pulled up his jeans and ran for the nearby work.

Bang—Bang—Bang.

"Police...open the fuck up!" they were heard shouting.

Soul knew he had to move quickly. Lucky for him, the apartment door had heavy-duty, reinforced steel doors that were able to slow the police sudden barge into the apartment. With Keisha's help, they snatched up the keys off the table and ran for the bathroom to flush it.

They were racing against time, knowing that each key could fuck them over.

Bang—Bang!

Soul continued to hear, knowing that the police were relentless and were soon coming into the crib to fuck shit up. They managed to tear open three keys and flush shit down the toilet and wash away the powder into the sink and bathtub. Keisha was sweating and panicking, her fingers were covered in cocaine residue. Soul was on a mission and that was not to get caught, so he moved like the Flash and tore open the key of Ecstasy and tossed that shit into the toilet.

He suddenly remembered the *.9mm* on the table and went to go recover it. But when he got into the living room, he was too late. The steel door finally gave way after unrelenting pounding from the police and they rushed in—Glocks out and cocked and flashing badges and papers, and being clad in their blue flight vest that read **NYPD**.

"Get down...get down...get the fuck down!" they screamed, running through the place like a swarm of ants.

They piled up on Soul and forced him to the floor and restrained his arms around his back and handcuffed him quickly. Moments later they were dragging Keisha from out the bathroom as she kicked and screamed and tried to fight the cops.

Within minutes, they were both in police custody and watching police ransack the entire apartment. The only thing left for them to seize was the loaded *.9mm* and the key of Ecstasy that Keisha wasn't able to flush.

A Sgt looked at Soul with his beady eyes and said, "You going to jail muthafucka. You fuck with us, we fuck with you…get this nigger out of my sight and book him for gun possession and drugs."

Soul sighed, knowing he had fucked up. But the only thing that was on his mind as the police carried him away in iron bracelets was, *what the fuck I'm gonna tell my girl, America?*

2006 Jamaica, Queens…

Today is finally the day. I thought about this day for four long years, and now it's finally arrived. I lingered in the shower, having the water cascade off my natural brown skin. My nipples were erect by just thinking about his touch, and the way his hands used to caress me night after night had between my thighs tingling and pulsating with excitement.

I wanted to become fresh for him again, and I kept myself pure for years just because I love him. My girlfriends thought that I was crazy, going without dick for so long. But when you're in love with a man so strongly, then why allow for another man's penetration when I was longing for only one to push himself into me. I didn't want to corrupt what belong to him. Just the thought of him coming back to me soon was sexual satisfying for me. But don't get me wrong, I love sex, but if it wasn't with Omar, then I was cool and remained celibate until his return.

Omar captured my heart the very first time we met. He was from the streets, no doubt, but he had such a strong aura about him, that I was able to look past that and accept him for who he was. He took my virginity soon afterwards, and from then on. I wanted to marry him.

They called him Soul on the streets, because the man had a future in whatever he took part of. He could rhyme and play the piano and the guitar. His musical gifts were phenomenal. He could dance like no other before him. He could play ball just as good as the players out of Rucker's park in Harlem, and he was a gentlemen. Despite his street reputation, my baby knew how to take care of me in the bedroom and out. And I was able to talk to him about anything.

But Omar wasn't perfect, like every man on this planet, he had his flaws too. He loved the streets, and sometimes hustling and hanging with his homeboys got in the way of his talents.

He sold crack. He got into fights. He drank. And there was even a rumor floating around the hood that he cheated on me. But being his woman, I looked beyond his flaws and wanted us to be one. I wanted us to be together till the day we became old, gray, and wrinkle like crumpled paper. He was the only man that I became intimate with. He was my first, and I wanted him to be my last.

I met Omar when I was fifteen. He was seventeen at the time. He used to hang out with his boys in front of this corner bodega on Supthin and South Road. He did what majority of the youths his age did in the neighborhood, hustling and getting into trouble.

But he was cute. And he used to carry himself different from the rest of his friends. His style was different from his peers. His friends wore their pants low and sagging off their asses; Omar used to sport khakis and wore his jeans above his ass with a belt. Niggahs sported timberlands, which he did too, but every now and then, you would catch him in some loafers, soft bottom shoes, or even a suit and some wing tips. His niggahs sported cornrows and wild hair, Omar kept a low cropped style and took a trip to the barbershop once a week. His niggahs wore clad in big bulky chains and jewelry looking like they took advice from Mr. T and the only jewelry Omar sported was a thin gold chain and a small cross which his mama gave him.

He had caught me coming out of the bodega carrying groceries for my aunt. We had locked eyes for a short moment when I came out. But I remained silent and walked passed the same group of boys that lingered in front of the same store on a daily basis.

As I walked down the block, Omar came jogging up to me and said, "Hey hold up, youngin'."

"Youngin'?" I had snapped. "Niggah, you ain't that much older than me."

He had chuckled, and then replied with, "Yo let me carry that for you."

I was reluctant. "Why?"

"Because it would be the polite thing to do, and besides, you're too small to be carrying that big of a bag."

"I've been doing fine for half a block without your help. Did I look like I was struggling?"

He smiled and then said, "Yo, you got some mouth on you. How old are you anyway?"

"Old enough," I had said.

"Damn, you kinda feisty. I like that," he had countered.

"Whateva!" I said, and began walking away from him.

But Omar was persistent. He then said, "Being a man, I'm not going to let you carry these bags to your crib by yourself. My mama raised me better than that."

"Oh, she did, huh," I had said. "And did your mama teach you about harassment too?"

"Harassment? Yo, why you tryin' come at me like that, shorti, when I'm just tryin' to help you out?"

I had given off a grim stare.

"You don't trust me, I don't look like a nice guy to you?" he had said. He gave me a warm smile. His smile was so contagious that I couldn't contain mines any longer.

"See, there's a smile I was lookin' for," he had said.

"Shut up," I had said jokingly.

He proceeded to remove the bags from my grip and we walked side by side to my home. I was attracted to him. He was tall, about six-feet. He was slim, but was outlined with a six pack and well defined arms. I remembered that day he sported some jean shorts, a wife-beater, and he had the brand new red and white Jordan's on.

"So what's your name, beautiful?" he had asked me. His eyes were a dark onyx, and his lips were full like the rest of him.

I remembered not wanting to tell him my full name because I was embarrassed. My mother before she passed named me *America*. I know it sounds patriotic, but I dreaded the first day of school when the teacher would call out the names on her list. When they would get to America, I could see the look on their faces, perplexed as if they weren't reading it right.

"America?" teachers would call out incredulously. And all the kids would laugh. The first week of school, my name would be the butt of every kids joke. But that was the only thing they could joke about on me. I was cute, and despite my name, the boys loved me, and some of the girls took a liking to me.

I had looked at Omar and said, "My name is America, okay?" I was waiting for him to laugh like all the previous ones who had heard my name before him. But surprisingly, he didn't laugh. He looked me square in my face and said, "I like that, America…it's different. God bless America," he had said.

I smiled. We got to my crib and he lingered around after I took the groceries in to my aunt. We talked for hours and from that day on, Omar and I became inseparable. He became my heart. We would spend days together, talking, laughing, and just being us.

Every day without him, it felt like part of me was missing. I thought about him everyday since his incarceration. I went to visit him often, trying to keep his mind at ease and remind him what he had waiting for him when he got out. I couldn't wait to nestle in his arms again. I yearned for his touch, and to feel his breath against mines. I hungered for our souls to entwined, and for him to devour me like a strong appetite.

He's been on my mind so much that with every passing thought of him, my pussy would throb uncontrollably, and my panties would get saturated with juices escaping from my lips.

I tried to cool off in the shower, but it got no better for me. I was horny. I was so fuckin' horny that there was an ache in my body that just wouldn't leave. I was like this because I knew that in less than twenty-four hours, my baby would be home and with me again, loving every curve, shape and inch of me until my pussy puts him to sleep.

Four fucking years of waiting, and being faithful to my boo, I was ready to explode. I lost count of how many times I masturbated alone in the dark, either with toys I had purchased over the years, or with my own free hands—thinking about Omar grinding and gyrating between my legs. I lost count of how many sleepless nights I had thinking about Omar with a pillow clutched in between my thighs as I fondled my own breasts. I lost count of the long cold showers I had to take because being horny and alone without my man around was sometimes too unbearable to think about. During the days and evenings, I would pour my heart and soul into songs or poems I've written, some so emotional that after I would repeat them from my own lips, tears would form in my eyes and a sadness would overcome me.

I removed the shower head from above my head, placed one leg up on the cast iron porcelain tub and neared the shower head to my animated kitty cat. I set the water speed just right for pleasure and moaned as I felt every bit of the water rushing against my pussy. I moved my other hand in between my thighs and started masturbating by moving my fingertips in a circular motion against my clit. With the sensation of the water smacking against my lips and my own fingertips against my clit, I cried out feeling the full effects.

"Aaaaaahhh.....Aaaaaahhh.....Aaaaaahhh....Aaaaaahhh...oh shit...oh shit...Mmmmmm....Mmmmmm. I missed you baby. I missed you so much," I cried out as I came. I had Omar so deep in my mind that if felt like he was right next to me.

Tonight was finally my night. There would be no more pretending, because he was coming home after four grueling long years of abstinence, just to keep what was his pure and tight.

Augustuspublishing.com / Info@augustuspublishing.com

ORDERFORM

Make All Checks Payable To: **Augustus Publishing** 33 Indian Road Ny, Ny 10034

Shipping Charges: Ground One Book $4.95 / Each Additional Book $1.00

Titles	Price	Qty	Total
Ghetto Girls (Special Edition) / Anthony Whyte ISBN: 0975945319	14.95		
Ghetto Girls Too / Anthony Whyte ISBN: 0975945300	14.95		
Ghetto Girls 3: Soo Hood / Anthony Whyte ISBN: 0975945351	14.95		
A Boogie Down Story / Keisha Seignious ISBN: 0979281601	14.95		
Booty Call *69 / Erick S Gray ISBN: 0975945343	14.95		
If It Ain't One Thing - It's Another / Sharron Doyle ISBN: 097594536X	14.95		
It Can Happen In A Minute / S.m. Johnson ISBN: 0975945378	14.95		
Woman's Cry: Llantó de la mujer / Vanessa Mártir ISBN: 0975945386	14.95		
A Good Day To Die / James Hendricks ISBN: 0975945327	14.95		
Lip Stick Diaries / Various Female Authors ISBN: 0975945394	14.95		
Spot Rushers / Brandon McCalla ISBN: 0979281628	14.95		
Hustle Hard /Blaine Martin SBN: 0979281636	14.95		
Crave All Lose All / Erick S Gray SBN: 082307885X	14.95		
In Ya Grill: The Faces of Hip Hop SBN: 082307885X	21.95		
	Subtotal		
	Shipping		
	8.625% Tax		
	Total		

ame

ompany

ddress

ty State Zip

one Fax

nail